The Cupid Chronicles

The Cupid Chronicles

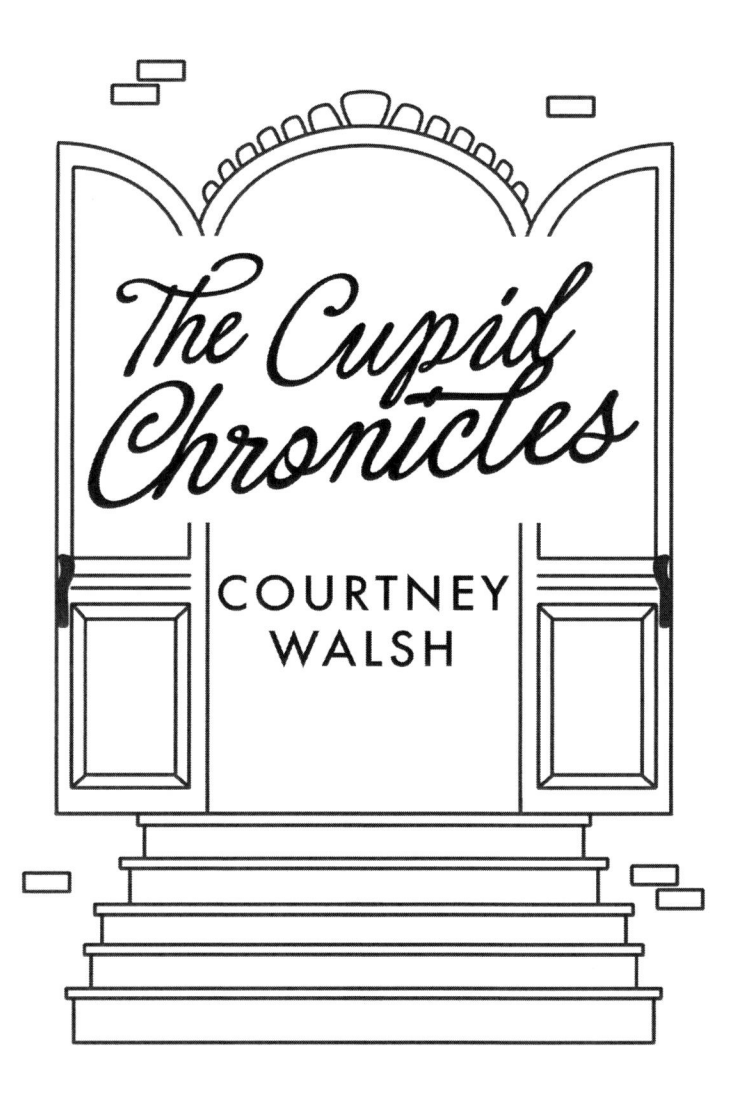

COURTNEY WALSH

Visit Courtney Walsh's website at www.courtneywalshwrites.com.

The Cupid Chronicles

Copyright © 2025 by Courtney Walsh. All rights reserved.

The author is represented by Kristy Cambron of Gardner Literary.

The Cupid Chronicles is a work of fiction. Where real people, events, establishments, organizations, or locales appear, they are used fictitiously. All other elements of the novel are drawn from the author's imagination.

For information about special discounts for bulk purchases, please contact Sweethaven Press at courtney@courtneywalsh.com

Printed in the United States of America

Book cover design and Illustration by Melody Jeffries

For Becky Nelson
Who knew how to turn ordinary things into magic.
You will be missed.

Prologue

A wisp of cool air flutters down the hallway, with no apparent source. A faint tinkle of bells, like wind chimes heard from three blocks away. A perceptive adult might hear it, though they may wonder if there was even a sound at all.

Children can hear it, plain as day.

As quickly as the wisp and chimes are there and then gone, something is left in their wake. Something that wasn't there . . . and then, all of a sudden, was.

But this time, it's different.

This time, it's new.

This time, the magic lands in front of a different door.

Chapter One
Iris

JUST ANOTHER MANIC MONDAY.

Ever since my mom sang that old Bangles song to me when I was a kid, I've woken up at the beginning of every week with it stuck in my head. She'd walk into my room belting it out, office-party-karaoke-night style, as if this is how everyone should wake up.

It stuck. And now I'm stuck.

They say in order to get an earworm out of your head, you have to listen to the whole song, front to back . . . but I don't have it in me.

Yes, Susanna Hoffs, it is manic. And yes, I do wish it were Sunday.

I've got to start going to bed earlier.

But how can I sleep when I'm so close to finishing my third re-watch of the latest season of *The Great British Baking Show?*

Some people have hobbies. They bake, or whatever.

I have Paul Hollywood.

Oh, and crochet. I took that up last year, when I put

myself on a forced hiatus from dating. Given my history, the hiatus probably should've turned into a sabbatical.

Toothbrush in my mouth, shirt hanging at a crooked angle, one hand through the sleeve, the other tugging at my pants. I'm like a Picasso if it overslept.

As I move toward the sink to spit, my foot thinks it'd be hilarious to get stuck in the leg of my pants. I tumble forward with a foamy "Ack!" and land in a pile on the floor.

I lift my head, and out of the corner of my eye I see a glob of blue toothpaste on the bathroom rug.

Yep. That'll stain.

Just another manic Monday, indeed.

Get it together, Iris.

I flip onto my back, slip my arm into my shirt, push my rebellious leg into my pants, and scramble to my feet. "One thing at a time," I moan out loud, mouth full of toothpaste, so it sounds like "Wha fing anna nyme."

I sigh at the ridiculousness of this scene before spitting the toothpaste into the sink.

I run my hands through my hair, fingers tangling in the waves, put on just enough makeup to look awake, hustle to the kitchen to grab my coffee, my bag and the stack of projects I spent last night grading, then fling open the door of my apartment, running through a mental checklist in hopes of remembering anything I might've forgotten.

This exercise is interrupted as I step into the hallway and nearly step *on* something laying on the floor outside my door.

"What the . . .?!"

I maneuver my line of sight around the armload of things I'm holding and see a rolled-up newspaper sitting on my welcome mat.

That's weird. Who reads the newspaper? And one rolled up with a rubber band?

I glance up and down the hallway, looking for someone who could have left the newspaper in front of my door.

I huff out a breath and bend over to pick up the newspaper, which is definitely not mine. I could leave it for later, but what if this neighbor—I find a label on the outside of the sleeve—*Matteo Morgan*. The name interrupts my thoughts.

Matteo. Probably an old guy, if he's getting a newspaper. And this is probably part of his morning ritual—coffee, paper, crossword puzzle, that kind of thing.

If I had a morning ritual, I'm pretty sure I wouldn't want it interrupted.

The image of an older man forms in my mind. He looks like Gerry, the guy who fixes Woody in *Toy Story*, same pointy nose and bald head, and in my imagination, he's gracious and kind, and when I show him I've gotten his newspaper by accident, he invites me in for a cup of tea. Maybe he has a British accent and a million stories to tell.

All at once, I want to meet Matteo. Maybe he'll become a friend, a wise old neighbor who can give me life advice. The father I've always wished I had.

I moved into The Serendipity at the beginning of the school year, but I've been so consumed with my new teaching job, my new students, and my promise *not* to fall into my old habit of inserting myself into other people's lives that I haven't gotten the chance to meet many of my neighbors. I suppose now, on a Monday morning, manic or not, is as good a time as any, right?

I turn in the opposite direction of the elevator and double-check the address label again.

Matteo Morgan. Apartment 3J. Two doors down from me.

The corner apartment. Lucky. He probably has two full walls of windows. As I move down the hall toward his door, I find myself wondering—not for the first time—what the other apartments in this old building look like.

Maybe kind, old Matteo will give me a tour, not just of his apartment but of the whole building. I have a thing for old buildings and the secrets they hold. Think of all the people who've lived here—the love, the loss, the stories. These walls have probably seen plenty, first when it was a college dorm, then later, when it was converted into these beautiful apartments.

When I moved in, I didn't get a grand tour. My space and the common areas—the courtyard, the rooftop garden, the big kitchen, the library—are the only spaces I've seen. It's definitely unique—after all, I don't know of any other apartment building that has a community kitchen *or* a library—which is one of the things that drew me to The Serendipity in the first place.

I knock on the door of the corner apartment, trying to tip my wrist to see my watch, and stifle a "Gah!" as I'm instantly scalded. The wrist I decided to tip is attached to the hand holding my coffee. And I didn't close the lid of my travel mug.

I hold my hands out from my chest as the hot liquid trails down into my bra, and I groan an *"Oh, come ON!"*—loudly—just as the door flings open.

I come face to face with a glare so intense that for a second I can't remember why I knocked in the first place.

Okay. So . . . Matteo Morgan isn't a cute old man who fixes toys.

He's maybe in his early thirties, tall, with olive skin and dark, brooding eyes—brown with flecks of hazel. And it looks like someone ran a filter over his face to make those eyes more vibrant.

He momentarily glances at the coffee in my right hand, then back to my eyes.

I try to laugh.

I must look deranged.

Also, I'm not one to be knocked sideways by a good-looking guy. People are people. I'm good with people. I like people.

I'm a full-on adult now. With adult conversational abilities.

I'm just not sure where they've gone because right at this moment, my brain is a whiteboard that's just been erased.

"Can I help you?" I don't miss the annoyance in his tone.

I force my gaze to lock onto his.

"Uh, hi." I paste on a smile that I hope erases the nerves and distracts from what I am sure is a large brown wet stain down the front of my shirt.

It doesn't succeed at either. He glances down, and then up again.

Get it together, Iris.

His brow gives way to the slightest quirk. Why did I knock on his door?

"Hi. I'm Iris?" I say it like it's a question.

"Are you?" he responds. It's like having your serve returned at a hundred miles an hour.

"Yes! Hah!" I clear my throat. "I live—" I lift my hand to point toward my apartment and coffee drips from my wrist down my arm to my elbow, where it clings for a dramatic second before hitting the floor.

He notices but doesn't say anything.

"I live down the hall, and this—" I try to juggle the dripping travel mug, my keys, and the art projects I desperately wish I'd stuck inside my bag, which has fallen from my shoulder and is now dangling in the crook of my elbow.

First impression. Nailing it.

Finally, I inch the paper forward and nod to it. "This was delivered to my door by mistake."

His face immediately changes. He looks surprised, and . . . caught? He shakes it off and returns to what I'm starting to guess is his default scowl. "Where did you get that?" His tone is accusing, like I've done something wrong.

Did he not hear me? "I don't know. I didn't steal it, it was in front of my door. Sorry it's crinkled. I stepped on it."

He still looks completely confused, glancing down and side to side, as if he's calculating something in his head. He shakes his head for a second time, then reaches up and slides the paper out from under my arm.

See? He's just a guy. And apparently, not a very nice one.

I decide to give him the benefit of the doubt. Maybe he had a bad morning. Maybe he's been wondering where his paper was. I meet his eyes. Or maybe he's just a jerk.

Unfortunately, jerks are my kryptonite. I'm now curious enough to find out what his deal is. And yes, some part of me wants to fix him.

No, Iris. Do not go there. Not again.

I smile, determined to win him over, or maybe to get him to quit glowering at me. "So, you're Matteo?" I ask. "I just moved in this past fall, and I—"

"Yeah. Great. Thanks for this." He holds up the paper, steps back, and shuts the door in my face.

Wait.

Wait, did he . . . ?

I'm so stunned, I stand there for a solid ten seconds, staring at the door like a child who's been sent to time-out in the corner.

Okay. Wow. What a jerk.

"Hey, uh, *you're welcome!*" I call out, hoping he's still within earshot.

Finally, I make a stupid face at his door, confident he can't see me, and after a few more stunned seconds, I turn and stomp back down the hall.

So much for being a good neighbor.

At this point, I'm certain that even if I had a teleporter, I still wouldn't make it to work on time.

Matteo

I squeeze the familiar newspaper, peeking through the hole in the door.

"*You're welcome!*"

She wanted me to hear that. Can't blame her. I was a jerk.

I stand stone still, watching, hoping she can't see the shadow through her side of the door. She makes a face (pretty funny, actually, made even funnier by the fish-eye lens of the peephole), and I hold my breath as I wait for this woman to *finally* walk away.

After what seems like an hour, I hear her footfalls disappear down the hallway.

I let out my breath and knock my head slightly against the door. My mind races, trying to decipher this latest move.

Three years, I think. *Not in three years.*

Three years is exactly how long I've been receiving the newspapers.

Never once has one been delivered anywhere but my apartment.

Is it some sort of glitch?

A change?

Wait. A change.

Things might actually be changing. Finally.

As usual, the newspaper has arrived at the worst possible time.

"I don't have time for this!" I call out into the emptiness of my apartment.

My schedule doesn't matter. Not to The Serendipity.

I hold up the latest delivery, turn it over a few times in my hand, and scoff.

I know there's going to be a task typed somewhere in this stupid paper, something only I will be able to complete.

Harold needs a distraction. The distraction is named Margaret. They need to meet at a certain time on a certain day. *Samantha* is the ideal mate for Brent, who needs to order coffee from her to get the ball rolling.

And I'm the one who has to make these meetings happen.

Connector of people. Maker of matches. Arranger of happy endings.

Because I'm the *perfect* one for that job. The irony isn't lost on me. I don't even believe in "happily ever after." I assume that five or ten years down the road, all these "happy couples" are going to come to their senses and realize that real-life romance doesn't work out like it does in the movies.

I should know.

I start to mentally replay my reaction to the woman who knocked on my door.

I sigh. *Such* a jerk.

It's not her fault the paper landed on her doorstep. She was just trying to be nice. She has no idea what a strain this rolled-up burden brings.

I stare at it again.

Looks like my plans for the day have once again been derailed. I'll have to find another time to test the new recipes I've been trying to perfect so I can add them to the menu next week.

I close my eyes and start to count to ten.

I get to four when I start to scold myself. *Did you have to slam the door in her face?*

I blow out a breath. It doesn't matter. I don't want or need new friends, and I don't care what she or anyone else thinks of me.

Alone. I'm better off alone.

I walk over to the counter, take a deep breath, and begrudgingly spread the newspaper out. To everyone else, it's just a vintage newspaper, headlines written in a script-y font over innocuous stories about people they don't know.

To me? It's a curse.

I scan the text and black and white images neatly arranged under the banner that reads, *Serendipity Hall Ledger*.

Finally, I spot it. Near the bottom of page three. The article with my marching orders. Now, I just have to interpret the directive and carry it out.

Again. Like I've done for the last three years.

But it didn't come to me this time.

Maybe this is it.

Maybe since it was delivered to someone else, The Serendipity is finally getting the hint that I suck at this.

Maybe it will finally be over.

Then maybe, just maybe, I'll get a little peace and quiet.

Chapter Two
Iris

"Okay. Yes. Fine. He was good-looking, Brooke, but you're ignoring the most important part."

We're standing in the teacher's lounge, me waiting for my single cup of coffee to brew, and my co-worker Brooke wasting her one precious free hour. The things she'll do for even the hint of gossip.

I arrived at work coffee-stained, sticky, and twenty minutes late, and attempted to slip into the staff meeting already in progress. I tried to be stealthy so I didn't disrupt the principal, Mr. Kincaid—Charles—I have a hard time calling him by his first name, though he insists—but I might as well have been wearing a headband with sparklers on it. Everyone turned to look at me the second I opened the door.

And now, half the day has passed, and Brooke has been waiting to get what she expects is the salacious scoop about why I was late. Save for the coffee, the truth is, unfortunately, utterly lukewarm.

"I can't think of *anything* more important," Brooke says, still expecting drama. "Come on! You're hot and single."

"Ha."

"*He's* hot and single."

"Nobody said that—"

She continues like I'm not even talking. "The universe is practically forcing you together. You can't ignore that. *His* paper on *your* doorstep? It's the building. Has to be."

"Brooke, come on."

"I *knew* that place is magic." She spins in a circle. "Are there any apartments for rent? Or do you have a spare room? I just want to see it for myself."

I groan and roll my eyes. "It's *not* magic." I pick up my cup from under the spout of the Keurig machine, move down the counter, and pour in so much creamer that it hardly even tastes like coffee anymore. "And what kind of magic would it be? The kind that makes me late for work? The kind that makes me spill coffee all over my shirt?"

"The kind that brought you face-to-face with a hot neighbor." Brooke opens the refrigerator and pulls out two cups of yogurt, waving one in front of me.

"I can just dump this right on your shirt if you want, save you the time," she jokes.

"Hilarious," I deadpan.

She puts one carton back in the fridge, closes it, then removes the foil from the top of the other. "You're refusing to see what's right in front of you."

"Okay. Let's just say you're right, for argument's sake. If 'magic' brought me face-to-face with that jerk, it was only to remind me that just because someone is good-looking, it does not make them kind."

Even as I say it, a question enters my mind: Why is he so rude? Did something happen to make him that way?

Brooke must've seen the question on my face because she points her spoon at me. "Ha!"

"No. *No*, Brooke, I have zero interest. None."

She doesn't know that I'm determined to break my cycle

of picking the wrong guys. Of trying to talk someone into feeling a certain way about me. My new friends here don't need to know that I'm trying to be *less* . . . me. Less open. Less all-in. Less dramatic. Just . . . less.

You're a lot, Iris.

"Zero interest in who?" Liz Ridgeway pops in the lounge from the hallway but stops short and glares at the yogurt in Brooke's hand. "It's *you*." Her tone accuses.

"What's me?" Brooke's face is all innocence.

"You've been stealing my yogurt!" Liz shakes her head. "I thought it was Joyce."

Brooke slowly holds out the half-eaten cup to her, but Liz rolls her eyes. "Forget it. You owe me two Boston cream pies, one strawberry, and one of whatever that is." She takes a K-cup and moves toward the Keurig, then looks at me. "Did your building finally come through and find your soulmate?" Her eyes brighten.

"Oh, good *grief*," I groan. "Not you, too." I expected this reaction from Brooke, but I thought Liz was more level-headed.

"Look, Iris." Liz sets a cup under the spout of the machine and turns it on. It whirrs to life as she and Brooke exchange a glance. "If you were mysteriously brought together with someone, you should pay attention. That place is magic. Everyone says so."

I'd heard rumblings of magic in the building, but those are just silly superstitions, right? Despite Liz and Brooke's earnest expressions, I have to stick with logic. I'm trying to be more practical, which is why I need to save the magic for the movies. Would it be *so cool* if a mother and daughter really could switch places to gain a new perspective on each other's lives and struggles? Of course. But my life is not a Lindsay Lohan movie.

I'm not sure if I'm happy or sad about that.

"I don't believe in magic." I toss my stir stick in the trash. "It's not real! And if it were, it would be the kind of thing that happens to other people." I take a sip of my coffee, hearing the pathetic *nothing cool ever happens to me* in my own voice.

No. I do not need a *magic man* right now. Or any man. I promised myself I wouldn't make the same mistakes I've made a hundred times before. That's why I moved. That's why I'm here.

Mostly.

It's not like I left town because I ran through all the men there and needed a new hunting ground. But I did need the chance to figure out how to let logic—and not emotion—be the thing that drives my choices. "Emotion" would have me believing that I've magically stumbled upon a unicorn of a guy, the one person on the planet who might actually stick around. "Logic" knows better.

Logic knows that people leave. Or—maybe more to the point—people don't stay. Those might seem like the same thing, but they absolutely are not.

Which is why I cannot buy into the "magic" or "romance" of a building—*a building? Really?*—because if it *were* true—which it obviously isn't—I would hope it would try to match me with someone nicer.

I turn and add a little more creamer to my cup.

"Why do you even bother with the coffee?" Brooke stares at the near-white liquid in my mug. "You might as well just pour some sugar in a cup, stir in some cream, and drink it like a shot."

"Ooh, good idea," I say, faux-happy. "I'll do that tomorrow."

"Don't disregard The Serendipity, Iris," Liz says, stuck on this. "You can look it up. Whole articles have been written about it." She points at me. "*Magic.*"

I lean against the counter as Brooke shoots the empty

yogurt cup at the garbage can, missing and hitting the wall. "And the thing about magic is . . ." She walks over and picks up the cup, steps a few feet back, shoots . . . and misses again. "You don't have to believe in it for it to be real."

I frown. "Oh, my gosh. You're *actually* serious."

Up until now, I thought this was a *wink, wink* kind of suggestion, but I realize I was wrong.

Brooke picks up the cup one more time and, this time, does a little move and tosses it into the garbage can. She whips around and points double pointer fingers at me.

"*First try,*" she says in a funny voice.

I roll my eyes, but I smile and shake my head.

Liz holds up a hand. "I know you're not from here—"

"I'm not from Zimbabwe, I'm from like an hour away," I interject.

"—*but*," she continues, leaning on her tone, "there is plenty of evidence to back up the claim. My uncle met his wife because of that building."

I give her a look. "Because of a *building*?"

"Yes. Absolutely."

I muse. "A building told them they should meet."

She nods and shrugs. "That's the story. She lived there when it was a dorm."

"The Serendipity is special," Brooke says. "If you were lucky enough to get an apartment in that building, it's because the building has a plan for you, you know—"

"Romantically," Liz says, finishing the thought.

I laugh. "Okay. Pause. I love a good folk tale as much as the next girl . . ." They lean in. "But as much as I hate to disappoint the *magic building*"—my words drip with massive verbal air quotes—"I'm not looking for romance."

Liz purses her lips and tilts her head at Brooke. "Huh. They never are."

I shake my head at them. "You guys. I'm not just saying it. I really am *not* looking for romance."

Looking for romance has only ever gone horribly wrong for me.

"Why?" Brooke asks. "You don't want to fall in love? Love is awesome."

I think about the string of relationships I've had, each one a carbon copy of the one before. Always going all in. Jumping without looking. Believing each one is *the* one. Too much, too fast, too quick, or too deep never occurred to me.

But it was exhausting. It *is* exhausting. And last summer, I finally realized something needed to change. I realized the easiest way to stop heartbreak is to stop falling for the wrong guys.

Since "the wrong guys" were—and are—the only ones I seem to be drawn to, I've quit. Or . . . paused. New job. New city. A fresh start.

This is a cycle I'm determined to break.

"It's just not for me," I say. "I've tried it before—" I look at them. "Didn't go my way."

Brooke opens the fridge and takes out another cup of yogurt. She turns to Liz, eyebrows up, and Liz slowly shakes her head. Brooke, without breaking eye contact, slowly nods and peels up the corner of the lid.

Liz sighs. "Fine, thief. But now you owe me five."

Brooke pumps a fist and rips it open. Then, to me, she says, "Maybe this guy—this *hot neighbor*—is the one to change all that."

"Yeah, no. Hard pass. Matteo Morgan is not the kind of guy I'd be looking for even if I *was* interested in a relationship."

"*Matteo?*" Liz says this on a sigh, as if his name conjures anything other than annoyance. "Sounds like a hot guy name."

She looks at me. "Sounds like a hot guy name, and the building is telling you that you shouldn't just dismiss him."

I shake my head. "I have to go. I have fourth graders."

I do have to go. And I do have fourth graders.

I turn to leave, and as I do, I hear the two of them chant a sing-songy "Ooh, *Matteo*...!" behind me.

"I'm calling HR." I toss a look over my shoulder as I head to my room.

Chapter Three
Iris

I LOVE TEACHING ART.

I also love fourth graders. Sometimes people can't handle that age, but I think they're hilarious. And brutally honest. When do people lose that trait, I wonder.

Sometimes people give up on a "big dream" and become a teacher because there was nothing else for them to do, but not me. I always wanted to be a teacher. I've always believed that everyone is an artist . . . until age and work and the grind of the real world beats it out of them.

My goal has always been to keep kids creating as long as possible.

I've only been here at Spring Brook for a few months, and I am still finding my footing. But I already have a soft spot for a few kids—usually the ones everyone else has given up on—and some who still think art is dumb and they're too cool to finger paint. I'm also getting used to the fact that the point of this job change is to also change my direction in life.

"You're in a holding pattern, Iris," my best friend Charlotte said on one of our FaceTime calls. "Stuck. Doing the same things and expecting a different result. That's the definition of insanity, you know."

I groaned. "You sound like one of those twenty-year-old influencers trying to be a life coach."

She smiled. "You know I'm right."

And I did. Because she was. I was in a rut, and while I had a decent job in the Boston suburbs, it was too same-y. Too routine. No inspiration. Plus, my personal life was a mess. Searching for the right person while surrounding myself with the wrong ones.

"Maybe it's okay to take time and figure out what you really want," Charlotte said. "Stop trying so hard to fall in love and just be open to whatever life brings your way."

I suppose she would know. Over the past year, she'd married the love of her life and moved to Chicago to start her dream job. I was happy for her, of course, but I couldn't deny that a part of me was feeling sad for myself. Charlotte was like family to me, and while I wanted her to go and live her life, it still seemed to prove what I'd believed since I was thirteen—people always leave.

As I watched her drive away in the U-Haul, I thought about what she'd said. I thought about how staying where I was felt . . . repetitive, somehow. A hamster wheel.

So, I made a decision.

Time for a change. Not just a mental change, but a location change too. This time, I'm doing things differently. No more jumping into relationships. No more desperate pleas for love and attention. No more believing I can love someone enough for the two of us or inventing excuses to make cruel people seem sympathetic.

So far, my plan hasn't exactly worked. I still feel like the old Iris, and I still feel the pull to be everyone's friend, and I *definitely* feel the urge to find out more about Matteo.

Blech. Thinking about his jerky face makes me mad that I like thinking about his jerky face.

Do not make up reasons for his behavior, Iris. Some people are just jerks. Full stop. I've spent years excusing bad behavior like his—and I'm not doing that anymore.

Still, I wonder if it's lonelier to keep everyone on the perimeter, at arm's length, or to try really hard to pull someone in and never quite succeed.

I'm so lost in thought as I walk down the hall toward my classroom that I don't see Mr. Charles Kincaid—I guess I'm calling him by all of his names now—until he says, "Alarm malfunction this morning, Iris?" He's standing in the doorway of his office, holding a cup of coffee and watching me.

Charles is an older man who started as a math teacher, and his promise to stick up for his staff and his dedication to value his teachers were the reasons I felt comfortable taking this job.

Also, he told me he knew nothing about art and gave me permission to pretty much do whatever I wanted to do in class.

He has a smile on his face, but he has every right to point out my tardiness, especially since it interrupted the staff meeting. I haven't worked here long enough to know whether it will go on my permanent record.

"Mr. Kincaid!" I swipe my mental whiteboard clean and focus. "I'm so sorry I was late this morning. It was an off morning, for sure. There was a pant leg issue, and a rogue travel mug, and . . ." I point at my stained shirt.

He holds up a hand, chuckling. "Fair enough. Just wanted to make sure you're doing okay," he says kindly. "I should've checked in sooner to make sure you're settling in and have everything you need."

"I am, and I do." I say this in my most professional, reassuring voice. I really have been loving my job. Big feelings are welcome in elementary school, so it's a good fit.

Sometimes it feels like the only time I'm really myself is when I'm talking to my students.

I force myself to smile at Charles. "It's just another . . . manic . . . Monday." I manage to stop speaking before adding the "oh-ay-oh."

Mr. Charles Kincaid might be from the right era, but by the blank expression on his face he never had a Bangles poster in his room. He studies me, and I can practically feel him trying to convince himself I don't need a mental health day.

He gives his head a little shake, then says, "Have you landed on a date for the art show?"

The words are so uncomfortable, it's like I'm being fed through a high-powered sewing machine. "Oh, no, not yet."

"Still not convinced the students need to display their work?" He takes a sip of coffee.

"No, it's not that, they're brilliant—a few who are actually really, *really* talented." I already tried to get out of this, but clearly it didn't work. Spring Brook likes to have a dedicated art show. I should be thrilled. They want to celebrate the kids and art! How many schools do that anymore?

A memory resurfaces. I'm standing in the lobby outside my high school gymnasium. The one day all school year when this space isn't about sports. I'd been awarded first prize in a local art competition, so my teacher, Mrs. Akers, created a whole section dedicated to the pieces in my senior portfolio. Every single piece I'd created was on display.

Mrs. Akers was so proud. And so excited. It was the first time someone from my school won this award, which came with a scholarship and a beautiful blue ribbon.

I stared at the ribbon as my classmates and their parents wandered around, the quiet hum of "This is amazing" and "You're so talented" filling the air.

Charlotte looped her arm through mine and squeezed. "It's incredible, Iris."

I smiled, but my eyes clouded over with tears. Because while all the other kids were showing off their hard work to their parents, I only had Charlotte. And while she was the best kind of friend, she wasn't my family.

I really wanted to make my parents proud.

My mom had already told me she'd be coming right from work and might be late, but I'd heard nothing from my dad. I pulled out my phone to see if he'd texted, but there was nothing.

I shove the memory aside and look at Mr. Charles Kincaid, absently thinking I should call my mom. She and her husband Richard moved to Toledo when I was in college, but Toledo sometimes feels like another planet. Our relationship is good, but it's hard to stay close when you're miles apart.

I look at my boss. "I'll look over the school calendar and get you a date," I say with a firm nod. Because this art show is not about me.

I just don't want what happened to me to happen to another kid.

"By the end of the week," he says.

"Yes, sir."

He nods, and before he can say anything else, I smile brightly and inhale a sharp breath. "Well, I'm off. Lots to do!"

I wave quickly at Joyce, the school receptionist, and rush down the hall, into the quiet of my classroom. Once I'm safe inside, I let out a heavy breath and take a seat behind my desk, willing myself to focus on my students, their art projects, and my much-needed job.

But for some reason, as the kids file in from the hallway, the only thing I can think about is the intensity in the very dark brown eyes I encountered this morning.

And a single word zips through my mind: *Magic.*

Chapter Four
Iris

DID anyone ever write a song about Tuesdays?

A quick search on my phone doesn't show many, but "Tuesday Moon" by Neutral Milk Hotel sounds fascinating.

I stumble through another strange morning. I start to question whether I was ever a competent, put-together adult, because I seem to have become someone who can't make it out of my apartment on time or unstained.

I may have finally reached the age where I'm not able to stay up after midnight and still function the next day.

Tragic.

I vault through the process of getting ready, grab a package of Pop-Tarts from the cupboard, and rush into the hallway.

I take one step out the door and I feel something beneath my foot.

There, now creased in half, is a rolled-up newspaper on my welcome mat.

Again?

I let out a frustrated groan as I narrow my eyes, like

there's a tiny Matteo Morgan inside the pages and he can see how annoyed I am that *his stuff* is on *my mat.*

A tiny piece of me is intrigued that I might get to see him again.

But only a tiny piece.

I lock my door and storm down the hall, dramatically dropping the paper on the floor outside of his probably fancy corner apartment, hoping there is a hidden camera somewhere recording my overacted release.

As the paper drops, I notice *he* does not have a welcome mat.

Figures.

"Nice to meet you *too*, new neighbor who took time out of her busy morning to return something that *belongs to me* . . ." I mumble the words under my breath as I adjust the strap of my bag and start back down the hall toward the stairs.

I'm about to walk past my apartment when something stops me.

There's a rolled-up newspaper on my welcome mat.

Wait. Is that . . . ?

I lean back and peer down the hall toward Matteo's apartment. The newspaper I've just dropped outside his door is gone.

I look back at the one in front of my door. Then at his. Then at mine.

Surely that can't be the same paper.

I didn't hear his door open, but maybe he grabbed it when I had my back turned?

But that doesn't explain why there is another newspaper at my door. I'm certain there hasn't been another person in this hallway since I walked out of my apartment.

I pick it up and turn it over. Like the others, it's wrapped in a plastic sleeve with an address label stuck to the outside. Also like the others, it's addressed to Matteo Morgan.

Super hot chef and owner of Aria, a little Italian bistro down the block and around the corner.

Ok, so, *maybe* I googled him. And yeah, *maybe* I lingered a little too long on the photo I found of him in his chef's whites, turned to the side, holding the knives. And *maybe* I will deny that with the full force of the Acting 101 class I took in college when I was trying to figure out what I wanted to do with my life.

I look once more toward the door of his corner apartment and tromp back down the hall. I drop it again in front of his door and stare at it.

Stay. There.

I wait a good ten seconds, then turn away to walk back down the hall and stop again.

There's a rolled-up newspaper on my welcome mat.

I look back at his, and the one I left there is gone.

Okay. Okay. Now I'm bewildered and annoyed.

I march back to my apartment, grab the paper, march back to his, and set it in front of his door. Again.

Instead of turning, I walk backwards down the hall, eyes locked on the paper, until I'm right in front of my door. The paper stays put, as papers should.

"Ha-*HA!*" I say, triumphantly. I relax my shoulders and look down.

There's a rolled-up paper on my welcome mat.

I whip my head back to his apartment, and the paper I just set there is gone.

What?!

If this is some kind of joke, it's really not funny. But I don't have time to figure out what's happening. I can't be late for work again.

Mr. Charles Kincaid will not be happy.

I grab the paper, and this time, I walk halfway down the hallway and chuck it overhand toward his door. While it's still mid-air, I turn back to my door in time to watch a rolled-up newspaper *appear* from *nowhere* and drop in front of my door as if someone has just thrown it.

I gasp. *What. Is. Happening?*

Magic, my brain says.

"Shut up," I retort.

There's no such thing.

"Fine," I say out loud, to no one. "*Fine.* Think you can outsmart me? Ha! I'm an *art teacher.*"

I take the paper from my door in one hand, and in the other I grab my phone. I confidently walk down to Matteo's door.

If there's someone playing a trick, I'll catch them, I think.

I open the camera, zoom in on my welcome mat, and hit record. Holding the camera pointed down the hall at my door, I drop the paper in front of his.

Looking at the screen, I see there isn't a paper in front of mine. I look down, and the paper still sits right in front of his door.

"Ha! There! See?" I keep the camera on my mat as I walk back to my door. Still aiming the camera on it, I look back at his door.

The paper is still there.

I start narrating.

"So, someone has been trying to play a prank this morning with a stupid newspaper that keeps appearing in front of my door. It must be a magic trick or something, but I think I finally outsmarted whoever is pranking me. See?" I whip the camera down to Matteo's door, and there still sits the paper. "Paper. By his door. *His* paper, *his* name, *his* problem."

I turn the phone back to my mat . . . which is still empty. "And there! Look! No paper!"

I swing the camera around at my face.

"Take that, *magic building.*"

I click off the camera and look down.

There's a rolled-up paper on my welcome mat.

I cover my mouth and stare at it in disbelief. My eyes are wide as I search the halls for some sort of hidden camera or something—anything—to explain what is happening.

But no. There's not.

There's just a rolled-up newspaper on my welcome mat. There has to be a logical explanation for this.

Drugs? No. Gas leak causing hallucinations? Plausible.

I start sniffing around the hallway, trying to find a tell-tale rotten egg smell. That *has* to be it. I angle up and down, moving around like a bloodhound having a breakdown. I don't realize what I'm doing or how I look until my elderly neighbor opens her door to find me on all fours, nose pressed against her door jamb.

I look up at her face, which is a mix of surprise and confusion.

"Oh! Ha, ha, I was . . . erm . . ." I frantically look around and pretend to grab something from the floor. ". . . I was just looking for this, uh . . . pen cap! Found it!"

I try to shrink as I get up and plaster on a huge smile.

"Are you having an episode?" the woman asks me.

"I'm all good!" I wave at her. "Gotta go!" I turn and shuffle down the hallway.

Brooke and Liz have gotten in my head. That's all this is. I'm imagining things. Or maybe I'm still asleep. Stuck in a dream state. Right? That's it. I'm still stuck in a dream.

MAGIC, my brain insists.

"I said, shut *up* already," I tell my brain.

I pinch the thin skin of my wrist. It hurts. So . . . definitely awake. Definitely think my mind is playing tricks on me.

That happens sometimes, right?

As I briskly walk down the hall to the stairs, I glance at the rolled-up newspaper on my welcome mat.

I try to tell myself that when I get back home after school today, the newspaper will be gone.

I walk outside toward the parking garage, and when I get in the car and turn on the engine, the radio, turned up at full blast, shouts at me, *Do you believe in magic?*

I flip it off and force myself to take three slow, deep breaths.

But as I pull out of my parking place, I can't help but thinking . . . *maybe I do.*

Chapter Five
Matteo

THE NEWSPAPER DOESN'T LIKE to be ignored. I learned that the hard way three years ago.

And just saying that makes it sound like the newspaper—or more to the point, this building—actually has a personality.

It does. And it's comically vindictive.

I've been inadvertently coerced to orchestrate happiness for dozens of people who have lived in this building over the years—and dozens more who only stumbled into the building to visit a friend or family member. People who never realize I've done anything at all.

This building? It has a mind—and a plan—all its own. And yes, I do realize that this doesn't make sense. But I gave up on trying to figure it out a long time ago.

What I know is that the newspaper brings people together—long-lost lovers, rekindled romances, fractured families—and it uses me to do it. The Serendipity has made me into some kind of tailor for trauma, sewing the pieces of people's lives back together.

It's ironic. Maybe even cruel.

Thankfully, it's not always about bringing lonely, lovelorn

people together. Once, the newspaper practically turned me into a detective to figure out a crime was going to be committed at a local tea shop so I could set things up ahead of time to prevent it.

How the building knew the future is beyond me. Those are the kinds of questions that never get answered.

Another time, I had to rescue a German shepherd from an abusive owner. And a few months ago, with the paper's prodding, I found the perfect tutor for a dyslexic teenager. And nobody knew I'd been involved at all.

Thanks to this paper, I make people happy. While remaining just barely north of miserable myself. After all, I know how fleeting happiness really is.

Not that the newspaper cares what I think.

I hate that I think about "the magic" and "the newspaper" as if they were people, or a tangible thing. I know how it sounds, but it's just something I've accepted: I live in a magic building. Magic newspapers land at my door.

The worst thing? If I don't carry out the wishes laid out in black and white on the pages of this mysterious newspaper, there are consequences. Nothing sinister—more like practical jokes. Like I said, the newspaper has a personality, and it seems to fancy itself a prankster. But its "pranks" are so disruptive that I'm better off doing what it tells me to do in the first place.

If I'd known the apartment would come with this bonus job, I wouldn't have taken over the lease from my grandpa when he announced he was headed off on what he called "a grand adventure." I was happy he was going—he deserved to do something fun. But when he mentioned he wasn't sure how long he'd be gone, I got a little concerned.

"Don't worry about me, Teo," he'd said. "I just need a change of scenery." My grandma hadn't been gone long, and I knew the apartment was full of reminders of her. I also knew he wasn't ready to let go of this place, so I wasn't surprised when he asked me to move in and "keep an eye on the place."

I needed a change of scenery too.

I soon realized that my grandpa had left out some very important details about living in this building.

We all assumed his "adventure" would be short-lived and he'd come home after a few months, but he met an Italian woman named Elena and moved to Tuscany.

That rascal.

I picture him sipping coffee on the terrace of a pristine beige and tan villa, next to a sprawling chianti vineyard, breathing in myrtle and cypress, eating the food of Tuscany—the *panzanella*, the *castagnaccio*, the *cantuccini*—and living his best life.

I glance at the photo he sent—him and Elena, smiling broadly on a gondola in Venice. I stare at the image, stuck to my refrigerator with a plain black magnet. I don't have to turn the photo over to remember what he wrote on the back:

It is possible to love again.

Uffa.

I open the refrigerator and pull out the coffee beans, then move over to the counter to start my morning ritual. Grind beans. Boil water. Make breakfast—today, an omelette with some leftover *prosciutto*, mushrooms, and tomato—and sit down at the table and eat.

Slowly. I like to taste my food. And I've learned to appreciate the slow morning when I know what kind of chaos will come later. For me, mornings are sacred, which is why the disruptive nature of a newspaper that shows up whenever it wants to feels like plain old bad manners.

Which is why I often think about moving. I'm not sure if I've been hanging on to this apartment because of its proximity to the restaurant or because I'm too sentimental about the summers I spent here with my grandparents to let it go—but my life would be a heck of a lot easier without the constant interruptions.

I think of what my grandpa said when I finally got up the nerve to ask him if he knew what was happening—and why. He chuckled, almost like he'd been waiting for this, and told me to "be open to whatever the building brings you, Teo."

Open? To a building?

"It chose you for a reason," he said. I argued with him, telling him *he* was the one who'd asked me to move in.

He smiled and handed me a newspaper.

On page six, circled with a highlighter, was a small pull quote in the middle of a larger story.

If you're looking for someone to trust with all you've done, look no further than your grandson. He needs to find himself again.

Cryptic and plain at the same time.

He added, "And it won't let you go until you've figured it out."

The memory makes me pause because I don't think I've figured anything out except that I'm not a good matchmaker, I still don't believe in love, and I really don't need people complicating my life.

I look slightly past the photo on the fridge, the one of him and Elena in Venice, and I see, stuck under the same magnet, the highlighted section of that very paper, ripped out.

Someone to trust, I think. *More like someone to dump on.*

I'm better off alone. Life decided that for me, and I don't need some magic building to remind me of it.

After I drink my first coffee, eat my omelette, and finish getting ready for the day, I head downstairs and walk outside, inhaling the chilly January air as I walk down the block and around the corner to work.

The sign on the front of the building comes into view, prompting another morning ritual. "All for you, Aria," I whisper to myself, pushing back memories of late nights and quiet dreams and the way she convinced me that one day, I could open the restaurant I'd always dreamed of.

She was right. I did it.

I grit my teeth and will away the memories that try to surface. It happens every time I realize I'm talking about her in the past tense.

She isn't here to see it. And I know the pain of that will never go away.

I let one memory slip through.

At night, after a long shift, we were unwinding with a glass of wine, in pajamas, snuggled under heated blankets, talking the dreamy talk only soulmates can indulge in.

As usual, she prodded me to talk about what I'd do differently if I finally had the chance to run my own kitchen.

In my mind I can see the light of the fireplace in her eyes, the way she tipped her head down and raised her eyebrows, and I knew exactly what she was thinking.

Stop. Stop it.

I shake myself to the present and look up at the logo on the front of the building.

This place is the result of those late-night conversations. Aria, the restaurant—*our* restaurant—is exactly what we intended it to be—small, intimate, and sought-after, featuring the special family dishes my grandma taught me to make in the kitchen of the very apartment where I live now.

"Food brings people together, Teo," she said, hands floured, pinching *tortellini*. "Don't forget that. And don't underestimate how important it is."

That's why I started cooking. I was a young, idealistic chef with a mission to *connect people through delicious food.*

But that's not why I cook now.

Now I cook because the kitchen is the only place where life makes sense.

I walk the familiar path around to the back of the building and enter through the kitchen. My manager, Val, is standing near a counter next to our pastry chef, Nicola, and their best friend, the espresso machine. It's the smaller one, mostly used by staff, relegated to the kitchen when we upgraded to a much larger, fancier machine last year.

Nicola convinced me that genuine Italian espresso was an essential part of the dessert experience, and she was right. The machine has paid for itself two times over already.

"Chef!" Val calls as I walk in.

I wave as she holds up what will be my second coffee of the day. It's routine by now, a rite of passage, as if the only way to gain access to the kitchen is to accept the fine gift of espresso.

It's the same every day. And I like it that way.

No surprises.

Nicola faces me. Her blond hair is pulled into a tight ponytail, and she's wearing an expression I instantly recognize —the look of success.

I don't say anything as she produces a small plate from behind her back. On it sit three cannoli, the recipe Nic's been trying to perfect for months.

I can see the flakiness of the crust, the creaminess of the filling . . . *wait*. That's custard. Not ricotta. It's also baked, not deep-fried.

Venetian. Not Sicilian.

Judging by the smug look on her face, she's confident she's finally done it, but she and I both know I'm the only one who can judge whether she's figured out Grandma Vivi's recipe.

I motion for her to hand it over, and when I take the first bite, I'm instantly transported back to big family dinners and holiday parties, to hiding under the kitchen table when my parents thought I'd gone to bed just to sneak another cannoli when nobody was looking.

Ever since she started at Aria about a year ago, Nicola has had one task—to perfect Grandma Vivi's cannoli. I gave her no recipe, only a blindfolded taste, and finally, after many *nearly there* attempts, I think she got it.

But I let her sweat for a few more minutes as I slowly chew another bite.

She and Val are both staring at me now, wide-eyed and hopeful.

"Come *on*, Teo," Val says. "Did she get it?"

I pause, letting the flavors settle as I look for every key ingredient, including the Marsala wine she's left out so many times.

She stares at me, hopefulness on her face, waiting, until finally, I reach out and give her a Paul Hollywood handshake. "You got it, Nic."

Nicola gasps, grabs my hand and shakes it, then picks up the rest of the cannoli and finishes it off in one bite. "I got it!" she says, mouth full. "Woo-hoo!"

She and Val do a celebratory dance as I take a sip of coffee, then pick up another cannoli and take a bite. It's Grandma Vivi in a dessert. My heart pangs with grief, a reminder of the love I've lost.

Food has a way of awakening things, bringing the past into the immediate present.

"Did the produce arrive?" I ask, setting down the mug.

Val stops dancing and looks at me. "You know, you *could* celebrate for a tiny second."

I frown. I don't celebrate. She should know this.

Val widens her eyes with a weird nod toward Nicola, then back to me. There's a hidden message here I'm supposed to pick up on, but I have no idea what it is.

She sighs. "Really proud of you, Nic. You are amazing." She says in what I'm guessing is an impersonation of me.

"That's what I sound like?" I muse.

"No," she quips, "because you never give compliments."

I shrug. People don't usually deserve them.

She scowls at me. "Yes, the produce arrived. It's all ready for you." She motions for me to hand over the empty plate, and as I do, I don't miss the disappointed expression that seems to indicate I'm going to get an earful later.

I look at Nicola, who's moved on to washing raspberries. I feel a nudge in the back of my mind that feels like Aria. I walk over to Nicola. "Good job, Nic. Really."

She looks over at me, eyes wide. "Well, thank you, Chef!"

Val quirks a brow that seems to ask, *Now, was that so hard?*

I make a mental note to be more complimentary.

It's not that I don't value the staff—I do—but I get busy and distracted and forget to let people know. It's something Val has brought up more than once. It's why she's here—to keep everyone on task and point out shortcomings, even mine.

She's one of two people in the world I trust to do that.

The other is most likely tanning on a veranda in Tuscany.

I walk over to the counter where Val has stacked the produce. I look through the carrots and potatoes and leeks, making sure we'll have what we need for today's lunch and dinner service.

"So, Chef . . ." Nicola says from behind me.

"Yes, Nic." I don't turn around. Instead, I pull a small notebook from my back pocket and look over one of the new recipes I've been working on at home—*maiale al latte*—a milk-braised pork loin.

"Val and I were, um, we were just talking . . ."

I don't even have to look at her to know where this is

headed. I can tell by the cautious tone of her voice. "Not interested," I say.

"You don't even know what she's going to say," Val says in a reprimanding tone.

"Did you call in extra help for the weekend?" I ask, moving the potatoes from a basket to a colander.

"Don't change the subject," Val says.

"We have that big bridal party," I say. "We're going to need more wait staff."

"Yes, I called in more help," Val says. "Can you just listen to Nicola for five seconds?"

I sigh. "I don't need to listen. I already know what she's going to say." I look up at Nic. She looks back, eyebrows raised, face hopeful.

"She's wonderful," Nicola says. "I promise."

"Not interested." I move the colander to the prep sink and run water over the potatoes.

"Why?" Val asks. "Just go out for a drink. You don't have to marry her."

At that, my jaw tenses. "I don't have time." It's technically true, but it's not the reason I don't date.

They know this.

"We both find time," Nicola indicates to herself and Val.

"You don't own a restaurant." *Or have my history.* I turn the water off, then repeat the process with the carrots. "And Val doesn't date."

"I date," she says.

"You're married," I counter. "And Bear works here."

"Yeah." She gives a shrug, as if to say, "What's your point?"

"When was the last time you actually went out on a date?" I turn the water off and face her, waiting while her eyes scan the air overhead. After an appropriate pause, I say, "That's what I thought."

The back door opens, and Bear walks in, as if on cue.

Val shoots him a look, and he freezes. "Whoa. What's that look for?"

"You need to take your wife out more," I say.

Val crosses her arms as Bear's gaze jumps from me to Val and back again. But then, as if to prove my point, he holds out his arms and says, "When would I have time for that?"

I shoot Val a *See?* look and go back to prepping while Nicola moves around to the opposite side of the counter to face me. Val whips a towel at Bear, and they walk out of the kitchen, presumably so he can apologize.

I settle in and prepare for whatever sales pitch Nic is about to feed me.

"So, Danny's sister is going through a divorce—"

I hold up my hand without looking at her.

"She's really great, just in a bad situation—"

"No." I feel like I'm repeating myself.

"She's not falling apart or anything. Just . . . lonely."

The word is like a shock to my system. Because I know a little something about lonely. But I've grown comfortable with my solitude, no matter how much my employees—or a stupid magic building—try to force people on me.

And here I thought I could go a good half-hour without thinking about the building.

"Nicola, I appreciate you wanting to take care of me, really. But let's stick to desserts and espresso and leave my love life out of it, okay?"

Her face falls. "I'm sorry, I don't mean to push, I just . . ." She pauses. "I'm worried about you, Chef," she says. "We aren't meant to be alone."

"Apparently some of us are," I mutter, grabbing my knife roll.

I don't have to glance up to feel how her face looks. I can be a real piece of work sometimes.

Hiring Nicola changed our relationship. We'd been friends

back in culinary school—she and her then-boyfriend, Mark, and Aria and me. Good friends, actually.

But now that she works for me, she's not a friend anymore. At least, I can't see her as a friend anymore. She's an employee.

The problem is that she might be right, and I don't like it.

I try to soften. It's difficult when people are constantly pressing on an open wound.

"I apologize. I didn't mean to brush you off like that. I'm actually good with it, Nic," I say. "This is how I prefer it."

"Yeah. I know," she says, with an *oh, ooo-kay* undertone. "I know you've convinced yourself you're better off alone." She chews the inside of her lip thoughtfully. I'm about to change the subject when she says, "I know you miss her."

The sting of her words sparks something inside me.

A mental image of blue and red lights surrounding an overturned car flashes through my mind.

I look up.

"I do. But I'm not doing this right now. Let's drop it," I say.

She goes still. I look back at the vegetables on the counter, relying on muscle memory to chop them because my mind is elsewhere.

Nicola walks around to the side of the counter and lays a hand on mine.

I stop cutting.

It might be the first time someone else has touched me in months. It reminds me of what I'm missing. It reminds me how it felt to connect to another person. Even on a purely platonic level.

"It's been six years, Matteo," she says. "And I know Aria wouldn't want you to spend the rest of your life miserable and alone."

"Miserable?" I scoff.

She raises her eyebrows at me as if to say, *I mean* . . .

"I'm good, Nic," I repeat. "I promise."

"But—"

Enough. I can't talk about this. A familiar mental gate slams shut.

"I said I'm good." I cut her off with a stern look, pulling my hand back. "I need to get everything ready for lunch service."

Her smile looks more like a wince as she nods, makes a fist, gently knocks it twice on the counter, then walks out of the kitchen.

Finally, I'm where the universe has decided I should be.

Alone.

Chapter Six
Iris

I DIDN'T TELL Brooke and Liz about the newspaper.

They would've jumped at the chance to talk about magic and matchmaking and my so-called mystical building.

The problem is that I thought about it all day today.

As I sit in my car at a red light a couple blocks from home, I'm still a healthy mix of intrigued and freaked out.

I muddled through work, struggling to concentrate as I tried to find a reason for what I thought I saw that morning. Because if what I think I saw was what I actually saw, then Houston, we have a problem.

Either I've started hallucinating. Or my building really is magic.

Hallucinating is more likely, right? Concerning? Sure. But more likely. I'm sure my mind was playing tricks on me. One of my exes, a guy who called himself *Ace*, convinced me for months that he wasn't cheating—I just had an overactive imagination.

Maybe that's all this is.

Only . . . Ace really *was* cheating. So, that theory doesn't hold.

Normally, I stick around the school for at least an hour after the final bell, but today, I bolt like I am avoiding a behind-the-school fight. I *need* to see if the newspaper is still outside my door.

My leg starts bouncing in anticipation as I park my Toyota Corolla in the parking garage next to The Serendipity. If I get upstairs and that newspaper is still outside my door, I'll march straight down to my grumpy neighbor's apartment and demand an explanation.

How exactly will that go?

I tried to throw your newspaper, and it basically teleported back to my door. It only moves when I'm not looking, so what's the deal?!

I groan. Here come the men in the little white coats, asking me to remain calm.

I only now notice that my leg is still bouncing. I put my hands on my knee to try to quell my obvious nervousness.

"Okay. Let's do this."

I hop out and grab my bag and water bottle from the back seat. I contemplate calling Brooke. She's been begging for an invite to my place, and maybe I shouldn't be alone right now. I pull out my phone and start to dial but change my mind and click it off.

If I'm having a breakdown, I need to have it on my own.

That's great advice, I think.

I try to act natural as I walk into the entryway, but I can feel my eyes darting around and the small hair on the back of my neck standing on end. Once I see that there's no one else around, I race through the lobby and straight into the stairwell. I bolt up three flights of stairs, skipping every other step, and when I reach the third floor, I stop, hand on the door handle and draw in a very slow, very deep breath.

"Everything is okay." But I hear the shake in my voice as I open the door to my floor. It's weird, but a small, tingly part of me wants it to still be there.

I peek around the corner and down the hall, squinting like a child watching a horror movie, not really wanting to see the scene in front of me but compelled to keep looking.

But when I sort out which door is mine, my eyes whip to the floor in front of it, and I let out a relieved sigh.

It's gone.

My sigh turns to laughter, and I shake away thoughts of delusion.

Hallucinations. My eyes *must* have been playing tricks on me. That or Matteo noticed it and picked it up on his way out of the building that morning.

"You need more sleep, Iris," I say out loud as I stick the key in my door, vowing to forego Netflix tonight in favor of actual rest.

I push the door open, and all the good feelings in my body disappear.

On the floor, just inside my door, is a rolled-up newspaper.

Inside my apartment.

Behind the locked door.

I stare at it.

I cock my head and stare at it longer.

In a daze, I slowly turn, close the door, hang up my bag, and then kneel down and gently reach out and pick up the paper.

Not a hallucination. It's real. I can feel it.

I turn it over and see the same name—*Matteo Morgan*—on the outside label. I run a finger over it, unsure what I'm looking for. Do I expect the words to come to life? Are the photos going to start to move? Is this paper like some kind of magic fortune cookie, rhyming riddles or predicting the future?

Ooh. Will it make me travel through time? Because I'd really love to find out who Jane Austen was imagining when she wrote Mr. Darcy . . .

Stop it, it's not real.
I shake it. I stand and move it around like a wand. Nothing.

It's just a paper. It's not exploding in my hand or playing music or turning me into a newt. The only thing special about it is that it's here, in my apartment.

And while I'm sure there is a logical explanation, I'm also sure that the only person who might know the answer is the man this newspaper belongs to.

I open the door, walk down the hall, and raise a fist to knock. But then I remember my first encounter with him, and I pause. I don't want to get a reputation as "that deranged single woman who moved in last fall."

I also don't want to handle rudeness right now.

I drop the paper at Matteo's door and pivot back the way I came, thankful when I don't see anything on my welcome mat. I go inside and close the door behind me. "Not going to try to figure out how that thing got inside," I say out loud as I open the refrigerator and pull out a Dr Pepper. "I'm sure there is a perfectly logical explana—"

But as I close the refrigerator and turn back around, I freeze. Because there, on the counter, is a *stack* of identical rolled-up newspapers.

What. The.

I back away from the fridge and go to set the Dr Pepper on the counter but completely miss, and it hits the floor—remarkably not exploding or spewing soda everywhere. I leave it, walking around the stack, studying it.

Then, in an impulsive rush, I gather all of the newspapers in my arms, fumble to open my door, and haphazardly toss the armload into the hallway and slam the door shut.

I feel a slight wisp of cool air move behind me—*were those chimes?*—and I tense up. Holding a breath, I close my eyes and spin around to face my apartment. I stand there for a second, not sure if I should listen to the part of me that doesn't want to open my eyes, or the part of me that *really does*.

Finally, I give in, and the second I do, I stare at what I see —newspapers everywhere.

On my couch. On the side table. There are newspapers stacked on my chandelier. I look over toward the kitchen table, and there is a stack of newspapers on each chair, staged in a mock family dinner.

I barely notice that my Dr Pepper is back on my counter, upright.

I blindly reach behind me and fumble for the door handle, kicking newspapers now stacked around my feet. Pulling open the door, I stumble out into the hallway to confirm that the newspaper I'd just set in front of Matteo's door is, in fact, gone.

It is.

Something inside me switches.

I'm not scared. I'm not freaked out.

I'm curious. And determined.

I want to find out how this is happening, and I decide that he must have the answers. I leave my door open as I head toward his apartment. Is he some sort of Harry Houdini? Is he the one playing tricks on me?

I answer zero of these questions before impulsively knocking—loudly—on his door.

It's the middle of the afternoon. There's no way he's actually home. Don't chefs work 24/7? And live in the kitchen? I feel like I read that somewhere.

I take a step closer to the door and lean in, as if I'll be able to hear anything in what I assume is an empty apartment. As I do, I glance down the hall and see newspapers sticking out of my doorway.

I bang on the door again.

Nothing.

After at least thirty seconds, I give up and walk away. It's probably better this way. What would I have even said to him?

I walk back down to my door and look inside.

They're everywhere.

I kick a pile of them back into the entryway of my apartment. As I do, I hear the sound of a door opening down the hall. I spin around and see Matteo step out of his apartment.

Seriously? He could've waited another minute before leaving after he just pretended not to be home.

"Hey, did you not hear me knock? I was—"

He nonchalantly locks his door and starts down the hall in my direction, eyes focused on the phone in his hand. My breath catches in my throat. He looks like he just stepped out of an ad for luxury clothing. Or high-end watches. One of those salons specializing in making people look extra hot. That's a thing, right?

I'm suddenly self-conscious, which is my least favorite way to feel. I absently run a hand over my shirt and stand up a little straighter, cross my arms, then uncross them and cross them back, trying not to think that he must be a pretty successful chef.

He *looks* expensive.

By contrast, I look like I work in an elementary school. There's a very good chance I have peanut butter in my hair.

Matteo doesn't seem to notice. In fact, he doesn't seem to notice me at all. In *fact*, he walks right past me without so much as a nod of acknowledgement.

This guy!

I'm so stunned, it takes me a slow three-count before I realize that yes, he really did that. He really was that rude to me. Would it have killed him to say hello? That's just basic human etiquette. Does he think he's too good to at least *wave* at his neighbor?

Yes, we're essentially strangers, but honestly. Would a simple "hello" have killed him?

I spin around on my heel and rush down the hall behind him. "Hey!"

No response.

"HEY! Excuse me?!"

He doesn't stop. He keeps walking toward the third-floor lounge area, reaching for the door to the stairwell.

"Hey!" I call out before he disappears. "Do you want to tell me what kind of trick you're playing?"

Now, he stops, hand still on the doorknob, and finally—finally—glances my way. He reaches up and takes AirPods out of his ears.

Okay, fine, while that does make his lack of acknowledgement a tiny bit more understandable, he does have eyes. Couldn't he see me standing in the hallway?

He frowns. "I'm sorry?"

His voice is low and deep, and it almost makes me forget that I'm really, really annoyed with him.

"Did you not see me? I was standing right—" I shake my head and scratch above my eyebrow. "Your newspaper?"

His eyes flicker, but he gives no indication that he understands.

"The newspaper. The *newspaper!*" I'm repeating it like he should just know what I mean. It's like someone playing charades who repeats the same motion over and over and expects you to guess something different.

He still looks confused.

"Putting it in front of my door was one thing, but *inside* my apartment?" I scoff. "I feel like this might actually be a felony. I don't know that for sure, but I'm going to find out. Do you have keys to my apartment? Do you know the owner of the building or something? I mean . . . I don't know how

48

you're doing it, but you need to stop, because that is a *total* invasion of pri—"

"I did what?" He cuts me off. The frown line deepens in his forehead. It's so deep, I assume it's a permanent fixture. I've known rude people before. I always—always—win them over. It often becomes a little bit of an obsession, which has only come back to bite me once.

Or maybe five times.

I try to remind myself at this moment to not do what I always do.

We'll see how that goes.

I soften a little when he drops his hand from the stairwell door and takes a step toward me. "What do you mean? What do you think I did?"

His voice is laced with genuine concern—whether it's for me or something else, I'm not sure—but by the way my body is responding to it, I must have decided it's for me.

I sigh, realizing in that moment that this is a really stupid thing to accuse him of. I'm blaming my desperation. I *need* that logical explanation.

"I . . ." I start, but then stop, trying to figure out how to explain this without raising red flags. But Matteo is the only other person who seems to be connected to these newspapers.

Who else am I supposed to ask about them?

I pinch the bridge of my nose and close my eyes so I'm not distracted by the weight of his attention.

"I put the paper at your door this morning," I say. "But it didn't stick."

"It didn't . . . stick?"

Now, I look at him. "It didn't stick. It didn't stay where I put it. I turned around and it was back at my door."

There's that look again. It's like he's caught or . . . guilty, somehow, and I know immediately he knows something but isn't saying it.

"I didn't have anything to do with that," he says flatly, changing his demeanor.

"I don't believe you."

He studies me, a little too intently, then shrugs. "Sorry."

I persist. "You have to know something! Your name is on the paper. Is that even normal? For there to be an address label on a newspaper?"

He shrugs again.

This is infuriating. I can *feel* that he knows something. Why won't he just tell me?

"And is it normal for me to come home from work and find a whole *stack* of newspapers on my kitchen counter?"

At that, his eyebrow twitches. "A stack?"

"A *stack*," I say again. "Was that you? Are you playing a joke on me? Seems a little strange since we just met and you *really* don't seem like the joking type, but you know, weirder things have happened. Probably."

His eyes narrow. "I've got to get back to work."

"I can prove it to you!" I motion for him to follow me back down the hall. He hesitates so long, I'm actually shocked when he starts walking in my direction.

I reach my still-open apartment door and say, "Here, Mr. Know-Nothing, how do you explain . . . *this!?*" Without looking, I hold up my arms as if it's *The Price is Right* and I'm displaying a brand-new car.

He peers past me, then looks at me.

"Nice apartment."

I scoff. "Nice?! What about all of the—"

I turn around. My apartment is completely empty.

Except for a Dr Pepper on the counter.

"What?!" I exclaim. "No, no, no, this was all covered, there were newspapers *everywhere*, and they just *appeared*, and they all had your name on them, and . . . ." I rush into my apartment, frantically moving things around, pulling up couch cushions.

"Can I go, or . . .?" He's standing in my doorway, motioning toward the stairwell.

I stand in stunned disbelief. "Great. Okay. Fabulous. Go back to work." I push my hands through my hair, frustrated when, as expected, my fingers snag on the peanut butter from Eliana Watson's sandwich. That's what I get for leaning in to help open fruit snacks at lunch. The kindergartner thought my hair was pretty, and when she reached out to touch it, she transferred a glob of Skippy straight to it.

I unglue my fingers from my hair and glance up to find that Matteo has disappeared from my doorway.

I sprint over and lean out just in time to see the stairwell door slowly closing, his footfalls retreating down the stairs.

I blow out a tense breath, closing my eyes and shaking my head at the ceiling. I know he knows what's going on. And even though he seems fixed on not telling me, I now have a new obsession . . . er, project.

Matteo Morgan.

I turn back to my apartment, glance at the counter, and let out a rueful laugh.

There, next to my Dr Pepper, is a neat stack of rolled-up newspapers.

Chapter Seven
Iris

SARCASTIC MAGIC. Lovely.

I can't get the fun, wrinkle-your-nose-and-a-pile-of-money-appears magic, no. I get the kind that makes you look like a buffoon.

It's fine. I'm fine. Everything's fine.

A part of me is freaking out—but it's offset by the other part of me, which is genuinely intrigued.

If my rude neighbor has the answers, he's not sharing them. Which is why I'm back in my apartment, pacing and staring. Back and forth, wearing out the boho rug I'd been so happy to purchase for my new apartment.

With hands on hips and a scrunched-up face plastered with determination, I blow out a breath and stare at the newspapers. "Okay, I just need to get rid of you. How hard can that be?"

I pick up the stack, shove them in a garbage bag, and take them outside to the dumpster. When I get back to my apartment, there is a new stack on the counter, only this time, they seem to have doubled in number, spilling onto the floor.

I can't have another newspaper tsunami. Maybe hiding them will stop them from multiplying. I pick them up and stuff them in the front closet. One falls out, but I kick it in and slam the door shut.

"There."

I turn around to find three new stacks surrounding my Dr Pepper.

With one solitary rolled-up newspaper on the end of the counter, pointing at me.

What is happening?

"I tried delivering these to the guy they're addressed to," I shout to my empty apartment. "It didn't work!"

I look down at the one newspaper on the end of the counter, and it moves, ever so slightly, toward me.

And then it gives a little wiggle.

Like *"Hey. Hey, buddy. Pick me up."*

I'm stuck inside a cartoon. I'm Aladdin, trying to figure out how a rug can have a personality. Finally, I give in and start talking to the newspaper like it's a person. "No. I'm not picking you up."

It wiggles again.

"*I said NO.*" I fold my arms. "Go bother someone else."

Then, moved by some unseen force, the paper launches at me and smacks me in the forehead.

"Ow! Hey!"

It flips back down onto the counter and wiggles again, and I get the distinct impression it's laughing at me.

"Okay, fine. Good grief, you didn't have to hit me," I say, rubbing my forehead.

The paper turns slightly away, like it's ashamed.

I frown. "You want me to read you?"

The paper spins around quickly, pointing at me and rolling back and forth.

I roll my eyes. "Okay, okay, calm down."

It raises up, mid-air, and rears back as if to launch at me again, and I quickly hold up my hands in defense.

"I'm sorry! I'm sorry! I'm sure you have, uh . . . a really nice font!"

It slowly lowers to point at me again and—still mid-air—moves at me twice and wiggles.

I heave a sigh, look up and around at the ceiling, certain someone must be watching me—then I pluck it out of the air. Like this is a completely normal occurrence.

As I turn it over, there's no more movement, like it's gone back to being just a newspaper. I glance up and see that all the other newspapers have disappeared.

"Guess I only need one, huh?" I sit down on the floor of my living room and open it.

It's not a thick paper, and it doesn't even seem to be connected to the town of Serendipity Springs. The banner at the top says *Serendipity Hall Ledger*.

I frown. Serendipity Hall?

I knew this building used to be a dorm and was converted into apartments in the 1960s. What in the world am I looking at right now?

I start to read the headlines.

Winnifred Waller Marries William St. George in Ceremony by The Springs

Advertising Mogul William St. George Credits Wife Winnifred With Award-Winning Campaign Idea

Weird. These seem to be all about the same person.

Beloved Philanthropist William St. George, Dead at Age 52

Yikes.

Winnifred St. George Will Die of Loneliness if Someone Doesn't Intervene

My mind trips on that last one.

I re-read it, noticing that unlike the other headlines,

which seem to recap what's happened in the past, this one seems to be written about something that hasn't happened yet.

I read on:

Winnifred St. George first came to Serendipity Springs as a young girl. She fell in love with the town, its architecture, and what she calls "the magical feeling that's always in the air." That magic was certainly at play when she first met William St. George while attending school at Spring Brook College.

While the two married and had a rich and full life, Winnie is now alone, living on the fourth floor of what was once Serendipity Hall, the same building her mother lived in as a student. Winnie's charitable donations have contributed to bettering several areas of her beloved town, with a special focus on the animal shelter, as Winnie is a devoted cat lover.

For years, Winnie has been very comfortable living on her own, but in more recent months, "alone" has turned to "lonely," leaving her mourning the many losses she's experienced in her life. This loneliness has made the once spirited lover of opera, swing dancing, and Italian food quite withdrawn. She no longer feels needed, and the absence of meaningful connections is causing her to give up.

Lately, she's been especially distraught over the loss of her beloved cat, Lenny, who was black with white paws and a white circle around one eye. Lenny was Winnie's constant companion, and this loss has felt like the final straw. Winnie hasn't left her apartment in weeks, and while she's certainly lived a lot of years, she still has many more to live . . . On Thursday of this week, Winnie should receive assistance.

Before it's too late.

A chill runs down my spine.

Before I set the newspaper down, I notice that all the other articles have vanished from the pages. I flip through, and the entire newspaper is blank, save for this one article.

This is what the newspaper wanted me to read.

But why?

I skim the article one more time, piecing together the life of Winnifred Waller St. George, getting a clear picture of not only her past, but—weirdly—also of her future.

I don't understand how this one story can predict things that haven't happened yet. And why did it land on my doorstep?

Wait. This had the brooding chef's name on it. Was it meant for him? If it was, it's not like *he's* going to do anything about an elderly widow who happens to live in the same building.

A thought hits me.

That's why the newspaper came to me.

Because it knows that unlike a cold-hearted man who can't even be bothered to say hello in the hallway, there's no way *I* can ignore this.

Magic.

I find I'm starting to settle down with that word, to not dismiss it out of hand.

As I cut out the article, the leftover pieces shimmer and dissipate, sparkling into tiny fragments of golden light until they disappear.

"Okay, that was kind of cool," I admit out loud, and the cut-out article flutters in my hand, as if it agrees.

I take the clipping and stick it to my refrigerator, my gaze lingering on the image of a lonely old widow who may or may not need help.

My eyes snag on the words "before it's too late."

I frown, again trying to apply logic to what is most definitely not a logical situation.

A magical disappearing newspaper addressed to someone else bullied me into reading an article about saving some old woman's life.

Am I doing this? Like, *really* doing it?

The question is rhetorical, of course, because unlike the chef, I actually like people. No way I'm not going to help.

The problem is, I don't know what to do. I don't know *how* to help Winnie.

And that is the thought that keeps me from falling asleep until very, *very* late.

Chapter Eight
Iris

SMACK

I get shocked awake, slurring a mealy "Whassthebig . . . hey . . .!"

My forehead hurts, and I crack my eyes open and peer at the side table where my alarm clock sits. A rolled-up newspaper obstructs my view of the time.

I open my eyes wider. "Did you just hit me again?"

The newspaper disappears with a wispy tinkling of chimes, leaving behind a golden, misty shimmer.

I can now see my clock.

Holy heck! I have twenty-six minutes to get to work. I jump out of bed and holler a quick, "Thank you!" to the magic building, because apparently, I'm going all-in on this now.

Somehow, I manage to get to work only two minutes late, and I'm immediately met at the back entrance by a woman with a dog.

"Is this the way we should go in?" she asks.

I look down at what appears to be the bestest girl and wonder why I don't have a pet. "With the dog?"

"We're doing a presentation?" the woman says. "Letting the kids meet the dogs?"

I stare at her for a moment, and it finally clicks. "Therapy dogs!" I point at her and the dog simultaneously with both hands.

The woman gives me a quick nod. "Yes! I'm Darla Graves. I'm giving a quick talk about the dogs, what makes them special, how they help with stress, anxiety, and anger, and then each class will spend time with one of our trained emotional support animals." She smiles.

"Right!" Emotional support sounds like a dream. I might need some one-on-one time with these dogs myself, this floofy one especially. "We're so glad you're here. *I'm* glad you're here! The kids have been so excited about this."

I've been excited about it too, but with everything going on, I completely forgot today was the day.

Darla is a plump woman with dark, wiry hair, and the kind of glasses that tint when you're outside. She's holding a leash attached to an adorable tan dog.

"This is Shandy," Darla says. "She's a sweetheart."

I bend down and pet the dog with both hands—behind the ears, under her chin, scritching her shoulders—and I decide that yes, I absolutely need a support animal.

This support animal. Like, right now.

"I feel less stressed already." I kneel and look Shandy straight in the eyes. Hers are big and chocolate-brown, and they radiate kindness. I hop up and hold open the door. "Come in! If you don't, I'm going to take Shandy to my classroom to hang out for the rest of the day."

Darla smiles as she leads the dog into the back hallway.

"She helps with all kinds of things—stress. Anxiety. Loneliness," Darla continues. "We take our dogs into retirement homes and schools. Colleges often have them round the clock, especially during finals week." She reaches down and ruffles Shandy's head. "Dogs are such a gift."

I consider this as an idea forms. "Do you think a cat could help with those things too?"

"Sure," she says brightly. "Cats get a bad rap because they're pretty independent, but I know several people who rely on cats as support animals. Animals are so much better than people," she chuckles. "Better comfort, I mean. But also"—she shrugs—"just better."

I sit with that for a second.

Should I get Winnie a cat?

I wasn't allowed to have a pet when I was growing up, and I don't know the first thing about how much time, work, or money is involved. Feels risky to buy a cat for a stranger. But the paper was really detailed about the cat she lost. Lenny—black with white feet and a white circle around one eye. Those details must be important.

I walk Darla into the main office and find two other dogs (and their people) have already arrived.

Mid-morning, the entire school gathers in the gymnasium for Darla's talk. While she introduces the dogs to all the kids, I google local animal shelters, hoping to find a black cat with white feet. Surely, there must be one somewhere.

But I come up empty. Lots of gray cats. Several white ones. One that's all black. And several orange ones with descriptions like "Not the brightest animal, but still loveable" which feels like a blatant lie.

Hmm. Maybe a cat isn't the move.

If you wanted to be more helpful, I think, *you could've been a little more specific.*

Why I'm thinking that this magic newspaper can hear my thoughts is beyond me. And yet, maybe it can. It *is* magic . . .

At lunch, I'm sitting in the teacher's lounge, eyes glued to my phone, having expanded my black cat with white booties search, when Brooke plops down in the seat across from me.

"You're getting a cat?" she asks, leaning over and looking at my phone.

I turn to her as I click my phone off, the image of a gray and white kitten disappearing as the screen goes black, and frown. "Uh, privacy."

She opens a Chipotle bag—which may or may not be hers—and my stomach growls. I glance down at my sandwich, wishing it was a burrito.

"Every time I've seen you today you've been on your phone." A frown. "And you look terrible."

I fluff my unruly hair with my fingers and lean back in my chair.

She winces. "That didn't help."

I scrub a hand down my face and groan. "I didn't get much sleep."

"Please tell me the hot neighbor kept you awake," she says.

I shoot her a look.

"Fine. Don't kiss and tell, I don't care." She shrugs as she opens her chips, scoops up a healthy pile of guac, and looks at me. "Tell me what's going on."

I take a bite of my PB&J and chew, trying to figure out how *not* to freak out about this. How *not* to let my big feelings creep in.

But honestly, this is a big feelings kind of thing, right?

I have to tell someone what's happening—and Brooke and Liz will eat this up. They might even make me feel like I'm not losing my mind. Maybe they can even help me figure out what to do next. Even if talking about it out loud makes me feel a little ridiculous.

I inhale a slow breath, then say, on an exhale, "Do you actually believe my building is magic?"

"Uh, *yeah*." Her eyes go wide. "Wait."

I wince.

Her eyebrows shoot up. "Do you? Did something happen?!"

I pause. "Maybe?"

"Oh, my gosh. Tell me everything." She doesn't hide the excitement in her voice. "Wait, we need to get Liz." She pulls out her phone, shoots off a text, and less than twenty seconds later, we're a trio.

She doesn't say anything when she comes in, and I can only assume this is because Brooke's text revealed enough for her to know that we're talking magic—a subject they take very seriously if their expressions, a mix of somber and bursting, are any indication.

"Okay," I say, trying to choose my words. "I know how this is all going to sound."

Liz waves me off. "Just tell us what's happening. Is it the hot chef? Did you run into him again?" She looks at me, deadpan. "Is *that* the kind of magic we're talking about here?"

"Oh, my goodness, *no*," I say, shaking my head. "I mean, yes. I did run into him again—"

They both hold in a squeal.

"—*and* that only confirmed what I already knew. That man is a serious jerk."

They exchange a glance and a shrug, acting like his completely off-putting nature doesn't matter.

Then Brooke takes my hands and says, "Tell us *everything*," so dramatically, I almost forget how ludicrous this is going to sound.

I inhale a slow breath and then unload the entire story. I soften the parts that make me look like a total halfwit. I also leave out how I felt when I first saw Matteo, with his runway-worthy looks.

I don't want to admit that I *really* liked what I saw. But I *really* liked what I saw.

The whole thing is awkward, and I feel a little silly. It's one thing to say you believe in things like magic, but something else entirely to say you're *experiencing* it first-hand.

When I finally stop talking, I lean back in my chair and wait for their judgment. "Well?" My eyes bounce from Liz to Brooke and back.

Finally, Brooke stands. "This. Is. *Awesome*." Her eyes are wide, her mouth agape with delighted anticipation, while Liz leans back in her chair, apparently processing.

"It's really not," I groan. "It's confusing. And weird. It's weird, right? It's weird."

"Weird as it may be, Iris, it's obvious," Liz states matter-of-factly.

"What is?"

"You need to get Winnie a cat."

"Yeah, I thought about that," I say. "But I don't even know if she wants another cat."

"Oh, she wants a cat," Brooke chimes in. "The article said she was struggling because she lost Lenny."

"And you saw the kids with the dogs today—animals keep people from being lonely. That's not a coincidence," Liz says. Then, after a slight pause, "Actually, *you* should get a cat."

"Me? Yeah, no, I definitely don't want a cat," I say, brushing her off.

"A dog, then?" She offers.

"Maybe the whole point of this was to show you that you need a dog," Liz suggests.

"Or that you and Winnie have something in common . . ." Brooke sits back down. "You're both alone."

I shoot her a look. "Okay, thanks for that."

Brooke scrunches up her nose. "Oh, I didn't mean it like

that, but . . . you know. You're both . . . without people right now."

"There has to be a bigger lesson we're not seeing here," Liz says. "Or a romance brewing behind the scenes? Most of the stories I've heard about your building have to do with romance." Now she stands. "Somehow, I think this might have to do with the hot chef."

"It doesn't," I say, though I'm not all that convinced.

"It might."

"Might not."

"His name is *on* these newspapers, right?" Liz says. "That's not an accident."

I shake my head. "I've got that figured out. I'm thinking the newspaper thinks he's too much of a tool to actually help anyone else other than himself. I'm a different kind of person than he is." I pause. "I love helping people. The newspaper knows I won't rest till I figure out how to help Winnie."

Brooke chuckles. "You're talking about the newspaper like it's alive."

My hand reflexively moves to the spot on my forehead where it's been smacked by a flying newspaper. Twice.

"Yeah. Silly me."

"We *told* you that building was magic, Iris!" Liz says, practically bouncing. "Can we come over? Can we see it for ourselves?"

"Ooh! You can text or call when it starts happening again!" Brooke adds.

I throw away my trash, then zip up my lunch bag. "Look, I don't know if this is going to keep happening. I don't even know what I'm supposed to do. I'm still having a hard time wrapping my brain around this. It doesn't make sense." I start toward the door, but Brooke blocks my exit.

"Magic is like *love*," she croons. "It doesn't have to make sense."

I hold in a chuckle. "How long have you been holding on to *that* one?"

She shrugs. "Eh. A while. But it's still true!"

"All we're saying is that your building chose you for a reason. The magic *chose you*. It's up to something," Liz says from behind me. "And whatever it is, you don't want to miss out on it."

I stop. "You're right. I kind of don't," I admit.

They exchange another glance.

"It *is* exciting, right?" Strange, yes, but still exciting.

"Uh, *yeah* it is," Brooke practically shouts this at me. "And who knows? Maybe you can, you know . . . *exchange papers* with the chef."

Heat rushes to my cheeks at the mention of Matteo. "Okay, that's my cue." I try to escape and push past Brooke, out into the hallway.

She follows me. "Oh, come on, Iris. This would be way more exciting than crocheting those weird little animals on Friday nights while you watch reruns of *New Girl* and *The Great British Baking Show*."

"Ouch! Below the belt, Brooke!" I whip around, mouth agape and smiling, mostly because I know she's right. It's possible I've *over*-corrected my tendency to insert myself into other people's lives.

And it's also possible I'm suffering for it. That doesn't mean I should get overly involved in whatever is happening with my building. One time . . . and then done. No more. That should be enough to satisfy my curiosity—then Matteo can deal with things.

His frowning face flashes through my mind, and I wonder what he would look like if he smiled.

Be careful, Iris.

Brooke holds up her hands, as if in surrender. "All I'm saying is . . . maybe this could be a good thing."

"For whatever reason, the building is opening a door between you and your neighbor. You should probably pay attention." Liz looks so certain, as if any of this is normal. "Maybe you are exactly what *he* needs."

I can't imagine that man needing anything, least of all, me.

"Okay, stop. This isn't about the chef, or even about me. This is about my lonely old neighbor who needs a sort of . . . intervention." I frown. "And yeah, maybe a cat. I researched shelters all day and found zero black cats with white feet." I glance over. "Should I just get any old cat?"

Liz shrugs. "I have a turtle. I don't know anything about cats."

Both Brooke and I turn to Liz. "You have a turtle?" I ask.

"Yeah. Donatello."

I love Liz a little bit more now that I know that, and I make a mental note to crochet her a turtle.

"Can't it be about *both* your lonely neighbor and the hot chef?" Brooke asks, ignoring me.

"No." I start walking, and they both follow. "If this does have something to do with magic"—I glance over at her—"and I'm not saying it does—I think the newspaper found me because it knew this guy . . . Matteo Morgan"—I say his name like it leaves a bad taste in my mouth—"couldn't be bothered to help anyone other than himself."

"Mm-hm," Brooke says, making it clear she doesn't believe me.

"*Matteo Morgan*," Liz whispers, as if saying something sacred.

I leave them swooning in their adolescence and head back to my classroom and find a note on my desk. It's from Mr. Kincaid.

Please send Joyce your proposed date for the art show and let us know how to best support you and your students! —CK

The art show. *Right.* This is just part of my job. And I

decide in this moment that the best way to handle it is to go all in. We'll make the event feel special. We're not just hanging pictures in the hallways. We're going to turn the gymnasium into a gallery. How? I have no idea, but I'm determined to create new, wonderful art show memories—for my students *and* for me.

I open my laptop, scroll over to the calendar, and choose a Thursday evening in April with nothing scheduled. I email the date to Joyce, copy Mr. Kincaid, and put it in my own personal calendar.

I try to brainstorm more ideas to make the art show special for the kids . . .

. . . but I can't stop thinking about the newspaper article stuck to my fridge.

Chapter Nine
Iris

WHEN I GET HOME, no more newspapers. No more antics. My apartment is nice and quiet.

My brain, however, is not.

The absence of magic only raises more questions, and while it was nice to tell Liz and Brooke what happened, romanticized speculation doesn't really help.

The only person who might be able to help . . . won't. That thought sparks annoyance all over again.

Twice, I've marched down the hall and stood outside Matteo's apartment, *almost* knocking, *almost* ready to demand answers. Twice, I've decided against it, turned abruptly, and marched right back to my apartment without going through with it.

Mad at him and mad at myself.

Once, I trekked up to the fourth floor after locating Winnie's apartment number via the mailboxes near the stairway on the first floor.

I didn't knock on her door either.

I don't know her. What would I say? "Hey, Winnie, a

magical newspaper told me you might be feeling lonely. Here's a cat I rescued for you."

I need a plan.

Once again, I don't fall asleep until pretty late, and in the morning I'm met with a—

THWAP

"What the—"

I fumble around for a second, disoriented, and rub my eyes open just in time to see a disappearing golden wisp.

The newspaper hit me again.

"Oh. Oh! Oh, *yeah?* That's how it's going to be now?"

I can't be sure, but I think I hear a soft tinkle of wind chimes, maybe from outside. I immediately sit up and look around for another newspaper.

There are none.

I hop up and look in my drawers, under the bed, but nothing. It's weird, but I'm a little disappointed.

That feeling of disappointment is quickly replaced by the overwhelming feeling of helplessness. The article said something needed to happen by Thursday.

That's today.

A weird pit forms in my stomach. Time is running out.

I've imagined every worst-case scenario my overly active imagination could conjure, and by the time I've made my morning coffee, I'm so worked up I almost call the school and take a personal day.

I mean, not to be overly dramatic here, but was the newspaper suggesting that without some sort of intervention Winnie might die?

It's the *"Before it's too late"* bit at the end of the article that gets me.

Menacing? Macabre? Or just an added punch at the end to show it's serious, but not to be taken verbatim?

I'm not going to chance it either way. I have to figure out how to help her.

I spend most of the day hiding out in the art room, eating lunch in my car, and calling all the animal shelters one more time on the off chance that a random, black and white cat came in last night.

"We have an orange tabby that would love a new home," one woman tells me on the phone. I tell her, "No, I really do need a black one with white booties."

"That's a very specific request," she says.

And I agree, then hang up questioning whether I'm being too literal. I truly have no idea why the cat *needs* to look like her old cat, but would the newspaper have mentioned that detail if it wasn't important?

My brain is in run-on sentence mode.

I head home after work, planless, cat-less, hopeless. Even so, I'm determined to knock on Winnie's door and at least say hello. I'll just check in and make sure she's okay. Tell her I'm new(ish) in the building, trying to meet all my neighbors, casual-like.

I will not mention magic.

As plans go, it's pretty basic, but it's the best I've got. The newspaper seemed to want more to happen, but I'm just not sure what.

I pull into the parking garage and navigate my way to my dedicated space but slam on the brakes when I see it. There, sitting right at the center of my parking spot, is a small, black cat with white feet. He even has a circle around one eye. I stare at it and blink.

It doesn't disappear.

I stare longer, like my mind conjured it from thin air.

It stares back, unmoving.

You've got to be kidding.

I put my car in park, get out, and walk over to the cat. As a rule, I'm not a cat person. I think they're weird and possibly demon-possessed. But I kneel down to inspect it, wondering if it's a figment of my imagination.

It makes a squeaking "meow" sound.

Okay, fine, that was sort of cute—for a little satanic animal.

Satanimal? I absently think, chuckling at the portmanteau, and I reach out to pet its head, then drag my hand along its back. It arches as I do this, squeaking adorably, and I think maybe I was wrong to judge cats so harshly.

This one, at least, doesn't seem to warrant a priest and a bucket of water.

First Shandy, now this cat . . . I understand Darla's comment about animals being such a better comfort than people. Still, I tried everything to find a cat for Winnie, and now one just appears?

Feels a lot like magic.

The unwanted thought sends a strange tingle down my spine.

The cat moves toward me, purring and brushing up against my leg. I pick it up, unsure how to hold it. Its claws dig into my coat, and I cradle it in my arms, petting its head as I check to make sure it doesn't have a collar. "Where did you come from, cat?" I say out loud. "Are you magic?" Then, I switch to baby talk, which I'm not proud to admit, and say, "Are you a magical kitty cat?" while continuing to pet it and —*oh, great*—now I have become its best friend.

It mews a soft reply, and I carry it back to my car, letting it sit in my lap while I park, doing my best to go with this weird turn of events.

It's perfectly content, curled up on me.

I'm sure there's a reasonable explanation that the exact cat I've been looking for would appear in my parking space at the exact time I was planning to show up at Winnie's door. Winnie, the old woman who has a special affection for black cats with white feet and who is probably going to be very concerned that she has a stalker when I pop in and gift her a *live animal*. I cradle the kitten, walk into the building, and go straight to the elevator.

"I hope she wants you, cat," I say out loud as the doors open and I step out onto Winnie's floor. "Otherwise, this is going to look utterly bizarre."

I reach Winnie's apartment and knock, petting the cat absently while I wait for her to answer the door.

In the pause, it occurs to me that I might be too late. Winnie may already be—

But then the door opens, and a tall, wispy woman stands on the opposite side. Her gray hair is pulled up in a loose bun with escaped strands framing her face, a lavender scarf tied up into it like a headband. Her long, billowy dress matches the scarf, and she's got on a full face of makeup.

Winnie St. George is beautiful. And regal. And elegant.

"Uh, hi," I say. "I'm—"

Her gaze drops to the cat in my arms, and she cuts me off. "Well, aren't you the cutest little thing?" With crooked fingers, she reaches out and pets the cat. "Is he yours?"

"Actually," I say. "I found him. He's, uh, looking for a good home."

"Oh, my goodness, really?" The trail of bracelets on her arm jingle as she motions for me to hand him over, which I do, watching as her face brightens the second he's in her arms. "He's homeless?"

"I found him in the parking garage," I say. "I took a chance knocking on—"

But Winnie doesn't need my lame explanation, which is good because I actually have no idea what I was about to say. She doesn't even seem confused by the fact that I *happened* to find this cat and then I *happened* to bring it straight to her, a woman I've never met.

Instead, she beams at me, then looks back to the cat. "I used to have one that looked just like him." She cradles the cat. "I miss my Lenny so much. I'll take him if you're sure he's homeless."

I stuff my hands in my pockets. "I'm pretty sure he is."

As most magic cats are . . .

"Oh, he's *darling*," she coos. "Let's call him Squiggy. Like in *Laverne and Shirley?*" She looks at me, but I only stare. I have no idea what she's talking about. "Are you a cat person?"

I grimace. "Honestly? Not really."

"Well, you *should* be," she says. "There's no more wonderful companion. They love you unconditionally. They're always there for you." She gives the cat a slight squeeze. "Are you sure you don't want to keep him?"

"Oh, I'm sure." I feel awkward, like I want to disappear. Is it enough to give her the cat and leave? "I'm not quite ready for the commitment."

At that, she laughs. "You young people. Always afraid to commit. Oh, here, come in! Can you stay a minute?" There's hopefulness in her eyes, and I unconsciously think about how easy it would be to become a lonely person. After all, you can be surrounded by people and still be lonely.

Winnie moves out of the way, and as I step inside her apartment, I'm struck by the overwhelming and delicious smell of garlic and tomato, and the overwhelming, equally delicious sight of Matteo Morgan.

Here. In Winnie's kitchen.

If my mouth is agape, I'm not fixing it because *what is he doing here?*

When he sees me, he stops moving, a sort-of-but-not-quite "caught" look on his face.

I narrow my eyes.

He makes a weird face, then goes back to what he was doing.

So, I was wrong about him not helping . . . but right about him knowing more than he let on. *Would it have killed you to clue me in!?* I think at him, loudly.

"I'm Winnie," she says. "And this is Matteo." She giggles to herself. "I don't even know your name. I just saw the cat and thought you *must* be a good person." Her brow knits. "Oh, wait. You are a good person, aren't you?"

"I'm an elementary school art teacher," I say, as if that's proof of my goodness.

She laughs and says, "Ah, well, to deal with children, you must have a good bit of patience and kindness in there somewhere."

I like her immediately.

The guy in the kitchen? Jury's still out.

"I have a good feeling about you." She leans in closer. "But I *would* like to know your name."

The newspaper gave the impression that Winnie St. George was depressed and lonely, but this woman doesn't seem to be either. She seems full of life, like someone it would be impossible to be sad around.

"I'm Iris. I live, uh—" I stop short of saying *down the hall from the hot chef* as my eyes snag on Matteo's dark gaze. He watches me with a quiet curiosity that simultaneously makes me want to shut down and spill all my secrets.

"Iris," Winnie says. "Goodness, what a beautiful name." She regards me for a moment. "It suits you. Have you met Matteo?"

He looks away.

"I have," I say with a pointed look in his direction.

And I thought he was the worst.

"We live on the same floor," I say.

"Oh!" Winnie lights up. "So, you're neighbors!"

"Yes," I say with a put-on smile.

"Matteo's a chef," Winnie says, almost mom-proud. "He's testing out new recipes, and—oh! This is perfect! You'll stay and eat with us." She looks at Matteo. "Table for *three*, Mr. Morgan."

He holds up a finger as if to answer her, but she doesn't wait for a reply. "Odd time to eat, I know, but Matteo runs that adorable little Italian bistro down the block, and he only has a couple of hours off between lunch and dinner."

I stop listening because my brain snagged on the fact that he has only a couple of hours off between what I assume are two busy and stressful times of day . . . and he's spending them here?

Cooking for Winnie?

The icy feelings inside me start to thaw. But only a little.

"So, how long have you two known each other?" I say, trying to figure out if maybe Matteo was rude because he felt protective of Winnie.

"Not long. We're new friends." Winnie smiles as she takes the cat over and sets it on a tall, carpeted structure, something I assume belonged to the aforementioned Lenny. After a brief exploration, orienting himself to the cat tree, the kitten leaps around it like it was born there.

"Look! Squiggy already loves it!"

Which is a relief, because I really didn't want to bring that cat home with me.

She continues. "Matteo and I have just been getting to know each other the past couple of days. We met in the lobby, and he asked if I'd be willing to sample some new recipes he's been trying out."

The past couple of days?

As in, the days since I gave him that first newspaper?

Winnie glances over at him. "He really lucked out because I have impeccable taste. Isn't that right, Chef?" She looks at him, so I look at him. Because how can I not?

Also because—is he serious right now?

Why was he so stand-offish and secretive? He let me think that some poor old woman was going to kick the bucket if I didn't bring her a cat, and he's in here, looking all . . . whatever . . . casually trying out new recipes?

What else is he keeping to himself?

"You do have good taste," he says, moving around the kitchen with decisiveness. It's hard to *stop* looking.

Winnie must notice I'm gawking because she leans in closer and says, "Oh, I know, Iris. I'm old, but I'm not dead."

I spit out a shocked laugh, and she nudges me with her arm.

I look at her, still surprised, and she winks.

The cat hops from the bottom to the top of the tree, and Winnie watches, a sad smile on her face. "I just lost Lenny last month. I didn't have the heart to get rid of his things. Now I'm glad I kept them."

I can tell by her expression that bringing the cat here was the right move, and my argument that this is all one big coincidence gets thinner and thinner.

"Maybe I'll let you two eat in peace?" Matteo says, but Winnie dashes the idea away with a scoff.

"Nonsense," she says. "You need fuel before you go back to work."

"I'll be okay, really," he says, clearly angling for an escape. "I can grab something at the restaurant."

"Young man, you sit down right this instant. You'll break my heart if you don't stay." Winnie paints an innocent expression on her face that makes it hard to call her manipulation what it is. "Besides, I want to hear more about this grandpa of yours."

At that, Matteo's eyes drift to mine, and I quirk a brow, certain that my presence is what's making him uncomfortable.

What I don't know is why.

He holds up his hands in surrender and says, "Okay, okay, but the dish I'm making gets cold quick. You'll have to eat it *before it's too late.*"

The words stop my breath for a second. I whip my eyes in his direction and see him subtly shake his head at me, as if to silently tell me something.

He *clearly* read the newspaper—and more than that, he understood well before I did what to do with the information found inside.

My insides are vaulting over one another.

Winnie puts a hand on my arm. "And of course, I want to know everything about you, dear Iris."

It's such a simple, warm thing to say, and it instantly calms me, pulling my brain from WHAT DOES THIS MAN KNOW?! to seeing that Winnie genuinely wants to hear about me.

It's been a long time since anyone cared to know anything about me. The comment lodges itself squarely in my chest, and I have to look away.

Actually, that's not entirely true. It's been a long time since I've completely spilled my emotional guts out to someone, thinking it was forever, only to find out it was fleeting.

New town. New me. New boundaries—like not leaping *then* looking.

Winnie ushers me over to the table and motions for me to sit while she fetches another place setting.

By all logic, I shouldn't be hungry yet—it's only been a few hours since lunch—but even if my mouth wasn't watering, I would still want to eat whatever Matteo is making over there. It smells like heaven.

Home-cooked meals weren't really a part of my childhood. After Dad left and before she met her new husband, Richard, my mom went back to work, and "trying to make ends meet" took priority over "family dinners." We existed on quick meals. Cereal for dinner. Pop-Tarts. Peanut butter and jelly. It wasn't fancy, but it kept me alive, and I suppose that was the goal back then.

As a result, I don't have high-end tastes when it comes to food. I still bring PB&J to school every day.

But the way it smells in this apartment? *Sweet mamma mia.*

Matteo goes back to cooking, cleaning each utensil as he goes. When he's finished, I get the distinct impression there will be no sign he was ever here.

"Tell me about you, Iris." The cat jumps off of the carpeted tree and starts off toward the living room as Winnie turns her attention to me.

Matteo doesn't turn around, but he's *right there*, so whatever I tell Winnie, I'm telling him too. It's a good thing I'm trying out my new skill of sharing without really sharing. *Nobody needs your whole life's story, Iris. It's too much.*

"Oh, there's really not much to tell," I say. "I grew up near Boston and moved here at the start of the school year."

"To foster the imaginations of children through art . . . what important work." Winnie is so earnest when she says this, I take the compliment as genuine.

I smile at the sentiment because I do think it's important work, but I'm aware that most people don't think so. Even in elementary school, the arts are the first things to go.

Winnie goes on. "You get to inspire kids to use their creative gifts. I don't think enough people recognize the importance of that these days."

I nod again. "I completely agree!"

"You get to be the teacher who tells a child they aren't wasting their time if they spend it learning to draw or paint.

You get to help them see the world in a different way." She squeezes my hand, looking proudly at me for a moment. "That's *important*."

I smile. "Tell that to the public school system," I nod ruefully, trying not to think about all the people who have belittled my own love of art over the years. How I always felt like a disappointment—just a little—because I didn't pursue something practical.

Winnie leans back and studies me. "Did you move here with friends? I don't see a ring, so I assume you're not married."

My cheeks flush, and I wince a *caught me* look. "Ah! Yeah. Well." I wiggle the fingers of my left hand at her. "No, not married. And no friends. I moved here alone."

Winnie claps her hands together in front of her face. "An independent woman! I love to see it. It must be nice to have a blank slate!" She leans in, eyes narrowing. "Were you just looking for a fresh start? Or did some scandal force you to look for a new life?" Her eyes flicker, and she reminds me of Brooke—always searching for the drama, regardless of whether there is any.

I glance up in time to see Matteo pause as he's stirring whatever is in the pot, pretending not to listen.

My laugh sounds nervous in my own ears. "Ha! Nothing so podcast-y as that, Winnie. I'm not running away. Just came for the job." It's not entirely true, but the truth is almost as boring.

I can practically see the disappointment in her face. "How's it going so far?"

I shrug and say, "Eh." I know I'm giving her nothing of interest, but what am I supposed to do, blurt out the myriad reasons why I left? The endless cycle of carbon-copy relationships where I fell for guys who needed fixing, whether they were good for me or not? Do I explain that I never got used to randomly bumping in to my father's new family, or the fact that I still, after all these years of trying, haven't found a place where I fit?

"I'm working on changing. You know, holding back a little instead of throwing myself into every—" My eyes dart over to the kitchen, then back to Winnie. I lower my voice, as if that's going to prevent Matteo from hearing me. "I'm just trying to stop getting my heart broken."

"Ah. Say no more." She cocks her head and smiles at me. It's like she's sliding the pieces of a puzzle into place, and I don't have to explain it. We've just met, and I feel like I could tell this woman anything.

Plus, it's a well-documented fact that having a big heart and big feelings only leads to big hurt. Because people leave.

Winnie reaches across the table and covers my hand with her own. "Iris. Our world has enough cynics. Having a big, open heart when you meet someone new is never a bad thing."

The words have an unexpected weight to them, and I'm suddenly looking at her through clouded eyes. She doesn't understand. She doesn't know me. That big, open heart has gotten me hurt. A *lot*, actually.

I want to tell her all the ways life has proven she's wrong. All the ways being super open and going all in causes big, messy problems.

"I think . . ." I pause.

I think I'm too much.

"You think . . . ?" Winnie's eyes are expectant.

"I think dinner is served." Matteo spins around and sets two plates in front of us. When I catch his eye, I see a hint of knowing, almost like he's intentionally rescued me but is trying to pretend he didn't.

My stomach swoops at the thought, even though it's completely unproven.

People show you who they are. Plain and simple. And Matteo showed me plenty.

Why do I have to keep reminding myself of that?

But as he sits down next to Winnie, across the table from me, I start to wonder if Matteo didn't show me who he really is at all.

Chapter Ten
Matteo

Iris read the newspaper.

She read the paper, and she . . . understood it? Did it move? Did it fly around? Did the words disappear from the page like they do for me?

Had to.

Had to.

There's a soft meowing at my leg, and I feel tiny pricks of claws on my sock. I reach down and gently pull the kitten from my leg and drop it, pointing it in another direction.

She read the paper, and it told her what to do, and she did something about it.

I knew things were starting to happen to her when she tried to stop me in the hallway. I recognized the familiar panic behind her eyes. Still, I thought I did a great job covering up the fact that I knew exactly what she was talking about.

But now? What the heck made me quote the last line of the article? I basically admitted out loud that yes, I am here because of the newspaper. And yes, I pretended not to know what she was talking about.

My mind spins back to my own introduction to these nuisances. I tossed the first newspaper in the trash, the same way I would any other junk mail. The next day, it was back in front of my door.

This went on for days, and every time I thought I'd finally succeeded in getting rid of the papers, they would multiply and reappear. On a table. On a nightstand.

One morning it was in the fridge.

Clearly, something was trying to get my attention.

Had the same thing happened to Iris?

Had to.

One time, when I was trying to make sense of what was happening, my grandpa paused on the other end of the phone, then said, "Some things about The Serendipity don't follow traditional rules of logic, Teo. Best to embrace the magic."

"I don't believe in magic," I said.

He laughed at that. "Nobody does . . . until they do."

Real deep, old man. Real deep.

But his words turned out to be true. I had no idea what to do . . . until I did. But I don't talk about it. Not with anyone.

Ever.

Because the few times I've broached the subject, I've been met with skepticism and concern, and I don't need to give anyone more reasons to worry about me.

Not only that, but people don't seem to remember anything I tell them about the magic, so what's the point? This magic, whatever it is, is not something that wants to be found out. Which is why I acted clueless when Iris asked about the newspapers.

But after all this time, the magic is suddenly including someone else—her.

Why?

I should probably be more sympathetic—after all, I

remember how confusing and terrifying it was when it started happening to me. But Iris's questions only raise questions for me. There's been very little change in the way this magic works . . . until now.

I've been turning over this whole conversation in my mind while I'm cooking in the kitchen.

Since Iris showed up with the cat.

A cat. *Why didn't I think of that?*

"Okay, Chef," Winnie says, a gleam of mischief in her eye. "I don't think we can eat without a proper presentation."

The day after Iris showed up with the newspaper, I spotted Winnie in the lobby. I'd already done a Google search so I knew what she looked like, and the newspaper had given me enough information for an introduction.

My plan on that first day was to prepare a meal and drop it off around dinner time, but Winnie mentioned she was tired of eating alone. She told me she would only give me her opinion on the food if I stayed and ate with her.

I knew better than to make up some reason why this wouldn't work.

If you try to outrun, outsmart, or outwit the magic, it will find a way to bulldoze, bury, or bully you.

So, I stayed. And Winnie bombarded me with questions about my restaurant, my favorite foods, how I started cooking, how long I've lived in the building . . . basically, my entire life story.

Not my favorite subject to discuss—but not wholly unpleasant, either.

Kind of nice, actually. No pressure. No expectations.

She's not trying to fix me or set me up with her granddaughter, which are major plusses in my book.

"You'll come back again, and we'll get into the *good* stuff," she said that first night when I was heading out the door. At my frown, she smiled. "Don't look so worried—I'm not talking about your love life. I have a feeling you won't indulge me." She laughs to herself. "I just know there's more to your story than you're sharing, Chef."

I felt a strange, unspoken kinship with her, knowing that, like me, she'd also lost the person she thought she'd grow old with. Life had stolen that from both of us, and now, here we were.

But she was right. I have no intention of telling her anything other than what you could find with a simple Google search, no matter how much she digs. And if there's one thing I'm certain of, Winnie is a digger.

For that reason, it's good to have Iris here, even if it is unsettling not to know the reason for the sudden shift in the way the magic is working. Maybe the old woman will be so interested in her she'll forget all about me.

I unfold my napkin and clear my throat.

"Chef," Winnie says, her tone chiding.

I look at her, and she motions with her hand for me to stand.

"Properly, please."

My eyes jump to Iris's, and she presses her lips together, like she's trying not to smile.

I nod to Winnie. "As you wish."

Winnie smacks Iris's arm. "Just like that guy from that movie!"

Iris giggles and then looks right at me, standing, staring back, waiting. She dips her head in mock surrender. "Farm boy. Fetch me that pitcher?"

Winnie lets out one single hoot of laughter. "Very nice accent."

"Thank you," Iris says.

Winnie must sense that I'm not amused because as she glances my way, she wipes the smile from her face and gestures for me to *carry on, please.*

I take a deep breath. Great. They're two peas in a pod already.

I place the napkin back on the table. And then, as if presenting my dish to a panel of judges, I look at Iris, then at Winnie, and nod again. "Today I've prepared for you a Sicilian classic, *busiate con agghia pistata*. This is a handmade pasta paired with a traditional Trapanese pesto. *Buon appetito.*" I gesture for them to begin eating, as Winnie claps her hands in front of her face like she's genuinely impressed.

"Wonderful, just *wonderful.*" She reaches over and squeezes my arm.

As I sit, my eyes flick up, and I find Iris watching me, curiously.

Her curiosity isn't something I'm interested in entertaining.

Winnie makes a show of unfolding her napkin and laying it across her lap, then surveys the meal on the plate in front of her.

If there's one thing I've learned about Winnie in the brief time I've known her, it's that she values well-made and well-prepared food. I've gotten the distinct impression she has a refined palate, which really does make her an excellent person to sample new recipes.

Iris, on the other hand, seems amused by the entire scene. "Oh, my gosh, this smells *a*-ma-*zing.*" She picks up the saltshaker.

"Don't do that." I nod to her hand.

She looks at the salt and frowns. "But I put salt on everything."

"Taste it first," I say, trying not to be annoyed.

She pauses. "Fine, but I reserve the right to add it." She sets the shaker down.

I nod.

She picks up her fork and starts winding the pasta around it. "So you made this by hand?"

"That's usually what 'handmade' means." I try to keep my tone light but not teasing. I don't want her to think I'm flirting. Unfortunately, the second I finish the sentence, I hear the sharpness in what I've said.

She deflates a little, and I look away. If they were here, Nicola and Val would both be kicking me under the table.

I'm not great with people.

Not anymore.

My "table side manner" is a topic of conversation in the kitchen more often than I want it to be, but I don't see the point. I'm not interested in widening my nonexistent social circle. I can be polite and withdrawn at the same time.

Politely withdrawn.

But now, thanks to my rude comment, there's an awkward silence in the room.

Winnie picks up her fork and turns her attention toward Iris. "Do you cook, dear?"

Iris coughs, then laughs. "Uh, no. Not like this. I do a lot of frozen pizza."

At that, I wince.

Winnie lets out a long, "Ohhhh. Your words have wounded the chef."

Iris pulls a face. "Yeah . . . sorry about that. My mom wasn't very good in the kitchen. I never learned."

I meet Iris's wide, apologetic eyes for a moment, then quickly look away.

"Chef Matteo learned to cook right here in this building," Winnie says.

Iris lifts her fork and looks at me again, one eyebrow raised. "Oh?"

"His grandma taught him," she says, as I lower my head, which is what I do when others are talking about me while

I'm sitting right next to them. Which happens often. Because I don't talk about myself. She turns to me. "I bet you have a lot of good memories of this place."

"I do." I take my first bite, the flavors of garlic and tomato and almond and basil settling on my tongue as I chew, slowly, assessing the flavor, the balance, the notes.

"Oh, my gosh." Iris's fork drops onto her plate with a clang. She goes quiet, leaning back in her chair. Is she choking?

"Are you—?" I stop short, frowning at her, worried she's allergic to pine nuts or something.

But she holds up a hand to silence me, still chewing, not waiting to swallow the bite before asking, "You *made* this?"

"Yes." I'm confused by the question.

She looks at me. "This. Is. Amazing."

I look back. The compliment is so genuine, it catches me off-guard.

Huh.

She takes a huge bite, and then, after only two chews, she mouths, "Ann you're righ, dis doesn't meed sall aht awl."

Winnie brings her napkin up to her mouth to stifle another laugh. "Iris, you and I are going to get along just fine," she chimes.

I'm shocked to realize I find her enthusiasm incredibly endearing. Iris doesn't seem to take herself too seriously, and it's refreshing. And she's funny. If I wasn't working so hard to remain straight-faced, I probably would've laughed too.

Chapter Eleven
Matteo

I FEEL EXPOSED EATING my own food with these two women —and a little embarrassed, given Iris's reaction. I get the impression she's been eating quick meals out of boxes, bags, and jars for most of her life.

She winds another long, coiled noodle around her fork. "Did you just come up with this on your own?"

I'd be lying if I said I didn't appreciate this animated response.

"It's a traditional dish," I say, with a quick glance at each of them. "My grandma used to make it, but she never wrote anything down, so I've been trying to recreate as many of her recipes as I can. I have to decide if I should add it to the menu."

"Yes," Iris says firmly, shoveling in another bite. "Add. This. Right now."

"It's delicious," Winnie says, in a much more dignified tone than Iris, who seems to have entered her own world.

"It's insane. I didn't know food could taste like this," Iris says around another very large bite.

"That's because you've been eating Tombstone pizza," I say dryly, then take another bite. "I think the balance is off."

"It's not," Iris says, mouth full. "I mean, maybe it is. I've never had it before, but if I had to choose a last meal"—she points at the plate with her fork—"this would be it."

I chuckle to myself but conceal my smile. It's nice. Even I can admit that. These days, I mostly stay in the kitchen rather than interact with customers, but I'd forgotten the joy of witnessing someone who appreciates my cooking.

Iris's reaction shakes something inside me. A memory of something my grandma always said. "There must be joy in what you do, dear Teo." She would move around her kitchen, tossing in spices, trying new things, tasting each dish with a kind of reckless abandon.

It's not how I cook.

Not anymore.

Now I cook with calculated precision. My goal is to elevate cooking to an artform.

But here, watching Iris devour this meal, is a reminder that once upon a time, I fell in love with my grandma's reasons for cooking. I wanted to carry on her tradition of bringing people together and making people happy. I wanted them to *savor* something I'd made.

I used to cook for the joy of it, spurred on by the memories of big family meals. Of sharing stories and loud laughter. Whooping and hollering over hand-spun Old Country delicacies.

With my grandparents, *everyone* was family. The table was always big enough for one more person, and there was always more than enough food for everyone. And always plenty of leftovers.

It's like they picked up some tips from the guy who shared loaves and fishes.

Every summer, I'd stay with them at The Serendipity

while my parents traveled. Even when I got old enough to go along on their trips, I always chose to come here. It's why this place has always felt like home.

Always felt special.

Meals weren't just something to "get through" with my grandparents. Food wasn't just fuel. It was *life*. Meals were events. Something to look forward to all day and talk about all night. Sometimes they'd open their apartment to anyone passing by. Other times, we'd spill out into the courtyard, bringing dishes and plates and glasses and wine and a lot of raucous laughter.

Everyone was always welcome.

Nobody was turned away for being a stranger.

"Did you know my grandparents?" I look at Winnie. "I just realized you might've lived here at the same time, and they liked to entertain." And then, I'm not sure why, but I add, "They used to host these big Italian dinners out in the courtyard."

My mind lingers on that memory because those were some of the best moments of my childhood . . . and also because life and communities aren't like that anymore. It's not something I actively miss, and yet, as nostalgia sets in, I can see the part it played in my upbringing.

Winnie seems to consider this for a long moment. "I do vaguely remember the very loud dinners out in the courtyard. I never attended one myself—I wasn't here nearly as much in those days, always out at charity functions with William, things like that." Her smile is fleeting. "But I wish I'd met them. I bet they are wonderful people."

I nod but don't say anything else. The realization that things are so different now—for me and for the world at large —hits me sideways.

Winnie must sense the pang of grief at the lost memories, because she glances at Iris and thankfully pulls the attention away from me. "I'd say that empty plate is a raving endorsement."

Iris wipes her mouth with her napkin, then tucks it back onto her lap. Her cheeks flush pink as her gaze falls to the plate in front of her.

It's been literally wiped clean, because she used bread to sop up all the sauce. If I did that, my grandmother would say, "Bravo, *ragazzo*! Bravo!"

Roughly translated, it's "Attaboy!"

She winces, a little sheepish, because Winnie and I are still working on our meals. "It was really good."

People compliment my cooking all the time but rarely to my face. For one reason or another, this simple sentiment sparks something inside of me. Something familiar but maybe forgotten.

I dismiss it, of course, because who gets sappy over a plate of pasta?

The kitten wobbles into the eating area, seeming to explore its new home, and I think about the article. It did mention that Winnie had recently lost her beloved pet.

I brought food, and Iris brought a cat.

For years, I've been sorting out the newspaper's demands, and in all that time, I've never had any help. Which makes me wonder again . . . why now? And why her?

I watch Iris as she serves herself another heaping portion of the pasta, and she looks up at me and gives a quirky little smile.

"Yeah, I'm not going to apologize. It's freaking good. You should feed this to the Pope, seriously."

Something odd happens.

I laugh.

And an unfamiliar rush of attraction zips through me.

I glance at Winnie and find her watching me watch Iris. She gives me a knowing smile.

And . . . that's my cue.

I've been around enough older women to know that the second they find out you're single, they turn finding you a love match into their full-time job. "I should go," I say.

"But you're not done eating," Winnie says. "And it gets my seal of approval too. I hope you'll add it to your menu immediately."

"I might," I say, still undecided. I stand. "I don't think it's right yet."

"So . . . you're a perfectionist," Iris says—a statement, not a question.

"When it comes to my grandmother's recipes? I feel like I have to be," I say. Again, odd that I'm even talking, but especially about my feelings.

Iris shrugs. "This seems perfect to me. If not perfect, then perfect-adjacent."

"I . . ." I stammer for a moment, then realize I'm being rude. "Thank you. It was a pleasure to cook for you." I clear my throat. "Uh, both of you."

Iris turns to Winnie and says, "I should go too, but . . ." She indicates the food she just heaped onto her plate.

There's an odd moment between the women, and Winnie then, all of a sudden, says, "I'll pack everything up and bring you a doggie bag. It's no trouble at all!"

Winnie scoots her chair back and heads into the kitchen to start rummaging through cupboards. I freeze where I stand, because Iris is now looking at me with a knowing look.

If her face were a body, it would have its hands on its hips.

I'm hoping to avoid another confrontation with Iris, like in the hallway, but it's obvious she's not going to make that easy.

She stands and, still looking at me, walks her plate over to the counter and sets it down.

"Oh, just leave it, dear," Winnie says. "You cooked. I'll take care of the mess."

Iris looks around the nearly spotless kitchen, then at me. "What mess?"

Winnie laughs. "Well, I suppose you're right. Chef Matteo left everything neat as a pin."

Iris watches me, and I can practically see the list of questions growing behind her eyes.

"You'll both come back again, won't you?" Winnie asks.

"I'd love to come back," Iris says. "Maybe you can show me a few of your favorite paintings?" She motions around the space. "Looks like you're a collector."

Winnie smiles. "I would love that." She looks at me. "And Chef? Will you be back?"

"I will," I say, "I have many recipes that need testing."

I like Winnie, which surprises me since I don't like many people. But more than that, I don't think my assignment here is finished. Sometimes, what the newspaper wants me to do is one-and-done—anonymously make sure two people enter each other's orbit, for instance. Other times, there's more. It seems like this is one of those times. I have a feeling there has to be more than a cat and a couple of meals to this one, I just don't know what.

I've gotten used to waiting to figure it out.

There's no rushing magic.

"Do either of you like to dance?" Winnie asks as I rinse my plate and file it into her dishwasher.

Behind me, Iris laughs, and I can't help but notice it's the kind of laugh that dances around in the air even after she's gone quiet. The kind that seems to catch her off-guard.

"Is that a no?" Winnie looks at Iris, eyebrows raised.

"What a left-field question," she says, still giggling. "Winnie, I *love* to dance. Just not in front of people." The kitten pads over and winds a figure-eight around Iris's ankles. She stiffens a little, almost like she's not exactly comfortable with cats.

Still, she brought it here.

For Winnie.

"You?" Winnie looks at me.

I frown. I don't remember the question.

"Do you dance?" She says this pointedly, as if she is speaking to a small child.

"Uh, no." The question conjures the image of the first moonlit night in that tiny apartment with Aria, the day we got back from our honeymoon. The moon was so full, Aria asked to keep the lights off while she turned on a slow, jazzy love song and asked me to dance right there in our living room.

With her, it was easy to try things I was sure I wouldn't be good at.

With her, everything seemed attainable.

It didn't matter if I looked foolish or even ridiculous. She had such a big, larger-than-life personality, it pulled me out of my shell.

When she died, I retreated. I have zero interest in those things anymore. I'm much happier to stick to what I know, to what makes sense.

Which is cooking.

"Why do you ask?" Iris looks at Winnie, and I feel the second her eyes are no longer trained on me. Something inside me shifts.

"The community center down the block offers square dance classes. I thought it would be fun." Winnie doesn't hide her disappointment. "I used to do it all the time with my husband. He didn't love it, but he indulged me." Her smile is wistful. "If I'm going to eat this much pasta, I'm going to have to find a way to keep my girlish figure." She shimmies, and Iris laughs.

I try to ignore it, but it's like a song that gets stuck in your head.

"I'd love to help, but I don't know the first thing about square dancing," Iris says apologetically. "But thank you both for letting me crash your meal." Then she looks at me. "I honestly haven't had food that good since I moved here." It's so kind and unexpected, especially given how rude I've been to her.

"He's good. I might keep him around for a bit." Winnie winks at her, then scoops up the kitten. "And don't be silly. You didn't crash anything. We were happy to have you." She pets the cat between the ears. "I haven't had this much company in . . ." Her voice trails off as if she's trying to remember the last time she entertained. "A long time. Let's just say that."

Iris looks at me, and I quickly look away. I don't need to be exchanging meaningful glances.

"I should go." I take purposeful strides across the apartment, hoping I can reach the door before Iris is ready to leave, but when I turn back to say a final "goodbye," I find her right behind me.

Same look on her face. I take in her features—the not-quite brown, not-quite auburn hair, the wide eyes, the trail of freckles across her nose. She's a great blend of adorable and pretty, and *that* is not something I should be thinking. I look away.

She clearly has no intention of letting me escape, and I brace myself for whatever interaction I'm about to have.

I know she's got questions.

I know I probably have the answers.

The last thing I need right now is to have to navigate a nosy neighbor on top of everything else.

So, I do what I always do—slip on my resolve, which feels a lot like armor, and prepare to drive her away.

Chapter Twelve
Iris

COULD HE *BE* MORE OBVIOUS?

Yeah, buddy, just try and duck out of dinner.

As if I'm going to let him go without explaining to me what is happening. Because he *obviously* knows, and he *obviously* lied to me.

Maybe not *specifically* a lie, but definitely an omission. He has answers. And I'm going to figure out how to get them.

Did I love helping Winnie? Actually, yes. It was really nice to meet someone new. And to help her. Plus, I *like* her.

Did I love getting to stuff my face with that *insanely delicious* homemade pasta? Also yes.

But I really need to understand how and why this is all happening.

He has the answers. And if the way Matteo cleans a kitchen is any indication, he leans toward practical. And practical is what I need right now.

Not that I need *him*. I only need to figure out *what he knows*.

If there's one thing I need to guard against, it's myself. I'm self-aware enough to know that even a year ago, in the same situation, I would've fallen head over heels by now.

The last thing I need is to develop a crush on this guy. The second we're in the hallway, I rush around in front of him. "Hey. You need to tell me what's going on."

He takes a step back, but not before I inhale the scent of pine mingled with garlic and note the flash of something unrecognizable in his dark eyes.

Man, he's handsome. Like, unfairly handsome. I feel like I'm at a disadvantage here—while I *need* answers, getting them is going to be challenging, mostly because I'm not sure I can form complete sentences if he's going to keep looking at me.

"You obviously read the same article I did, and you *obviously* came here to help Winnie, same as me."

He sighs again, looking caught, and says, "I don't know what to tell you. Like Winnie said, we ran into each other downstairs. I actually sort of know of her because of my grandparents."

"She said she never met your grandparents."

He pauses.

Caught ya.

"Right. She's . . . uh . . . kind of a legend around here. Must know her from that."

I narrow my eyes, then finally say, "You're a horrible liar."

He shakes his head at me. "I don't know what you're—"

I cross my arms over my chest. "Did you *know* that, or did the newspaper tell you that?"

He quirks a brow.

"I really do have to get to work." His voice is a low rumble, like a storm brewing just beyond the horizon.

"Are you serious?"

He can't expect me to just walk away when I obviously

know something—maybe mystical, definitely weird—is happening here.

"Oh, of course. You have to work. Sure, sure." I say, not meeting his eyes. "Big fancy chef who cooks amazing pasta *he made with his hands*. But this is my life! And it's being invaded, by . . . by *magic*!" My voice climbs an octave when I say this, and I know I'm being dramatic.

He whips his head around at me. "Will you keep it down?" he snaps.

I point. "*Aha!*"

He shushes me.

I whisper-yell, "I knew it!"

He tries to walk down the hallway, but I follow him.

"I *knew* you knew something! Why won't you just tell me what the heck is going on?"

He takes a breath, looking around the hallway as if to make sure no one is listening or watching, and just shakes his head, still moving down the corridor.

"Look. I don't want to be bothering you with this anymore than you want me to be bothering you, but . . ." I don't know what else to say to stop him but— "Matteo!"

He stops, and I see his shoulders sink.

"Please." I walk to the side of him, talking with my hands. "Please—I feel like I'm going insane. I don't know if I'm seeing things or losing it." I let out a heavy sigh. "And there's literally nobody else who can help me."

He stiffens, but he doesn't move, which I take as permission to continue.

I lay it out.

"For the past several days, I've been getting bombarded by these . . . newspapers. All with *your name* on them. I tried to return them to you, but it didn't work. Like, this newspaper keeps coming back. At first, I thought it was just a fluke, then maybe a weird sort of prank, but now, I don't know what to think. Plus, they show up *everywhere*. On my couch, in my chandelier. Stacks of them. They move by themselves. They even multiply." I'm starting to feel panicked, knowing how this sounds when I say it out loud. "One of them even floated up in the air, and flipped around, and then . . ."

Simultaneously we say, ". . . smacked you/me in the head."

He glances my way but doesn't exactly make eye contact. Something inside me settles. "What is going on?"

He looks past me, again, making sure—what, that we aren't being followed?—and then motions to the stairwell.

I follow him into the dimly lit space and blindly think that under different circumstances, it would be pretty hot to escape into a dark stairwell with a very good-looking man who knows how to cook.

When he turns back and looks at me, I feel my knees wobble because, holy heck, *those eyes*.

I want to look away. Looking away could be considered self-preservation. But it's like when someone tells you not to stare directly at the sun during a solar eclipse. Knowing you shouldn't do something sometimes makes it harder to do.

"You're not . . . seeing things," he finally admits. "Weird things happen. Sometimes. It's just part of living in this building."

I frown. Okay. A mention of the building. This is progress. "Is this place, like, haunted?"

"No, I don't think so. It's not . . . like that, exactly."

I pause. Am I really going to ask this aloud? Yes. Because I really want to know.

"Is it . . . magic?" My words echo in the cathedral-like acoustics of the stairwell, and I swear I hear the distant tinkle of chimes. Asking the question out loud makes me feel ridiculous, which is probably why I whispered it, even though we're standing here, just the two of us.

Just the two of us.
My brain makes more of that than it should.
"Do you believe in magic?" Matteo asks.
"Do you?" I counter.
He pulls a face. "I didn't used to."
"But now?"
He shrugs.
"Then explain the newspapers," I say, a little more forcefully than I mean to. "Because it doesn't make sense."
He squints at me, as if trying to place my face after having only met me once. "And you're uncomfortable when things don't make sense?"
"No, I'm perfectly comfortable when things don't make sense. Algebra makes no sense, and I survived high school," I say. "This mustache trend on guys in their twenties makes no sense, but that's never bothered me enough to make me lose sleep." I sigh. "*This* is making me lose sleep."
"I wish I could help more. I really do. I just don't fully understand it myself."
"But you read the paper! You showed up at Winnie's with Italian food!"
"And you brought a cat."
"Because of the newspaper."
He shifts, as if he's only now realizing he might've just proved my point. "Why a cat?"
"I thought she needed one," I say. "It's what the article talked about. I searched all over God's green earth to find a cat that matched the exact color as the one she had before, but I had no luck. And then, out of nowhere, this random black kitten with white feet was sitting in my parking space right before I was headed upstairs to knock on her door."
He looks antsy.
"Do you really have to get to work?"

"I do."

"Can you walk and talk at the same time?"

He pulls open the front door of the building and motions for me to walk through. As soon as I'm out the door, he breezes past me, walking at what feels like an Olympic clip.

I jog to catch up to him. His legs are longer, and if I didn't know better, I'd say he doesn't really care if I keep up with him. I zip my coat to keep out the winter chill, then reach out for his arm in an attempt to stop him.

"Look, I know we don't know each other at all, but for some reason, we both seem to be the target of some sort of strange . . ." My voice trails off because I have no idea what this is. A joke? A cosmic event? A dual mental breakdown? "I was just hoping you might be able to help me make some sense of it."

His eyes ping my hand, still on his arm, and I quickly pull it away, then stuff it inside my coat pocket. I'm just short of begging him for answers, which I'm not above doing.

He looks away, and I can practically *hear* his wheels turning. The only thing I don't know is if he's trying to decide how to explain this, or if he's trying to decide how *not* to.

"I get it," he says. "It's . . . odd."

"Odd." I huff out a laugh. "That's an understatement."

"And I'd really love to help you—"

I cross my arms and fix him with what I hope is an epic glare.

"Aaaand I will. But . . ." He pauses, then turns and looks behind him.

I lean to the side, peering in the direction he's looking, but I don't see anything.

"But what?"

"I have to get ready for the dinner service," he says, exasperated. "With any luck, the, um . . . newspaper delivery . . .

person won't get our apartments mixed up again." He starts walking again, like the conversation is over.

"The delivery person?" I stand there for a second before realizing that no, I don't want the conversation to be over. Because I've gotten zero answers to my ten thousand questions. "There is no delivery person. My co-workers think it's magic. They're convinced. Like our building has a personality or something."

"You told your co-workers?" He shoots me a look.

"Is that against the unwritten rules?" My tone drips sarcasm. "Because nobody included an instruction manual." I hug my coat tighter around me. "Also, why are you *walking* to work in this weather?"

He turns around and keeps walking.

I realize that I'm standing on a corner about a block from The Serendipity. If we make a right turn, we'll be in a small shopping area that looks like something out of a movie. The brick buildings are old with colorful awnings and faded murals painted on several of their walls. It's the kind of charm that makes a perfect backdrop for a photo shoot or a proposal.

I pause for a second and take it in. I've absently driven past here hundreds of times but never really *looked*. The school is in the opposite direction, and I haven't taken time to explore my new town yet. It's like my plan to overhaul my personality feels daunting outside of my apartment. It's easier to hold back when there's no one to hold myself back from.

My eyes settle on a hardware store across the street. Not a big chain store, a little mom and pop shop, and I suddenly want to go buy a screwdriver just to do what I can to keep them in business. "This block really is cool," I say, forgetting for a minute that I'm mad at him.

He's still walking and is now a good half a block away.

I huff and puff, then decide to run and catch up. "Hey, wait up."

When I reach him, he barely glances at me and asks, "What are you doing?"

I'm a little out of breath, and the cold has my lungs extra wheezy. "I just realized I've never seen this part of town."

He tosses a glance down the street behind him. "You haven't?"

I shake my head, stopping short of admitting that I have no social life. It's not like me, really. I've always been a social person. I've always liked meeting people and hearing their stories. I'm just trying not to share all of mine. In my experience, oversharing is a turn-off.

I draw in a breath, and that's when I see a sign coming up on our left. *Aria.* "Wait. Is *that* your restaurant?"

He keeps walking and nods, like he knows which sign I've seen without even looking up. "Yes. And they're probably wondering where I am, so, can we finish this conversation later?"

"What about Winnie?"

"What about her?"

"Are we going to keep up with her? I mean, one meal and a cat aren't going to solve her loneliness. What do we do next?"

"We?" he asks plainly.

I've had about enough of this. And him. "Look, you can be all '*I don't know what's going on, I'm going to be closed off and brooding*' or whatever, but this is serious. You might know what's going on—heck, you might even have been reading this newspaper for who knows how long, but I haven't. This is new and exciting and scary, all at once."

He makes a face.

"Please. Whatever wall is stopping you from helping me, just . . . peek around it for a second."

He softens. He takes a long, deep breath, then lets it out.

"I told her I'd be back," he says, simply.

"And you meant that?"

He frowns, as if he doesn't understand the question. "Well, yeah. Why would you think—"

"Because people don't always do what they say they're going to do."

"Well, I'm not one of those people. I'm a man of my word."

He meets my eyes, and all my internal organs rearrange themselves. Because I believe him. Or I want to.

It's just . . . in my experience, there's no such thing.

People always leave.

"I just don't want to let her down," I say. I might be working on putting some distance between my big feelings and everyone else, but that doesn't mean I'm going to become the kind of person I'm actively trying to avoid.

A person who can't be trusted.

"I'm not planning on letting her down," he says.

"Okay."

"Okay?" He looks like he wants to go inside with every atom of his being.

I nod. "Okay."

He spins and grabs the door as I blurt out, "But . . ." and stop him one more time.

He heaves another big sigh and slowly turns around. Again.

Might've done that one on purpose. Just to get a rise. Which is why there's a three-count pause before I come up with a new question. "Do you want to let me know when you have time to finish our conversation?"

"Sure," he says, lifting a hand in a wave.

"Should I give you my number, or . . .?"

"I know where you live," he calls over his shoulder, turning away and entering the restaurant.

The door closes on me.

"Right."

Apparently, that's that.

I'm getting used to this view. The outside of Matteo's door.

Maybe if I knock long enough, he'll let me in.

Chapter Thirteen
Matteo

"Who was that?"

Nicola is on me the second I walk in the kitchen. She's standing near the door, making no attempt to pretend she wasn't spying.

"Nobody," I say, because there is no story there, no matter how much Nic wants there to be.

"Didn't *look* like nobody," she says. "You stood there and watched her walk away."

Yeah, to make sure she actually left, I think but don't say.

I groan and trade my winter coat for my chef's coat, then move over to the sink to wash my hands. "She lives in my building. She was just—" I stop talking and look at her. "It's fine. No big deal. She's nobody."

Only, as I say it, something inside feels wrong.

She's really not nobody.

Though I'm not sure if I want her to be a somebody.

I can feel Nicola's eyes on me for a long moment while I try to pretend not to notice. When I finally glance at her, I watch her face switch from suspicion to a familiar pitying expression. "It's okay if you're interested in somebody, Tay."

"I'm not."

"Aria wouldn't want you to be alone for the rest of your life." She pauses, then laughs. "Actually, she probably would. That girl had a serious jealous streak."

I half-smile at the thought. Because it's true. Movies and books always make it seem like the person who's gone would *want* the love of their life to move on, but with Aria, I'm not so sure.

She once got mad at me because I cheated on her with a celebrity.

In a dream she had.

Of course I would never, celebrity or otherwise, but she still confronted me about it, asking me if I knew Zendaya personally.

I stifle a smile at the memory.

"I have to believe if she saw you like this, she'd want you to get back out there," Nicola says.

"Saw me like what?" I dry my hands and lean against the counter, studying Nicola as if she can telepathically answer my question.

I expect her to backtrack, but instead, she plows forward, almost like she's been waiting for a chance to tell me exactly what she thinks. "Look. I think of you like family. I remember the guy you were before."

Nicola is one of the few connections I still have to Aria. They were best friends, and while I do value her opinions, I prefer to hear her thoughts on cannoli. Not my love life.

"The night you and Aria met, she would not shut up about you. This ridiculously hot guy she'd met in her food safety class." She laughs softly at the recollection, and my insides are at war—part of me wanting her to stop reliving these memories and another part of me wanting to hear every single thing she remembers about Aria.

"But once she got to know you, it wasn't your beautiful face or your God-given talent in the kitchen she talked about, Tay." She waits for me to look at her, something I'm determined not to do but end up doing anyway. "It was how kind you were. How fun and happy. How much you loved people. How you cooked these amazing meals and presented them like a kid, super excited to share something you'd made."

I look down.

She continues. "Your whole reason for wanting to open this place was to bring people together, to pass down not only the food, but the feelings you have *about* the food." She straightens. "But now, it's almost like you're afraid that if you do anything that makes you happy, you'll betray her somehow."

I continue to stare at the floor. There's a chunk of tomato under the sink. Someone missed it when they were cleaning.

"Look, life kicked you in the gut. And me too—she was my best friend." Her voice shakes. I fight to hold back emotion, and this is exactly why I hate talking about this.

"I loved her too. She was . . ." She stops and shakes her head. "My point is, you're still here, and I'm still here, and I think it's okay to believe that Aria would want both of us to be happy and have good lives. You, especially. It's okay to move on."

Is it?

Is it okay?

My defenses kick up, and the wall slams down.

My eyes flick up to hers. "I love you, Nic, and I appreciate what you're saying, but I'm good. Really."

I'm not.

We both know it.

But I'm not interested in "moving on."

Loving someone the way I loved Aria isn't only unlikely—

it's impossible. I won't entertain even the possibility, because I can't think of anything that would dishonor her more than trying to replace her.

Life didn't just kick me in the gut. It hollowed me out.

And I'm going to do everything I can to make sure I never feel pain like that again.

Chapter Fourteen
Iris

THWAP

"Ow! Come *ON*—"

I barely force my eyes to focus through the sleep still in them long enough to see a disappearing wisp of golden shimmer.

I whip the covers off and yell, "It's not nice to bully people, you know!!" at the ceiling.

A tinkle of chimes.

"And I can hear sarcasm in those chimes!"

I rub my forehead, grumpy. It's the day after dinner at Winnie's, and thanks to my new surprise alarm clock, I feel instantly on edge.

Stupid magic. Stupid newspaper.

As I'm getting ready for work, I open every door to every room, cabinet, fridge, and vanity carefully, like I'm expecting a mass of newspapers to come rushing out.

But nothing happens.

I carefully open the door to my apartment and quickly look down, slightly relieved and a little disappointed when it's just a mat.

"Quit messing with me," I huff at no one.

I stare down the hallway, almost wishing I had a reason to walk down to Matteo's door and knock.

The truth is—and I'm only admitting this silently because no one else needs to know—I spent most of last night watching *Project Runway* reruns and crocheting a new stuffed jellyfish.

And thinking about Matteo.

At one point, I had to rewind the show because I wasn't paying attention and completely missed what the judges said about a very hideous couture gown made out of wrapping paper and tinsel.

He said he'd help. But he never said when.

And the not knowing is really messing with my head. Maybe even more than the bully of a newspaper.

I get to work, stash my things in my classroom, and decide to take a lap through the hallway before I'm overrun by first graders ready for art. I catch snippets of conversations coming from inside the classrooms as teachers usher their students to their desks for the start of another school day. I smile, say hi, wave to my co-workers and their students, then turn to go back the way I came as the hallways begin to empty.

I'm passing by the main office when the front doors of the school open, and I see a harried woman walk in, holding the hand of a little girl with big, wide eyes. They both look frazzled.

I smile brightly because, personal woes aside, I *am* on staff here, and I recognize her daughter, Alice, a very quiet, very artistic third grader.

"Good morning, Alice!" I say, in my brightest tone. To her mother: "I'm Miss Ellington." I hold up my lanyard to show her my school ID.

"We're so late," the mom says. "Alice hates it when we're late."

The girl's face falls.

"She never wants to make a scene." The mom pulls Alice a little closer, wrapping an arm around her shoulder. "We've got a lot going on at home."

My smile holds as I nod kindly, studying them a little more closely.

Their matching red-rimmed eyes seem to be visual proof that they're going through a hard time.

I smile at Alice, and for a flicker of a moment, I see something familiar in her eyes. A recognizable pain.

"Oh, my gosh, I get it," I say. "I've been late twice this week." I exaggerate my grimace and widen my eyes. "Thankfully I've got this great alarm clock that practically hits me in the face to wake me up!" I laugh, even though this is my least favorite thing about the newspapers. "I promise you aren't the only one who's late today. No need to apologize."

Still, Alice's worried expression holds.

"Alice, would you like me to walk you to class?" I ask.

Alice's shoulders rise and fall, as if she's just taken a very deep breath and let it out but without making any noise. Alice has probably gotten really good at making herself invisible.

Maybe I should take a page out of her book. I tend to jump in headfirst, whether anyone invites me or not. Always looking for my people. Never finding them.

It feels like if you don't have "people" by a certain age, you just don't find them.

At least, that's how it's been for me.

I suppose this latest move to Serendipity Springs is my attempt to accept that. And to change enough things about myself to avoid running people off.

I look at Alice. "Your teacher is Miss Ridgeway, right?"

Alice nods softly.

"I love Miss Ridgeway! She's a good friend of mine," I say brightly. "I think her class is in P.E. right now. I can take you down and get you settled." I look at her mom. "If that's okay with you?"

She looks at Alice, then back at me, and nods. "Of course."

I smile and reach a hand toward the girl, who studies it for a moment, then finally steps forward and slips her own little hand in mine.

I give it a squeeze, smile again at her mom, and say, "My classroom is just down the hall, through those doors." I point in the direction of the art room. "If you ever need anything, my door is always open."

Alice's mom nods. "I'm Joy, by the way."

I smile. "Iris."

She looks at Alice. "Have a good day, hon."

Alice looks away, and Joy's smile fades for a fraction of a second. Then, she pastes it back on, straightens, and nods at me.

I lead Alice back down the hall toward the gymnasium. "Did you get to pet any of the dogs when they were here?" I ask as we walk.

Alice nods.

"Me too," I say. "I *loved* them."

"Me too," Alice says quietly. "I liked the brown one."

She spoke! This feels like a major win. Since the beginning of the school year, I don't think I've ever heard her talk, and not for lack of trying.

I tell her about finding the cat yesterday—though I leave out the magic bits—explaining that it was such a happy *coincidence* because my neighbor had lost her cat and needed a new friend.

The second the words are out of my mouth, I can't help but wonder if Alice and her mom could use a new friend, too.

"Are you excited for the art show?" I ask, because I did finally set the date and tell my students about it and because I'm really trying to get them excited about it. I talked Liz and Brooke into helping me, and we've got a whole plan to do it up big, like a real art show, with stanchions and easels and placards and everything. The kids deserve to have a big deal made about their work. They deserve to be celebrated.

I deserved to be celebrated.

I shove the thought aside and give Alice's hand a squeeze. "You ready for P.E.?"

She shrugs.

"Oof," I say. "I know the feeling. We artsy types aren't usually fans of physical education, huh?" Her smile is fleeting, and then she tucks it away.

As we get closer to the gym, I can hear the muffled sound of upbeat, bouncy music. I open one of the double doors to see both third grade classes being placed in lines by a young woman I've never seen before. An older man stands on the stage, bobbing to the music, as if he's got an imaginary partner. He reminds me of a cartoon character, all arms and legs, with a wide grin that would seem fake if there wasn't so much joy radiating from it.

We watch for a few seconds as the kids bounce around, some of them paying attention to the man on the stage while others poke at each other, boundless energy zipping around the gym.

"What are they doing?" I ask, mostly to myself, but Alice hears me and says, "Dancing."

She lets go of my hand and walks, hands firmly at her sides, over to another little girl, a friend who waves excitedly, and I can't help but notice the sad expression doesn't fall away.

I watch them for a few minutes, staying out of the way, as the young woman joins the older man up on the stage. She catches the eye of the P.E. teacher, a guy all the kids call "Tiny," likely a football nickname he got in high school that just stuck. It's not the most respectful way to address a teacher, but Tiny is basically a big kid himself, and it's never seemed to bother him. He did somehow convince the kids to call him "Mr. Tiny" when Mr. Kincaid is around, which is kind of hilarious now that I think about it.

The woman nods at Tiny—who shoots her a thumbs up—and then she picks up a handheld microphone set up on the stage. She clears her throat. "Children! Good morning! My name is Christina, but you can call me Miss Chris, and this *young* man over here is my dad, Mr. Cromwell."

"He's not young!" one of the kids hollers over the smattering of applause.

"He's old!" another kid shouts.

Christina glances at Mr. Tiny for help, but he's sitting on the bleachers, staring at his phone.

Her dad steps up to the microphone and says, "Age is just a number, kids, and mine won't keep me from moving around the dance floor." He does a little shimmy. "We're here today to teach you all"—he pauses, like he's about to share an important secret—"how to square dance!"

The kids start cheering, even though I'm certain they have no idea what square dancing is, and once Christina calms them all down, she and her dad turn on the music and do a little demonstration of what the kids are about to learn.

They're third graders, so I'm pretty sure their version of square dancing isn't going to look anything like Christina and her father's, but I honestly don't really care because the only thing I'm thinking about is Winnie and what a great dance partner this man could be for her.

What a coincidence. Almost like . . .

This time, I let my brain finish the word.
Magic.

The kids start class grimacing when they're asked to hold hands and move around the circle, muttering variations of "Ew, gross" under their breath, but soon they move past the cooties and actually start having fun.

And it's all because of Mr. Cromwell's personality. This guy is hilarious and fun, full of energy and wit. It's my free period, so I stay to watch the entire class, and I'm floored at how this old man gets on the mic and calls out the moves, like a professional.

Hey there kids, now take it slow
Right and left on the heel 'n toe
Hands in the middle, now don't you wait
It's time for y'all t' star promenade!

The kids are loving it. This old man has taken a dance from I don't even know when—the 1800's? Earlier?—and successfully made third graders—*third graders*—fall in love with it.

When the class period ends and the kids line up by the door, they're still buzzing about it, mimicking his cadence on the mic and making up their own lyrics. And the big question they all seem to be asking is, "When can we do it again?!"

As they take their bottomless energy out of the gym and down the hall, I strike up a conversation with Christina and her dad, who insists that I call him Jerry.

I tell them about Winnie, and Christina gasps, because it turns out her dad has been looking for a dance partner ever since he found out about a local square dance competition.

"Wait," I say. "A . . . square dancing competition? That's actually a thing?"

They both look at one another and laugh. "Oh, it's a

thing," Christina says. "Dad discovered a group of people his age who absolutely love it."

"We need eight, so four couples," he says, "and I'm the only one without a partner."

I can't believe how this is all lining up, but I have a sneaking suspicion it's not a coincidence at all. I absently wonder if this kind of magic has been here the whole time and people just don't take the time to notice?

"With the right partner, we can win it," Jerry says, eyes gleaming. "How does she move?"

I shrug. "I'm not sure, but she's really fun. I think you're going to love her."

I might be overstepping, but when Jerry hands over his phone number, I feel like Emma Woodhouse. I think this is going to be the perfect match.

Chapter Fifteen
Iris

S*WING YER PARTNER, do-si-do* . . .

I'm still humming as I walk into the teacher's lounge. It's lunchtime, and I find Brooke making copies of a coloring page with a big letter M on it. I've managed to focus on the kids for the last three hours, but now, all I can think of is Winnie.

Which makes me think of Italian food.

Which makes me think of Matteo.

Which makes me think of magic.

I walk over to a table and sit down, silently opening my lunch box and pulling out my sandwich. It's not homemade pasta, but at least it'll calm the grumble in my stomach.

Brooke turns and looks at me. "You good?"

She and Liz are the only people besides Matteo who know about the newspapers. And since Matteo hasn't helped me yet, maybe Brooke can. I'm not feeling very patient.

Maybe I just want to talk about it again. To give her the update, which I only now realize I expected her to ask for.

She frowns. "What's wrong?"

I pause for a long moment, then stand and move closer

because Joyce and Mr. Truitt are eating lunch over a very quiet game of checkers, their daily ritual.

Brooke turns a coloring sheet over on the copier and starts it going again. "Are you okay?"

I press my lips together, then take a deep breath. "So . . . I went home last night, and there was a *cat* in my parking spot. Just sitting there. Staring at me." I watch her, waiting for her to make the connection.

She doesn't.

"A *kitten*, Brooke."

She cocks her head, studying me. "Did you . . . rescue it?"

"Yes," I say. "Of course I did. I took it to my neighbor, which is obviously what I was supposed to do."

Her eyebrows furrow, and she almost looks worried. "Okay . . ."

The door opens, and I freeze, feeling fidgety and rigid at the same time. When Liz walks in, I relax a little, pacing away from the two of them, wishing I hadn't had that third cup of coffee this morning.

I turn back in time to see them share a knowing, concerned, glance.

"What's wrong with you?" Liz asks.

"There was a *cat* in my parking spot, you guys." I look at them again, waiting for the lightbulb. Waiting for them to remember that *they* were the ones who told me to adopt a cat for Winnie *earlier this week*. Do they really not see the connection here?

They both just stare.

"Did you find its owner?" Liz asks. "Or are you a crazy cat lady now?"

What is happening right now? Do they not remember our conversation?

"I'm not crazy," I say, a little louder than I mean to because *I'm not*.

At my reaction, they both shift.

"Sorry, it's just . . ." I pause. My hands move with my words. "A *kitten*, you guys. It was the perfect color and everything. Black with white booties."

Brooke looks at Liz, then at me. "Is there some significance to the kitten?"

"Is there some . . ." I start repeating her question and then stop, now getting frustrated from the confusion. It's like I'm in *The Truman Show* and everyone is in on the social experiment but me.

I try again. Slower. "Remember, I told you about my neighbor . . . the one in the building . . . the one I read about in the newspaper . . ." Do they really not remember this? I look at Brooke. "You told me to get a cat for the lonely old lady in my building."

Brooke's eyebrows pull downward in a frown. "Uh . . . I don't know what you're talking about."

"My *magic building*," I hiss. "I got my hot neighbor's newspaper, and I kept trying to get rid of it and . . ."

But her face is blank. Like she doesn't know what I'm talking about.

"Ooh! I want to hear the story," Liz gushes, moving closer. "Just tell us what's happening. Is it the hot chef? Did you run into him again?" She looks at me, deadpan. "Is *that* the kind of magic we're talking about here?"

I freeze. A weird feeling of déjà vu passes over me.

That's exactly what Liz said when I told her and Brooke about the magic in the first place.

Word for word.

I stare at them both. They honestly don't remember.

Maybe this is how The Serendipity keeps its secrets.

I switch gears and fake-laugh. "Oh, gosh, I thought . . . I thought I told you." My laugh turns into a cackle because *they don't remember*, and I'm spinning out over here. "I met one of my neighbors, and it was like this really great coincidence because she'd just lost her cat, and I don't want a cat, so, you know . . . magic." I do soft jazz hands on that last word, like it's a perfect explanation for my strange behavior, something I think might be best to keep to myself after all.

I think about Matteo's question and wonder if I'm really *not* supposed to discuss the magic. Is that why he won't talk to me about it? Are there consequences if you do?

"So, this is about a cat. Not about the hot guy?" Liz looks disappointed. "Because if you were mysteriously brought together with someone, you should pay attention. That place is magic. Everyone says so."

I stare at her again, the memory of her saying that exact thing to me two days ago echoing in my mind.

"Well, I don't believe in magic," I say, almost robotically. "And I'm really not in the market for romance."

She shakes her head. "Famous last words."

I nod, watching them as they watch me back, and then finally, I grab my lunch, excuse myself from the lounge, and rush down the hall toward my classroom, inhaling a very slow, very deep breath because that's a tactic used to help people deal with anxiety.

And right now, my body is flooded with anxious thoughts.

How can they not remember? How far does this building's influence go? Am I being watched by the magic right now?

Will I forget?

And one last question that just pops in there without permission—*How long before I see Matteo again?*

Chapter Sixteen
Matteo

"Chef, there's someone asking for you."

I don't look up. I'm plating a *pasta carbonara*, and my staff knows I don't make a habit of talking to customers anymore. I'm not good at it.

That was supposed to be Aria's area.

"No time, Zeb," I tell the waiter, wiping the edge of the dish.

Across the kitchen, I can feel Nicola and Val staring daggers into the back of my head.

"She says it's important," he says. "She's a little, er . . . manic?"

At that, I stand upright as Val moves toward me and sets the plate up for one of the other waiters to take. "Go, Chef."

I glance over at her, and she's moved into the spot where I was, plating the next order without missing a beat. When I don't move, she adds, "I've got this."

And she does. Obviously. That's not why I'm hesitating.

After a beat, I look at Zeb. "I'll be right out."

Zeb disappears through the doors, and I wash my hands, knowing exactly who is waiting for me.

A part of me, weirdly, is hoping I'm right.

Seconds later, the kitchen door swings open, and I get my confirmation. There, striding into my kitchen, is Iris. Invading my space like she has a right to be here.

She really doesn't. Not here.

The magic of the newspapers has never shown up at my work . . . until now. Still, seeing her isn't as annoying as I thought it would be.

"Oh! Uh . . . I'm sorry, miss, you can't be back here," my prep cook, Dante, says, angling to get between her and me.

Iris doesn't seem to hear him. She's laser-focused, scanning the kitchen with a clear purpose, and when her gaze finally lands on me, she starts walking again. Behind her, I can see the worried expressions of my kitchen staff, and I hold up a hand, assuring them that she's not a threat. At least not a physical one.

I do find her emotionally disruptive, and that's something I have no intention of analyzing.

I hang up the towel. It's obvious she's not giving any of this up. Unlike the other people I've told about the newspapers, she's remembering. I don't know why the rules have suddenly changed, but I can't ignore the magic. It's to my own detriment. Especially if this really is my chance to be done with it once and for all.

That means Iris is also someone I can no longer ignore.

She stops right in front of me. "Hey."

I make a face. "Hi."

She purses her lips. "We need to talk, and I can't wait for you to decide when."

Bold. I respect that.

"Okay."

She looks up at the others in the room and leans over to make sure they can't hear her.

"It's about *you know what*," she whispers at me, then leans back, a pointed expression on her face.

Right. Okay. So . . . it's time to talk.

"Fine," I say. "But—"

Before I can tell her that the kitchen full of staff isn't the best spot to discuss this, she cuts me off.

"Today at school I met an old man who was—get this— teaching the third graders how to square dance," she says, and not quietly. "And you know my co-workers? The ones I told about—" She looks around for a second, the only indication she's aware that we aren't alone. "Everything? They don't remember the conversation." She throws up her hands. "Completely oblivious."

She takes a step toward me and points. "But you remember. Don't you?"

I straighten, looking around the kitchen at my staff. "I'll be back in five." I motion for Iris to follow me into the small office next to the back door of the restaurant. I walk around the desk then turn to face her, finding her standing in the doorway, eyes roaming over my workspace.

While I do have a business manager, I spend a fair amount of time in here, planning menus, booking events, paying bills, working on inventory. It's the business of owning a restaurant, and while it's not my favorite part, it's critical to Aria's success.

The longer Iris stands there, looking, the more exposed I feel.

Finally, she meets my eyes. "You're meticulous. This is the cleanest office I've ever been in."

I give the office a cursory glance as she steps inside.

"Close the door," I say.

She lifts her chin, as if to make sure I know she doesn't like to be bossed around.

"Please," I add.

She closes it, then turns and squares off with me.

"I like things in their place. It helps me keep things—" I stop. I don't want to get into this. I've been over my need for order with my therapist. *Control the things I can control.* I watch her. "What questions do you have?"

But she doesn't seem to hear me. She's too engrossed in the wall where Val framed and hung my diploma, business license, and the cover of a regional magazine that featured me as an up-and-coming chef to watch. A shelf of plaques and trophies—awards I've won.

"Chef of the Year?" Iris asks, studying one of the frames. "Most promising up-and-coming . . ." Her voice trails off.

I inhale. She's discovering information about me, and I don't exactly like it.

She turns back. "You're kind of a big deal."

"Not really."

"According to this magazine, you are." She points to the framed image, reading the headline next to that horrible posed photo. "And your restaurant is one of the top ten to visit in the entire northeast region? That's huge."

I don't look at her. I don't like this. I just want to get back to my kitchen.

"I get it. I tasted your pasta, remember?"

A picture of her talking with her mouth full, gushing about how good it tasted, flashes through my mind.

It's not an intrusive memory, the kind I have to shake myself to dislodge from my mind. It's the kind with a warm feeling attached to it.

It's been a while since memories felt like that.

"You mentioned something about a man you met?" I ask, hoping to get her—and me—back on track.

She takes a few steps toward the desk, then pauses, like she's not sure if she's allowed to sit. Which is funny considering she didn't employ that same caution when she barged into my kitchen in the first place. "I know I keep bugging you about this, but . . ."

And that's when I see the genuine fear in her eyes.

A familiar worry that her mind is playing tricks on her. That something is genuinely wrong with her.

And something I don't want to feel creeps in. *Empathy.*

I motion to the chair. "Sit."

She does, but she doesn't speak. Instead, her gaze falls to her hands, folded in her lap. I notice she's fidgeting, clasping and unclasping her hands, spinning a simple silver ring around her finger.

"Have you eaten?" I ask.

At that, she glances up, eyes wide. "Wait. That's an option?"

I tilt my head slightly.

"It's a restaurant."

She stares at me, like she's not sure if she can trust me, and after a moment, she shakes her head and says, "I'm sorry, I'm not sure how to process *kindness* coming from you."

I quirk a brow. "I can take it back?"

"No!" she practically shouts. After pretending to gather her composure, she adds. "No. Please don't take it back. I'm hungry." She smiles. "And out of frozen pizzas."

I groan.

"I do have Pop-Tarts, though. I might actually be okay." She smirks, and while I'm sure she is flush with Pop-Tarts, it's clear she's said this to get a reaction from me.

I hide how at ease she makes me feel.

Shaking my head, I stand and walk toward the door and into the kitchen, sensing the questions my staff isn't asking, and when I reach Val, I hold up a hand.

"She's a neighbor. She's got a few questions about our building. And she's hungry," I say, hoping to keep the questions at bay.

Nicola sidles up next to Val, and now I've got two pairs of wide eyes trained on me. "She's the same one who walked you to work."

"She walked you to work?" Val gasps.

"She did not walk to me to work," I say. "She followed me. She had a bunch of questions then too, and when I didn't answer, she wouldn't go away."

They look at each other. "That tracks," Val says. "But why is she here now?"

"I told you. More questions." I glance through the window and see Iris sitting there, looking around, patiently waiting.

"She's really pretty," Nicola says.

"But cute at the same time," Val agrees.

"Right," Nicola says, like the two of them are spit-balling. "Not intimidating—"

"More like a girl-next-door."

"Ooh, so convenient!"

"Just a trip down the hallway—"

"Bottle of wine—"

"Short walk of shame—"

"Are you two finished?" I ask desperately.

They both smile, extra-wide.

They're ridiculous.

"Do you *like* her?" Nicola asks.

I only stare.

They gasp.

"Chef! You do?!" Nicola exclaims.

I take an extra-long breath, gauging my dwindling level of patience before I speak. "I don't know her. I just want her to leave so I can get back to work." I scrub a hand down my face. "But she's going to eat Pop-Tarts for dinner if we don't feed her—"

They both let out a comical groan in unison.

"Exactly. So. Can you two stop acting like annoying teenagers and bring something back when you get a chance?"

Val's eyes narrow. "You want her to go . . . so you're feeding her dinner?"

"Pack it up in a to-go box," I say. "Maybe she'll get the hint."

"Uh-huh," Val says. "Okay. I'll bring back a chicken parm."

"Great." I start to walk away.

"And I'll bring back a dessert," Nicola calls after me.

I turn back. "I didn't ask for that!"

"Too late!" She disappears around the corner.

"I don't think you *both* need to deliver it," I shout after them, but there's no answer.

There's no point in arguing. Nicola and Val have an agenda, and it doesn't matter what I say. After all, Iris is the first person outside of vendors and employees to show up in the kitchen looking for me.

I walk back into my office and find Iris, still waiting, but looking worried. Maybe even scared.

I sit down, remembering how jarring it was when the magic first showed up for me. It feels overwhelming and confusing, and there is no way to just "go with it." And it took me months before I asked anyone about it. With the exception of my grandpa, nobody remembered anything I said. It was like . . . the same magic that delivered the newspapers, magic I assume the building generates, also decided who got to know about it—and who didn't.

Once my grandpa acknowledged it, I started to accept the fact that while the magic doesn't make sense, it is a part of living in our building.

Maybe that's what I'm supposed to do for Iris.

And maybe—hopefully, finally—that means the magic will move from me to her, like it did from my grandpa to me.

"Will you be straight with me?" she asks. "Like, will you just answer my questions?"

I pause for a three-count, then nod. It feels like the humane thing to do. But also—the realization that I could get my life back, free of magic, is too tempting to ignore.

Before she can say anything else, though, the door opens and Nicola walks in, followed by Val, who is carrying not one but two plated dinners. Neither of which is in a to-go container.

I frown, but Val is not looking at me.

"I thought you might be hungry too, Chef," she says. "Figured you guys could have a bite back here." She sets the plates down next to the two napkins, silverware, and a small tray of desserts Nicola has already placed on the desk. The only thing missing is a taper candle and a violinist. They are the opposite of subtle.

"I don't eat during service, Val," I say curtly, hoping that if my glare doesn't remind her this isn't a romantic dinner for two, then maybe my tone will. I add through gritted teeth, "You know this."

She waves me off. "I know, Chef, but there's a first time for everything."

"The rush is over, and we only have a few more customers out there," she goes on. "Figured it's good for you to see that we can handle things, you know, if you ever need some time off." She glances at Iris, then finally meets my eyes.

I've got my most annoyed expression pinned in place, though, and she quickly looks away.

"I'm Val," she says to Iris. "Sous chef."

"And I'm Nicola." Nicola beams. "Pastry chef."

They're like two annoying little sisters with a very obvious ulterior motive.

"First, you two are amazing and beautiful and I want to be best friends with both of you," Iris jokes.

They all have a laugh, and I want to chew my arm off.

"Second, you guys did not have to bring me this," Iris says. "I would've been happy with a piece of bread."

Nic laughs. "You're not a peasant."

And Val adds, "That's just not how we do things here."

Dante strolls in with two glasses of water, sets them down on the desk, and leaves without a word.

"You two have a nice dinner," Nicola says, moving toward the door. "Let us know if you need anything."

Val walks over and closes the blinds that cover the windows facing the kitchen.

I stare into the back of her head, willing her to feel my frustration, but she continues to avoid looking at me.

Probably as a means of self-preservation. As if I'm not going to address this little stunt after Iris leaves.

Once they've gone, I resist the urge to apologize for them but then give in. "They're . . . a lot."

"I like them," Iris says. "They seem really great."

"They are," I say. "Just . . . nosy."

She smiles and then glances down at the plate. "Is it . . . okay if. . .?"

"Yes, of course. *Buon appetito.*"

She picks up her fork and cuts into the chicken, dragging it through the sauce before taking a bite. She closes her eyes, inhaling as she chews, like she's tasting the food with all of her senses.

I watch as her brow furrows and she lets out a sigh of appreciation, like this is the best thing she's ever tasted. It's borderline inappropriate, but I don't look away. Nicola and Val are right. Iris is beautiful. And cute. A rare combination.

Watching her enjoy even the simplest things—like her food—wakes something up inside me.

She opens her eyes and finds me staring. "Aren't you going to eat?"

"I'm still working," I tell her.

Her frown deepens. "Sounded like your staff is going to handle things so you don't have to."

"Do you want to ask your questions?"

"Yes," she says. "But now I want to devour this entire plate of food and maybe part of yours, and I really want to do that before it gets cold." She picks up a loaf of bread and tears a chunk off.

I love that she's not shy about eating in front of me, but I don't say so. And once again, the way she shovels the food into her mouth but still takes time to appreciate it makes me like her a little more than I want to.

"I know what you're going to ask," I say.

"All the same thousand questions I've already asked but you've refused to answer, probably." Her mouth is full of bread, but I can still hear the sarcasm.

"Right." I squint at her. Am I really going to do this? I haven't talked about the magic in three years, and only ever with my grandpa. But it's obvious if I don't, Iris won't go away.

If the magic wants her to know, then I'll tell her, and maybe—fingers crossed—I'll be able to get rid of it for good. Besides, there's still a chance she won't remember anything I tell her tomorrow.

"I was in the same boat as you a few years ago," I say.

She stops chewing.

"You're not hallucinating." I meet her eyes. "The building we live in is magic."

Chapter Seventeen
Iris

I STARE AT MATTEO, mouth full, mid-bite.

I'm not sure I've heard him right.

Did he actually just tell me—out loud—that our building is magic?

I'm not sure what surprises me more—the fact that he admitted it or the fact that he's willing to talk to me at all.

I swallow my bite and wait for him to continue. When he doesn't, I say, "What do you mean? Like, for *real* magic? As in Merlin and casting spells and—"

"No, it's not exactly—"

I keep talking. "Who started it? Is there, like, a coven? Is it scary magic? Am I going to get turned into a frog? Or maybe it's more like Harry Pot—"

"*Iris.*"

It's the first time he's said my name, and when he does, I stop. A shiver runs down my arms. I force myself to ignore it.

"What I'm about to tell you isn't going to make any sense," he says.

"Nothing about this entire last week has made sense," I quip, stabbing another piece of chicken. "Have at it."

He picks up the loaf of bread, tears off a small piece and pops it in his mouth. After chewing thoughtfully for a moment, he says, "I'm trying to figure out the simplest way to explain this."

"Just say it. No matter how ridiculous it sounds."

He half laughs to himself. "No matter, huh?"

"And don't leave anything out," I say. "I don't want the abbreviated version here."

He swallows the bread and goes for another piece. "Fine, but are you prepared to leave here, after I explain everything, and still not understand what's happening? No—more accurately, not understand *why* it's happening?"

At that, my shoulders drop. Because no, I'm not. I want answers. The why. The how.

"Because I don't have those kinds of answers." He glances at my plate. "Is the chicken tender enough?"

I look down quickly. There's only one bite of chicken left. "It's perfect."

He nods, then arranges his own perfectly layered bite of sauce, pasta and breaded chicken on his fork. The bite looks as meticulous as this office, neatly stacked, as if *this* is exactly how it was meant to be eaten.

He sticks the fork in his mouth, and for a few long seconds, it's like he's assessing something. The taste? The flavor? The balance? I have no idea, but the way he chews is wildly different from the way I chew.

I eat like two seals fighting over a grape. Matteo, not so much. I absently wonder when was the last time he really enjoyed a meal. Without grading it or looking for ways to make it better.

After he swallows the bite, he sets down the fork.

"That's it?" I ask, going in for another bite.

"What's it?" He looks confused.

"You're not going to eat the rest?" I take the last chunk of chicken and do my best to assemble my own perfect bite, dragging it through sauce, swirling on a few strands of pasta. It's not nearly as neat as his, but it tastes way better. "You should eat."

"You should stop talking with your mouth full." He says this flatly, but I catch the slight smirk he's trying to hide.

"You should pack up your knives and go, because you're about to be chopped." I playfully hold up the knife at him.

Careful, Iris. This is what you do.

"If you're used to Pop-Tarts, I guess I can't fault you for reacting the way you do to actual cooked food." The corner of his mouth twitches.

I think he means to tease me, which is a sign that maybe I'm not the most annoying person he knows.

That feels like a win.

"Maybe the food is terrible and I'm just delirious with hunger." I take a sip of my water.

"It's not," he says, confidently.

I smile behind my water glass, and after I set it back down, I shake my head. "So cocky."

"It's all the awards," he says, dryly. "Remember? I'm a big deal."

And I start to think maybe there's an actual human behind that robotic facade.

The awards *are* impressive, but I'm not going to gush. That's the kind of thing the old Iris would do. Shower him with compliments in hopes of getting him to like her.

My superpower is oversharing. And over-asking. I want to know everything about everyone, which usually ends up suffocating the other person, and then they leave. Some for a few minutes, others for the rest of my natural life.

Enough about that. I'm here for answers about the magic. He's probably close to reaching his weekly quota of words spoken out loud, so I need to stay on track.

"Tell me what I need to know about our building." I push his plate closer to him, and after a pause, he capitulates, picks up his fork, and takes another bite.

Look at us, having a meal together.

Magic, my brain, the little traitor, whispers.

"My grandpa lived in my apartment before me. I used to spend summers with him and my grandma."

"The one who taught you to cook?" I ask.

He nods.

"The smell must've been otherworldly."

He cracks a small smile. "When I was a kid, I loved being there. My grandparents were very social, and there was always something going on. But I never saw anything to make me think The Serendipity was anything other than, you know, just a building." He pauses, takes another bite, methodically chews.

I do the same, though I'm eating at a much quicker pace than he is. "I think having the ability to make food like this whenever you want has desensitized you to how amazing it is," I say, a total non sequitur.

His eyes dart to mine, and he frowns.

"Sorry, go on."

He pauses, like my comment has thrown him, and I tell myself that interrupting someone who doesn't like to talk is probably not a great strategy for keeping the conversation going.

"After my grandma died, I started coming around more, mostly to check on my grandpa, but still, I didn't notice anything out of the ordinary." He takes a quick sip of water, and I watch the muscle in his jaw tense. It's a well-defined jaw, with just enough stubble to look sexy and not unkempt.

Not something I should be thinking right now when he's finally about to answer my questions.

Focus, Iris.

"But then, uh . . . a little over three years ago, my grandpa met someone new, got remarried, and moved to Italy."

"No way! How fun!"

He makes a pained face, and I can't tell if it's how I said what I said, or just *what* I said.

"Yeah, he's just living it up over there," he says.

I take another bite. "I would too. Italy? It's like another planet to me."

He stops talking for a moment, and I suddenly fear that's all I'm going to get out of him, but then he starts talking again.

"So, I took over the lease on his apartment. Not too long after that, things started to"—he looks at me—"get weird."

"Weird, how?" I ask, wishing I had more than one bite left on my plate.

He shakes his head, looking like he's trying to figure out the best way to say it. Finally, he says, "The newspaper."

I set down my fork and wipe my mouth with a napkin, waiting for him to go on.

"I got a newspaper at my front door. Big deal, right? Thought it was junk. Something everyone was getting and throwing away." He looks at me, eyeing his food and my empty plate, then quirks a brow. "Are you still hungry?"

Is it that obvious?

I lie and shake my head, holding up a hand because *good grief*, I just devoured another one of this man's meals, what more do I need?

Little does he know that if the plate were edible, I would have eaten it, too.

It's *that* good.

He sets his fork down and slides his plate toward me.

"I can't eat your dinner." I lean back in my chair.

"I'm good. I promise. Eat." He watches me as I take another bite. "Better than eating like a twelve-year-old."

"Don't knock the Pop-Tarts till you try them," I say, pointing my fork at him.

"You don't *actually* like Pop-Tarts," he says, making a face as if he just ate something sour.

"False. Brown sugar and cinnamon or strawberry. Or both, stacked on top of the other."

He indicates to his left. "Guaranteed Nicola's pastries will ruin Pop-Tarts for you."

I glance over at the small tray of desserts on the desk, then back to his plate, which is now fully in front of me.

"Ooh. I'll save room."

He leans back in his chair and watches for a few seconds while I continue to devour more than my share of this dinner. I can't help it. I have zero self-control. The only problem is, I'm never going to want frozen pizza again.

"So. Newspaper. What happened with it?" I ask.

"It kept coming back," he says, simply.

Ah. So the same thing that happened to me.

"Didn't matter what I did or how many times I threw it away," he says, sounding frustrated. "And then one day, I came home, and my living room was full of newspapers."

"Oh, my gosh, me too," I say, almost reverently. "That's what I tried to show you in the hallway the other day—my apartment was *full* of them."

He nods.

He understands.

Relief washes over me. Because for the first time since this started, I don't feel completely alone. Someone else has experienced the exact same thing as me.

"Why didn't you just tell me in the first place?" I ask, not hiding the accusation in my tone.

He looks at me like I just asked him to add Fruit Roll-Ups to his menu.

"Tell you? You mean, 'Hey, we just met, and oh, by the way, this building delivers magic newspapers'?"

I shrug. "Fair point."

"Plus," he continues, "all the people I talk to about the newspapers don't remember."

This makes me pause.

"They don't remember," I absently repeat in an awe-filled tone. "Like Brooke and Liz."

"The only other person I've talked to about them is my grandpa," he says, and then after a pause, "and now, you."

It's like I've just been let into a secret society, one with only a handful of very elite members.

"So, wait. Is this *real?*" I'm instantly giddy. "I mean, are we *really* discussing magic like it's something that actually exists?"

He sighs. "It would appear so."

"Okay. Okay." My mind is racing. There is so much I want to know. "How often do you get a new paper?"

"It depends," he says. "I've gone months without one before, but I've also gotten two in the same week." He glances over at the tray of pastries, almost like he's contemplating whether he should eat one.

I stack my empty plate on top of his now empty plate and move them aside, then pull the pastry tray to the center of the desk. "Do you want to share them?" I pick up one of the clean forks Nicola left with the desserts and hand it to him.

To my utter shock, he takes it, then cuts into a slice of cheesecake.

"It's like . . . when someone needs something, the newspapers show up," he says.

"Things like . . .?"

"Bringing a cat to a lonely neighbor," he says, smirking a little. "Which will ultimately lead to her meeting this swinger."

I laugh out loud. "He's not a *swinger.*"

"Swing dancer."

"*Square* dancer." I can't keep from giggling.

Matteo looks confused for a split second, and when he makes the connection, he hides his smile and looks away.

Endearing. My insides warm.

"Does that mean you think Winnie and my new friend Jerry are . . . soulmates?" I borrow Liz's word, but I don't do anything to hide the fact that I'm not buying in to the idea.

"If that's what you want to call it." He says it so easily, it catches me off-guard.

"Wait, for real?"

"Sometimes—but not always—that's where these things lead." He takes another bite.

"So . . ." I pause to taste a bite of cheesecake and wrap my head around this idea. "You're a matchmaker, and oh, my goodness, this cheesecake is amazing."

He harrumphs a reply, and I can immediately tell he doesn't like that title.

"A grumpy matchmaker with a sweet tooth." I close my eyes, now focusing on nothing but how this cheesecake tastes. "This is incredible." I open my eyes and find him still watching me. "Did you make this too?"

He shakes his head. "Nicola is the pastry chef."

"Right. She said that." I pause. "So that's why you're free to eat it like a human instead of a robot in charge of quality control." I move to the tiramisu and try a bite.

Heaven.

He frowns at me. "I don't eat like a robot."

"You do, but okay." I take a sip of my water, then smack my lips together loudly. "I need to cleanse my palate."

He allows himself a tiny laugh as he shifts in his seat. I'll take it. For a second, I think he's going to argue with me, but instead, he says, "I'm not a matchmaker."

I laugh at the disdain in his voice. "Oh, let me guess,

you're one of those guys who got his heart broken, and now you don't believe in love."

He reacts like he was just slapped, and there's a shift in the air.

I feel the mood change from light-hearted to tense, and I know I messed up. What I don't know is how. And I want the whole story.

Way to go. You don't need the story, Iris.

He sets down his fork and doesn't respond.

I desperately try to salvage the conversation.

"I'm . . . sorry if I said . . . I shouldn't have . . . sometimes I just, you know, open mouth, say stuff, and it's not always . . ." I tilt my head down a bit to try to catch his downward gaze.

He looks at me, and I can tell there is a really deep wound there.

"I should know better. If anyone knows about heartbreak, it's me." I hitch both thumbs back in my own direction. "Definitely the heartbreak queen." I frown. "That makes me sound super pathetic and—" I wince. "I'm just sorry."

I don't expect him to say anything back, and I mentally prepare myself to pack up my things and leave, when he says, "It's fine. It's just—" He stops. "But maybe we can stick to . . . you know."

Understood.

"The newspapers. Got it."

I pick up the plate of tiramisu. "And I'm not going to share this one." I smile, because I don't like the tension in here.

"Figures," he says, and I sense he's also missing the lighter mood. "It's our best-selling dessert."

"Is it your favorite too?" I ask.

He gives his head one quick shake. "For me, nothing beats cheesecake." He leans back but doesn't take another bite.

"How long has this been happening?" I ask, hoping we can move on. "The newspapers?"

"Started almost immediately after I moved in, three years ago."

"You've been doing this for three years?"

"Wish I could say no," he mutters. "But yeah."

Huh. So, he doesn't want to be a member of the secret society. Got it. Maybe that's why the magic has gotten me involved.

"You should give Nicola a raise," I say, holding up a forkful of tiramisu.

He chuckles quietly and says, "She'd love that," and picks up his fork again, almost like his attempt to set it aside keeps failing.

"So, three years of articles," I say, thinking. "How many couples have you matched?"

"I don't keep a scrapbook."

"But you're a part of people's stories." I watch him. "That's kind of amazing."

"If you say so," he says, again with a bite of irritation in his tone. "I think it's a huge pain." He pauses. "You'll see."

Right.

So, this hasn't turned Matteo into a hopeless romantic. I wish I could say the same. There's a part of me that will always believe in fairytales and happy endings, despite my experience.

"So, what do we do next?" I ask.

He shrugs. "I think you should introduce Winnie to—"

"Jerry," I say.

"Jerry."

"And then what?"

Another shrug. "And then you wait and see what happens. Usually, an introduction is all it takes."

"Right," I say. "I guess that's how it works with *soulmates*." I say this ironically, because what do I know?

I do love the idea of Winnie getting a second chance at love. And I like the idea of playing Cupid, even if my own love life needs an editor.

This could be great for Winnie. A friend. A companion. Someone to keep her from being lonely. Isn't that what we all need?

I think so, but if that's true and everyone is searching for the people who will just "get them," why are they so difficult to find?

I scrape the last bite of tiramisu from the plate, thinking that if I could figure out a dignified way to lick up every last smear, I would.

Matteo must sense this because he raises a brow and says, "I think you got it all."

I set down the fork and push the plate away. "And I'm stuffed." I turn and grab my purse. "Do you want to bring me the bill or . . .?"

He waves me off. "On the house."

I freeze. "Whoa! You don't have to do that. I wouldn't have eaten like a lion over a zebra carcass if I'd known you weren't going to charge me!"

He actually laughs.

I actually like it.

"I don't know if I should take that as a compliment or as a reason to avoid you altogether," he says.

I hang my bag back on the chair. "Eh. Maybe both."

With all the food gone, I don't know what to do with my hands. I fold them in my lap, not quite ready to leave. "So, are we partners now or what?"

He meets my eyes, confused. "No."

I feel myself deflate.

"I'm just hoping that if I tell you what I know, maybe this magic is going to finally leave me alone and become someone else's problem."

"Right," I say, acutely aware that that "someone" is me.

Chapter Eighteen
Matteo

THE MAGIC DOESN'T LEAVE me alone.

A few days later, I'm woken up by a newspaper to the face, that lovely old chestnut. I opened my eyes just in time to watch it disappear in its familiar way.

I wonder if Iris is getting woken up the same way, and I chuckle to myself, imagining her yelling at the air, rubbing her forehead.

Soon, I think. *Soon it will all be out of my life for good.*

Later that day, after my post lunch-service break, I'm headed back to work when I see Winnie in the lobby of The Serendipity. She's with a lanky, bald man wearing a brightly patterned sweater vest and holding his coat.

At the sight of me, Winnie throws up her arms and calls out my name. It catches me off-guard. I'm used to staying relatively invisible in our building.

Usually, the newspapers allow me to stay behind the scenes. Most of the people don't even know I've helped them at all.

That's how I prefer it.

With Winnie, that wasn't possible, and now every time I

see her, this is what I'm in for. Small talk. I force myself to be kind. To remember that I *like* Winnie.

There's no harm in letting myself like someone new.

That thought brings an image of Iris to my mind.

"I want you to meet my new friend, *Jerry*." Winnie says his name like she's showing a picture of her grandson who just got the lead in the school play. "Iris introduced us. We're going square dancing!" She looks at the old man, who smiles wide, deepening the lines around his eyes.

He reaches a hand toward me, and I shake it. "Good to meet you, sir."

Jerry laughs. "Oh, heck, you can call me Jerry. We're not formal around here." He looks at Winnie, and I see it, the spark I've come to recognize after years of bringing people together. Because while they didn't always see me, I usually stick around to make sure the meet-up actually happens.

Like the other couples, Winnie and Jerry will take it from here, and I have a comforting, almost gleeful thought.

Iris did great. This will be the end of my magical matchmaking.

But then Jerry says, "Winnie says you make the most amazing Italian food. We're going to come to your restaurant tonight after we dance."

"Great," I say. "I'll make you whatever you want."

"And you'll join us?" Winnie asks. "I hope that's not too presumptuous of me to ask."

"I'll be working, so I won't be able to," I say. "But I promise—we'll take good care of you."

"Then I'll make you and Iris a meal to thank you for finding me a dance partner." She smiles, and at that moment, as if summoned by the universe, Iris walks in from outside. When she sees us standing there, she stops.

"What's up, guys?" she says, caution in her voice.

My body tenses at the sight of her, and I remind myself of

the goal here—to share what I know about the magic so it fully transfers over to her and I can go on about my business.

By myself.

The sooner, the better.

"I was just telling Matteo that I'm going to cook a meal for you two," Winnie says, a smile taking up a good portion of her face. "I'll be in touch with details, but we're going to an early class, so we have to go."

"Sounds great!" Iris frowns at me as they pass by her and walk out the front door and onto the street, leaving us standing in the lobby alone.

"Well, they're cute," Iris finally says. She smiles. "We made that happen."

My disinterested expression holds.

"Oh, come on, Chef Crabby Patty, you can't tell me you're not a little bit happy to have found Winnie someone to hang out with and possibly given her a second chance at love," she says.

I stop and stare. Did she just call me Chef Crabby Patty?

"It's sweet, right? We made a real difference in her life."

When I don't respond, she starts fidgeting. Probably because I'm just standing here, mute.

She shoves her hands in her pockets. "What happens now?"

I shrug. "Now, they do whatever they're going to do, and I go back to my life."

"So, that's it?"

"Yep."

"You don't ever, I don't know . . . keep in touch with the people you've matched? I mean, you're basically Cupid, and it seems like they'd want to keep you around? The sentimental ones, anyway."

I start toward the door, and this time, I'm not surprised when she follows me. "No, I don't keep in touch with them, and no, I'm not Cupid. Usually I can arrange the meetings without being seen."

She suddenly laughs out loud.

I give her a confused look. "What?"

"I just thought it would be a hilarious movie if someone made Cupid totally against type. You think he's this round little cherub guy, diaper and a bow and arrow, but instead he's a hot chef who can't stand people and just wants to be left alone."

My bland expression holds.

"An anonymous, grumpy, *very* talented matchmaking chef. Obviously his last name would be Cupid." She stops and holds out her hands like she just had a huge *eureka* moment.

She slowly turns to me.

"*Chef. CUPID.*" She points at me, grinning and enjoying herself way too much.

I shake my head. "You're not calling me that."

"Chef Cupid! It's too perfect! Can't you see that as the title of a movie?!"

I ignore her and walk outside.

She follows. "So, C.C., how does that work?" she says with a lilt in her voice.

I cock my head at her.

"Okay, okay, fine," she surrenders. "I'll only use it in dire emergencies."

I take a breath and try not to be amused. It's getting harder to hide my smile around Iris. It's been a while since someone made me laugh, but her ability to amuse herself is contagious.

"Usually, I'm just the guy who initiates the meeting."

"The meet-cute," she says.

I glance at her. "The what?"

"The meet-cute. Good grief, how do you not know this?"

"Is that a real question?"

She ignores me. "In romance, they're called meet-cutes. The first cute meeting between two people." She bumps my shoulder with hers. "You're the meet-cute guy."

I roll my eyes.

"It actually makes sense that the magic chose you," she comments, almost as an aside.

"Why?"

She looks at me like I should know. "You're a chef. An amazing one, to be fair. What better way to bring people together than over food? That's like the whole point of food in the first place."

In all the three years of doing this, that has never once occurred to me.

Huh. Maybe she's right.

"Speaking of, you will come when Winnie invites us to dinner, right?" she asks.

"Sure," I say. "But after that . . ." I shrug. "She'll move on. I'll move on. That's the way this works."

Her forehead crinkles. "I don't know if that's true."

"Oh, really? You don't know if that's true?" I say in a repeated scoff. "In the seven days since you found out about the magic, you've figured that out?"

"I'm just saying—I don't *want* that to be it." She jogs to keep up with me.

"Are you going to barge into my kitchen again?" I ask, fully expecting her to realize I'm going to work.

"If you're lucky," she jokes as she falls into step beside me.

A pause.

"I want to see Winnie again. I like her. And think about what we did for her. I mean, she was so lonely, and now she has Jerry. *And* a cat. And us. Also, it's kind of nice to have people to say 'hi' to in the lobby."

I glance over and find her struggling to keep up with me. I have no idea why I'm walking so fast. I slow down, not so drastically that she'll notice, but enough so she can stop half-jogging.

She goes on. "I'm trying to figure out what to do now. I mean, do I just pretend this never happened? Wait for the next newspaper? You said it could be months, but I want one now. Now that I know I'm not hallucinating, I think this is kind of fun."

I stop walking and face her. "This isn't fun, Iris. It's disruptive and annoying, and yeah, maybe you give some old lady a cat and maybe you help two people meet, but it gets in the way. Of everything."

She frowns. "Right, but I actually like people, so to me, this isn't a chore."

I stuff my hands in my pockets and shake my head. She really doesn't get it.

"What about when you have to help someone during your regular work hours? Or in the middle of the night? What about when 'helping someone' requires you to put yourself out there in ways you don't want to—and it's awkward and uncomfortable?"

She seems unbothered. "I think it will be worth it."

I laugh and look away. "You're so naïve."

My insult lands. She looks away.

I instantly want to take it back.

"I like the idea of magic." She shrugs. "I like knowing it exists." And then a little more quietly, she adds, "For other people, anyway. It's nice."

There's something in the way she says it that makes me curious. And as a general rule, I don't get curious.

She pulls a pair of gloves out of her pocket and stretches them on. "Winnie is a good person, so if we can help find her other good people to spend time with, I think that's kind of great." She eyes me for a long moment. "Maybe that's why I'm here. Maybe I'm supposed to find people for *you* to spend time with."

"I'm going to go out on a limb and say probably not," I say.

She stops. "Did you ever stop to think how cool it is that you get to be a part of so many people's stories? Of helping so many people find happiness?"

I don't respond. Because what am I supposed to say? That helping other people find happiness leaves a bitter taste in my mouth when this kind of happiness is the last thing in the world I want to find?

"You're so closed off," she says. "No wonder you need my help with this."

I scoff and start walking again. "I don't need anyone's help. What I need is for someone else to be responsible for this junk."

She follows me. This time, I don't slow my pace. "Well, apparently, the building thinks you do. Maybe it wants to make sure that the person playing Cupid actually cares about who he's helping."

"I will gladly hand you my bow and arrow and let you take over," I say. "It's not like I asked for it in the first place."

"You really can't see how cool this is, can you?" she asks.

"I really can't. Because it's *not*." We've reached the restaurant, and I put my hand on the door as I stop walking. "But the sooner I share everything I know with you, then *hopefully*, the sooner I can be free of it."

She cocks her head, studying me. "Is it because you don't believe in soulmates? Or romance or whatever?" she asks.

"That sounds like a personal question," I say. "And those are off limits."

"Right."

I walk inside the restaurant and, like a lot of things I don't want to face right now, leave her on the other side of a closed door.

Chapter Nineteen
Iris

H<small>E</small> <small>SHUT</small> the door on me. Again.

Rude.

I pause, trying to decide if I pushed things too far, or if I'm being annoying, or if I'm going to do what normal Iris would do and dive in, headfirst, come what may.

I decide the latter and go to grab the handle, when the door opens.

It's Matteo.

And he's frowning. "I'm, uh . . . I'm sorry. I shouldn't have shut the door on you like that."

I'm shocked. He looks like he's chewing glass, but was that an apology?

He holds the door open. "Do you want to come in?"

I knew it. I knew there was a nice person tucked away underneath that hardened exterior. It makes me wonder what —or who—hurt him so badly.

"You're back!" Val doesn't hide the surprise on her face when I follow Matteo into the kitchen.

She's short, with dark hair pulled back in a bun, and she

isn't wearing a stitch of makeup. She's wearing black pants and a white chef's coat, which seems to be the uniform.

Despite my best efforts and his "nothing personal" declarations, I *am* curious about Matteo. Why did the building choose him as its Cupid? And why is it now choosing me?

We couldn't be more different. I don't know anything about his personal life, but I'm hoping it's not as bad as mine.

What's his story? And how do I find it out when he's definitely not going to tell me?

I stop my train of thought. That's not the point here. I don't need to know anything about Matteo—other than the fact that he knows how the magic works. I will think about *that* and not the fact that my torso turns into a cage of butterflies when he looks at me.

Those kinds of butterflies aren't real.

Val shoots Matteo a look, which he seems to ignore as he pushes past her and hangs up his winter coat. "She's probably hungry again."

He pulls his chef's coat down from one of the hooks and turns to face us, and only then do I realize I'm staring at the way his plain white T-shirt pulls across his chest, highlighting well-defined muscles and tattooed biceps that could easily carry a person from a burning building.

I would volunteer to test that theory.

I glance over at Val, who chuckles, and I quickly look away, embarrassed.

"Are you joining us for family dinner?" Val asks, hopeful.

"Uh . . ." I toss Matteo a helpless look, but he's inspecting a box of produce with that same careful consideration he seems to give to everything.

"Chef?" Val calls out.

"Yes, set an extra place," he says without looking at her.

Val wraps an arm around my shoulder and squeezes. "Welcome to the family."

My insides squeeze at the word.

Family.

I haven't had one of those since I was thirteen.

I can still remember waking to find nobody had gotten me up for school. My mom was still in bed, and my dad was just . . . gone. He'd left a note on the refrigerator that just said, *Sorry, Iris. Call you soon.*

I had friends whose parents had gotten divorced, but it was never something I thought would happen to my parents. We were close—a tight little circle, just the three of us.

And my dad was leaving? Didn't we matter enough to make him stay?

Didn't *I* matter enough?

Yeah, total cliché. People always say it "wasn't my fault," that there "wasn't anything I could've done," but boy, it sure feels like I somehow did something wrong.

People leave.

It turned out that my dad had met someone else. They were married a year later, and her kids became his. My mom remarried a year after that and had another baby with her new husband, Richard. She did her best to make me feel like a part of their family, but I was fifteen. Mostly grown.

And that's when I realized I'd always be an in-betweener. The biological child caught between two families. A disconnected connector.

After years of therapy, I finally realized that's why I've spent so many years trying to fit in. I'm trying to fill a void, and I try hard.

I give everything I can, as soon as I can, in the hopes that "this relationship will be the one that sticks," only to have that become the thing that ruins it. People don't like to be smothered, even when that smothering is well-intentioned.

Family?

I'm not sure I know what that feels like.

So, when Val says it so flippantly—*welcome to the family*—like it's not a big deal, something inside me twists.

I still want that. I still want to belong. And against my better judgment, the tiniest seed of hope is planted.

"So . . ." I look for a way to start a conversation. "What's family dinner?"

"Oh! Right! Sometimes I forget that normal people don't know our traditions." She leans up against the counter. "Before the chaos of dinner service begins, we come together as a staff—as a family—and eat a meal together."

"No way! I've never heard of that. Do other restaurants do it too?"

"If they don't, they *should*," Val says with a smile. "We share recipes, try new things, and rotate who cooks every day of the week. Gives us a chance to impress Chef."

I look around at everyone tying on aprons, wiping down prep surfaces, taking positions.

"Pick a seat," Val says. "We'll be ready soon! You're in for a treat because tonight is Matteo's turn to cook." She leans in. "It's always the best when Matteo cooks."

I smile, and before she turns to go, I ask, "How long has the restaurant been here?"

Val pulls a kitchen towel out from under the waistband of her apron and uses it to dry hands that I didn't know were wet. "About four years. It was a rocky start, but Matteo was never going to let it fail. It matters too much to him."

"He's really good, isn't he?" I ask.

"You have no idea," she says. "And I know he's got that whole gruff, rude thing going on, but he's one of the kindest, most thoughtful people you'll ever meet." She leans in. "Plus, he's *never* brought a woman here for family dinner. It's nice to see him back out there!"

"Oh!" I hold up my hands. "It's not like that, no, we're not—"

She dismisses my protest. "I know. But his food has a way of changing people's minds," she says with a glint in her eye, tucking the towel back under her apron. "Just know that he's worth the work it's going to take to knock down the huge brick wall he's built around himself. He's been through a lot." She pauses, nodding to herself, as if thinking about it, then smiles. "But he's one of the good ones."

I glance across the room just as Matteo looks up from where he's working. He straightens, clearly aware that our conversation is not about food. I want to ask Val all the questions—what's he been through? Why the brick wall? How do I knock that down?

But I don't ask any of those things. Instead, I flash her a smile and say, "He's just helping me with a project, that's all."

She studies me, then smiles. "Okay. We'll go with that for now."

She's quick.

My eyes flick over to Matteo as Val walks away. He studies me for a few seconds, and I realize that I want *him* to be the one to answer all my questions. Ideally, while he cooks.

I watch for a few minutes as the hustle and bustle reveals itself as perfect, routine choreography. To an outsider, it might look like chaos, but it's obvious that everyone has a job in this kitchen. They move in harmony, each filling in any gaps that might be left in the fray.

They have a shorthand way of communicating, too, foreign to me, but it probably comes from years of working together, of knowing each other.

And in the midst of it all, one thing is certain—Matteo is in charge.

It looks like they're prepping the food for dinner service at the restaurant while he cooks for the staff. It's a wonder to watch.

They carry on conversations, taste bubbling sauces, pinch

this spice into that bowl, pausing to respond to Matteo as he gives instructions or to get his approval on various things along the way.

Nicola and a big guy work behind one counter, while Val mixes up a salad dressing from scratch. A guy someone calls Dante chops vegetables, and a few other people move in and out of the space.

"How was Gio's basketball game last night, Renata?" Val asks a woman working on the opposite side of the kitchen.

"Oh, he fouled out in the third quarter," the tall, dark-haired woman says, shaking her head. "I keep telling him he needs to get his temper under control, but he's too much like his father."

They continue chatting while Dante, Nicola, and the bigger guy next to her talk about a trip to Paris Nicola and someone named Danny are taking in the spring.

"Is it a holiday or a work trip?" the guy asks. "Because you're going to need an extra week just to try all the restaurants on the list I sent you."

"Bear's right," Val calls out, joining their conversation. "You really need to eat your way through Paris to get the full experience."

Bear, I think. *Fitting name.* He looks like a linebacker.

Bear moves over to a sink to rinse out a bowl, and Matteo comes into view. He's isolated himself from the others, making quick, decisive moves around a workstation that is as neat and tidy as Winnie's kitchen after he finished cooking for her.

The noise of the kitchen fades away as I watch. I'm a little awestruck by the way Matteo moves. With everyone else on task, it's like he's completely blocked out everything happening around him, all the conversations, the noise—he seems oblivious to all of it. Every movement is deliberate and precise, and there's only one word I can think of to describe it.

Magic.

It's odd, though. I keep picturing his grandparents. When I think of them, entertaining and cooking and inviting people to eat with them, it's a lot louder than this.

This is quiet. Clinical. Precise.

I focus on Matteo and can't help but think it's all coming from him.

He needs fun, I randomly think. *I'm fun.*

I force my gaze to zoom out on the full picture of the kitchen. I can't fixate on him. And I certainly can't entertain the idea that this man's apple cart needs to be upset by someone like me.

I'm a lot.

I also can't just sit here, and I start to get antsy.

I need something to do. I stand and walk over to Val. She's way less scary than Matteo. "Can I help with anything?"

A voice from Matteo's corner. "No."

I frown. So I guess he *wasn't* oblivious. Still, he hasn't stopped working. He hasn't even glanced in my direction. I face him. "I can at least set the table or something."

"Dante will set the table," Matteo says, almost sounding like he's dealing with a petulant child, still not looking up.

I don't look at Dante, choosing instead to focus on Matteo and feeling a little slighted, even though this is his kitchen and he can obviously do what he wants. "Can I at least *help* Dante?"

"No," he says. "My kitchen. My rules."

I don't have to look around to know that the staff has heard this phrase before. And at the moment, they're probably all thankful they're not the one he's talking to.

There's just one difference. I don't work for Matteo.

Quietly, Dante moves over to a shelf and grabs a stack of plates, walking it out of the kitchen without another word.

I get an idea.

"Hey. Chef."

He looks at me, and I look back, and without breaking eye contact, I walk over to the shelf, grab napkins and bowls, hold them up and smile, and then walk out of the kitchen, all without a word.

"Wait! You can't—"

"Too late," I call over my shoulder as I walk out.

In the dining room, I find Dante setting a large table in a room marked "Private." I assume this is a room people can rent for small gatherings, and apparently it's also where the staff eats before they open for dinner.

I walk in and set the bowls and napkins down on the table. "So, you're Dante."

He grins a wide smile, "That's me. Dang, you totally ignored Chef's order." His eyes go wide, and he shakes his head.

I smile right back. "Yep."

He shakes his head. "You're playing with fire, you know that, right?"

I shrug. "I've seen worse. Is he always like that?"

Dante nods. "He's the boss."

"So, yes?" I pick up the napkins. "He's just got such a chip on his shoulder,"

"You'd be the same way if—" Dante stops talking.

"If?"

He shakes his head. "Ah. Nothing."

I stand there for a few long seconds, again wishing I could figure out why Matteo is the way he is, but Dante won't even look at me now. He takes the napkins from me and starts placing them around the table.

"Can I help?" I ask.

He freezes. "Chef said no."

"I don't work for Chef."

"You're right. But you're here as a guest." The deep voice comes from behind me.

I turn and find Matteo standing in the doorway.

"Guests don't help with prep," he says.

I frown. "Can you make an exception? I feel totally helpless. I'm just sitting back there, and you already fed me one meal, and I need to repay you."

"Two meals," he corrects me.

I give him an *exactly* sort of look, and say, "It's just napkins. Let me help."

"You're not an orphan. You don't have to earn your keep."

I shoot him a look.

"Just stay out here," he says. "Out of the way." He glances at Dante. "Can you get her a drink? She needs something to do with her hands. She fidgets when there's silence."

At that, I stuff my hands in my pockets, not sure how to process the warm feeling that spreads through me at this acknowledgement. It's stupid, really, but the teenager in me thinks, *He noticed.*

Dante shuffles around him, out of the room, and I find myself alone, staring at Matteo and horribly at a loss for words.

"Sorry, I'm not trying to get in the way—" I say, clearly missing something.

He looks at me. "I get it. You have questions about the building? About the newspapers? Great. I'll tell you what I know. But the rest?" His jaw twitches, and I'm not sure I want to know what else he has to say.

But then, his eyes find mine, and I very much want to know.

"No questions about me," he says. "No questions about my life, or my past, or the restaurant or . . ." He pushes a hand through his hair as Dante returns with a drink.

He hands it to me. "It's a Coke—is that okay?"

I take the glass and nod. "It's perfect. Thank you."

He goes back to setting the table, and I go back to feeling uneasy under Matteo's watchful glare. His whole attitude has shifted since we walked in from outside, and I'm not sure what changed.

He takes a step toward me. "I can't have you in my space," he says, his voice low so only I can hear. "I need to focus."

I nod, feeling off-kilter and a little weak-kneed at his nearness. "Okay."

Then, even more quietly, he says, "We're not friends, Iris. We're just getting through this weird situation and moving on."

The words linger, like a bad aftertaste. *We're not friends.*

I feel like such an idiot that I'd even for one second let myself think anything else.

But then I think about what Val said in the kitchen. That he's one of the good ones. That it's worth it to knock down his brick wall.

That I'm part of the *family*.

"We could be, you know," I say, knowing my vulnerability is showing. "Friends."

This is the exact opposite of what I should do.

His eyes flicker for a beat.

I add, "I don't have that many. It might be nice." *Careful, Iris, you're going to sound desperate.*

I shove the thought aside, and for a flicker of a moment, we connect. Like it wouldn't be so bad to open up, to get to know each other outside of the magic. Like maybe we aren't so different after all.

But then, as quickly as it came, the moment is gone, like a mist of golden shimmer.

He shakes his head. "No," he says. "I'm sorry. We can't."

I press my lips together and look away, waiting until, finally, he turns to leave.

I stand still, feeling the sting of his rejection, knowing this is my own fault. That, like always, I'm getting invested. I'm getting attached.

And that can't happen.

People leave.

Only, this time, at least Matteo didn't pretend to be anything other than what he is. It was me who got my wires crossed.

I glance up and find Dante actively trying *not* to look at me.

I set the Coke down on the table. "You know, on second thought, I'm going to go."

He looks conflicted, and I smile, hoping to put him at ease.

"I've got a lot to do, and I've only just now remembered." I nod. "Thanks for the drink."

"Of course," he says, disappointed. "See you next time."

My fake smile holds, and I duck out of the private room, moving quickly toward the front door, thinking that whatever spell I've been under where Matteo Morgan is concerned has been officially broken.

Two hours later, I'm curled up on my couch with my crochet basket, about to see who gets voted off of *Project Runway* and trying really hard to be thankful for the much-needed wake-up call.

I've finally got my emotions in check—*This is not a big deal. It's not like you want to be friends with someone like Matteo anyway. Better you realize that now rather than later, after you write a whole story about how you're going to be the one to pull him out of his shell*—when there's a knock at my door.

My heart skips.

I walk over, glance through the peephole, and see a teenager standing in the hallway. "Yes?" I say through the door.

"Delivery from Aria." He holds up a brown paper bag, and I see the logo of Matteo's restaurant printed on the outside.

I open the door, and he thrusts the bag in my direction.

"I didn't order that."

He shrugs. "Came through with your name on it."

I frown, taking it awkwardly, as if it's going to announce how it got here.

"Night, ma'am," the kid says, taking a few steps down the hall.

Ma'am? Ouch. How old does he think I am?

"Wait. Let me get you a tip." I wait to make sure he stops.

He turns. "Chef said I'm not allowed to take your money."

I stare at him.

"He already tipped me." A shrug. "Have a good night."

I watch him go, staring after him down the hallway, double checking to make sure there's no hidden camera, no newspaper, no other surprises waiting for me.

I take the bag inside and set it on the counter, torn between wanting to toss it in the trash—*Does he think he can make up for his rudeness by placating me with food?*—and wanting to devour every scrap in this bag.

I open it, and the smells of garlic, tomato, and basil fill my apartment—and my soul.

Inside, there's an entire loaf of bread, cut in half, and two large to-go containers.

I pull it all out and see there's a small piece of paper taped to the top of one of them. On it, in bold, black Sharpie, are five words.

Stay away from frozen pizza.

Sigh.

Why does the jerk have to be secretly nice?

Chapter Twenty
Matteo

SATURDAY MORNING, I wake up, thankfully, not to a smack on the forehead, but to a knock on my door.

Friday nights are late at the restaurant, and I prefer slow Saturday mornings. It's hard to jump out of bed on the weekend when I know I have to go in and do it all again.

Which is why I'm not quick to answer the incessant knocking.

In the three years I've lived in this building, nobody has ever knocked on my door, unless they're delivery people or maintenance people.

Which is how I know, even before I look, that it's Iris.

I haven't seen her since Tuesday, but I had a feeling that even my little "we're not friends" speech wouldn't really deter her. Something tells me that if Iris decides to make you her friend, there's really no escaping it, even if you're a big, fat jerk to her.

And I was.

I knew it *as* the words were coming out of my mouth, but it was confirmed when I walked back into the private room at the restaurant and she was gone.

Nicola let me have it. And rightfully so.

I drag myself out of bed, pull on a pair of sweatpants, grab a T-shirt from my dresser, and plod through my apartment to the door. The knocking never stops the entire time.

A part of me is relieved she didn't write me off. I think I've got the kind of personality that needs a second chance. Oddly, I want one with her.

What am I supposed to do with an intrusive thought like that?

"I'm coming," I say as I pull the door open, half-dressed and a little frustrated to be up this early on a Saturday. "What?"

Iris lets out a slight gasp and takes a step back, eyes dropping to my bare chest, before quickly looking away. "Were you asleep?"

"Yes." I pull on my T-shirt. "It's not even eight."

Finally, she looks at me. "Oh. Shoot. I've been up for two hours."

I can't even think about cracking 8 a.m. after Friday night service.

"Sorry," she apologizes. "I wasn't thinking."

I stare back, waiting for her to tell me what she wants. When she doesn't, I turn and walk away, leaving the door open as an invitation for her to come in.

She just stands there.

"I'm getting coffee," I call toward the hallway. "You can come inside."

Eventually, I hear the door close, then see Iris walking cautiously into the kitchen. She looks around the apartment, which I mostly left the way it was when I moved in. I got rid of the clutter, and my grandpa cleared out all his personal items, but this place felt pretty familiar already, so I left it alone.

It's unnerving, not knowing what she's thinking as she studies my space.

While I grind coffee beans, Iris walks into the living room, taking in the open floor plan and the large windows that flood the space with natural light. "Is this the apartment they use when new people need a tour?"

I pour boiling water over the ground coffee in the French press, pausing for a second to frown at her.

"No photos. No personal items. No clutter," she explains. "It's like the model they show to people who are thinking about moving in."

"I get it." I do a slow nod. "You're mocking me."

She walks over to the kitchen island, smirking. "Oh, no. I would *never*. I only tease my *friends*." She hangs an oversized bag on the back of the tall stool and sits.

I wince at the memory of my coldness. "About that—"

She holds up a hand. "I accept your apology."

I frown.

"You let the spaghetti and meatballs say you're sorry. I get it," she says. "Did Val make you do that?"

"No, I actually felt bad."

"Well, you should've felt bad," she says, matter-of-factly. "What you said stunk and made me feel like a loser."

I wince again. "You're right. It was uncalled for."

She narrows her eyes at me. "You're lucky I don't dwell."

"Yes," I say, "I am."

"We don't have to, like, have sleepovers and braid each other's hair or whatever, but I meant it when I said I don't have many friends here. I thought since we, you know, have something in common . . ." A shrug.

The admission surprises me. Shames me. But if she's looking for friends, she's in the wrong place. I'm just not in the business of letting new people into my life. "Sorry, it's just—"

"You don't like people, I know." Her eyes drift over to the refrigerator. "Are those your grandparents?"

I follow her gaze to the photos stuck to the front of the fridge. "Yeah, and then that's my grandpa in Italy. His new wife, Elena, took that photo."

I open the refrigerator and pull out a carton of eggs.

"That must've been hard for you," she says, but she doesn't press the point.

Instead, she lets me sit with her observation, and I realize that yes, it was hard. Partly because it felt like he was betraying my grandma by moving on.

Or maybe because he figured out a way to move on—when I can't.

Or won't.

I take two mugs out of the cupboard and pour us each a cup of coffee, then set cream and sugar out on the counter so she can make hers however she wants.

"Thank you," she says. "You're actually a really good host." A pause. "When your attitude doesn't screw it up."

I shoot her a look and start assembling ingredients—vanilla, nutmeg, heavy cream. "I'm guessing you haven't eaten."

"It's not even eight," she says. "Of course I haven't."

"I'm starting to think you keep showing up for the free food." I take a glass mixing bowl from one of the drawers.

"Well, shoot, I was hoping you wouldn't figure that out until next month," she says.

I chuckle at that, despite myself. I can't help it. Iris surprises me. Most people are so put off by me that they keep their distance. Iris was obviously hurt when she left the restaurant the other night, but she's clearly decided not to hold a grudge. There's something refreshing about that.

"But it's not just the insane food." She reaches into her bag and pulls out a rolled-up newspaper, setting it with reverence between the two of us. "It's also this. And before you ask, yes, it's addressed to you, so you're not off the hook yet."

Somehow, I'm not as disappointed by that as I thought I'd be.

She glances at the ingredients I've pulled out onto the counter. "Are you planning to feed the entire building?"

"Planning to make the best French toast in the city."

Her eyes brighten. "You're making me French toast?"

I feel the corner of my mouth tug at her excitement, and I do a bad job of hiding the smile. "I'm making *me* French toast."

She smiles back. "Can I have yours, then?"

I chuckle again, shaking my head. Out of the corner of my eye, I can see she looks pleased with herself.

"Did you make the bread?" she asks.

"Nicola made this. I bring a loaf home every week."

She shakes her head in disbelief. "Can I smell it?"

"How in the world have you been surviving all these years?" I ask, handing over the bread.

"You'd be surprised how long you can exist on straight sugar," she says, inhaling the fresh bread. "This smells insane. It should be illegal." She breathes it in again.

I remove my bread knife from the magnet strip on the wall above the counter.

"Okay, before we open this, I want you to know that what you said to me? At the restaurant? I heard you." Iris pushes the bread back toward me and folds her hands on the counter. "I won't ask anyone anything personal about you, and I will stay out of your space."

I look around my kitchen, and she gets my meaning.

"Your *work*space. Plus you invited me to come in, so . . ."

"You wouldn't stop knocking," I counter.

"Pssh. I never let facts get in the way of my point."

I smile again. Under different circumstances, at a different time in my life, I could see us being friends. And in another lifetime, maybe even more.

"Ah."

"From now on, we will keep things all about the magic," she says. "Aaand the food. Can we keep the food in there? Because I can't be expected to turn that down." She nods toward the counter.

"You do have a knack for showing up at mealtimes," I say.

Her face goes sheepish for a second, then turns serious. "Honestly. I'm sorry if I overstepped." Her gaze falls. "I can be . . . a lot." A pause. "Too much, really." And then, under her breath, she adds, "Or so people have said."

"You aren't, and no apology necessary. You didn't overstep." I want to take back everything I said the other night. Her presence in my kitchen was distracting, and it was an unfamiliar feeling for me.

I liked it so much that I didn't like it.

That's why I acted the way I did, which wasn't fair because it had nothing to do with her and everything to do with me. Not that I can tell her that.

"I did," she says. "You told me you didn't want me asking questions, and I asked questions." She squints at me. "You're just so *mysterious*."

I turn away to grab the vanilla and cinnamon from the cupboard, mostly because she's still studying me and I know she's going to find a way to slide the pieces in place if she keeps it up.

I turn back to find her still watching me. "But if you ever do want to tell me all your deep, dark secrets, I'm a really good listener."

I make a face. "Don't hold your breath."

She shakes her head but looks amused. "See? So mysterious."

I glance down and indicate the newspaper, anxious for a change of topic. "Should we open it?"

Iris tears off the plastic sleeve. "I thought you'd never ask."

I watch her, marveling at how excited she is to unroll that newspaper. It's always been such an inconvenience to me, but Iris is treating it like a gift. It's like she's a kid and this is exactly what she wanted for her birthday.

"Let's see whose life we're going to change!" Her tone reminds me of a game show announcer. She opens the newspaper and lays it out on the counter. Her eyes flick to mine, and I busy myself by pulling the griddle from the cupboard.

"I've never made French toast," she says. "Is it hard?"

"Eh, I think it's hard to get right," I say, considering. "Most people use white bread from the store. The trick is to use a thick slice that will absorb the maximum amount of liquid. And to treat that liquid like a custard."

She gapes. "A . . . *custard?*"

It's been so long since anyone's made me feel like what I do is special. It's just food. Big deal. But not to Iris.

It's been such a long time since I've seen someone react to my cooking like this.

"You have no idea what you're in for," I say, gaining confidence that this will be the single best breakfast she's ever had.

I also find myself *wanting* to cook for her. *Wanting* to see her response.

"You like things neat, right?" The question catches me off-guard. "Have you always been this way?"

I almost knee-jerk a "No," but manage to hold it in. My tendencies toward order and control intensified after I lost Aria.

I know Iris is one or two questions away from uncovering the truth, but I don't talk about what happened with anyone. Not even Val and Nic—and they knew Aria. Sure, her name comes up sometimes, but I don't have to tell the story. It would be exhausting—emotional—to explain it all.

"I like an efficient workspace," I finally say. "It's difficult to cook things, especially things that sometimes have to be timed down to the second, if you're constantly working around mess or trying to remember where your knife is."

She nods, considering. "You'd hate my place, then."

My eyes dart to hers, then back to the loaf on the counter.

"My place looks lived in." She looks around. "It's not like a dorm room. In here, you're definitely leaning in to a minimalist vibe."

I can feel her searching for common ground. A certain kind of person would take the hint, offer up something—anything—as a point of connection.

A kind of person who's not like me.

I cut the bread in thick slices and lay them out on a cookie sheet, then stick them in the oven. I glance at her, find her watching. Observing. "You want to know—"

"Why you put it in the oven, yes."

"Have you ever cooked anything?"

She shrugs. "Pasta. Scrambled eggs. Toast."

"Making toast is not cooking," I say, dryly.

"Tell that to the toast," she quips. "Sometimes I even burn it."

I let out a small laugh. I can feel myself relaxing—but part of me has been so closed off for so long, the relaxation borders on uncomfortable.

"So, tell me what you're doing," she says.

"Aren't you here about that?" I nod at the newspaper, and she quickly folds it and tucks it away.

"We'll do that after you give me a cooking lesson," she says.

I squint at her. "You're kind of bossy."

She shrugs, as if to say "Your point?" and then a smile spreads across her face.

"Why are you here?" I ask. "I was so rude to you the other day."

"You've been rude to me every time we've met," she says.

"And yet, here you are."

"Here I am."

"Right. Why?"

She steels her jaw, but the question seems to stump her.

And I realize in her silence that I don't know if I want to know the answer. I don't want to be the subject of her interest. If she's trying to figure me out or get my whole life's story, we're going to have a problem.

I'll teach her about the magic—but that's it.

We need to stay focused.

Which makes me wonder why I don't say so. Why instead I say, "If you want to make great French toast, the key is thick bread that's a little dried out. And lots of flavor in the liquid."

I add the heavy cream, vanilla, nutmeg, cinnamon, and orange zest into the bowl, then push it toward her. "Crack four eggs in there."

Her eyes go wide.

"You can't screw it up. Just keep the shells out."

She grimaces. "So, do you remember when I said I've made scrambled eggs?"

"When, three minutes ago? I was here for that, yeah."

She rolls her eyes, but the smirk on her face remains. "I sometimes get shells in there. And then I just cook them with the shells and pick them out later."

I stare blankly.

"It's why I mostly eat things that, you know, come in a package."

"We're fixing that. Right now."

I take out an egg on the counter, crack it with one hand, then toss the shell into the garbage.

"Show-off." She smirks as she picks up an egg and goes to tap it on the side of the bowl.

Instinctively, I reach out and cover her hand with mine. "Not on the bowl."

She freezes, and I pull my hand away.

I inch back and cross my arms. "Do it on the counter and the shells won't get in the bowl."

"Oh!" She glances at me, but I don't meet her eyes. "That's genius." She taps it gently on the counter.

"Don't be precious with it," I say. "Crack it."

"Now who's bossy?" She widens her eyes at me then hits the egg against the edge of the counter, and it explodes in her hand. She bursts into laughter, and I can't help but join.

The liquid spills out onto the counter, but there's a good amount on the floor too. I quickly swipe the mess away and toss her the towel.

She flicks the shell off her hand, wipes the egg away, and picks up another one, a determined expression on her face. She cracks it, this time, with more success than the first.

"So, I'm basically a chef," she preens. "You should plan on coming to my new restaurant where we serve only raw eggs."

I notice that I'm not tense. I'm not squinting. I'm not hunched over, looking for detail.

I'm . . . enjoying myself.

Once she's finished with the eggs, I pull out the immersion blender and plug it in.

"Whoa. Is that really necessary?" She gives me a look. "I feel like we could stir it with a fork."

"We could," I say. "But with dry spices like nutmeg in there, they're not going to distribute evenly." I shoot her a look. "Is the Pop-Tart Princess really questioning my methods here?"

175

She laughs and holds her hands up in surrender. "That's fair. Although Pop-Tart Princess isn't a bad nickname."

I hand her the blender and show her how to turn it on.

"Just, stick it in there? Mix it?" she asks.

"Yep."

She turns it on and sticks it in the bowl while I pull the bread from the oven.

Once everything is blended, I hand over a pair of tongs. "Time to soak it. Just take a few slices of the bread and dunk it, but make sure to coat it really well."

She does this, gingerly, like she's afraid she'll mess something up. She really is clueless in the kitchen.

It's kind of adorable.

She looks up, hands limp and dripping. "Now what?"

I pull out a timer and set it for twenty minutes. "Now we wait."

"For what?"

"For all the liquid to soak into the bread."

She frowns. "Oh, so this is, like, a process."

I laugh. "Good food takes time."

She sighs. "It better be worth it."

I pick up my coffee and catch her eyes over the edge of the mug. She's smiling. Teasing. Looking at me like she doesn't mind being here. Like maybe she even likes it.

And it hits me then that maybe I like it too.

Crap.

Chapter Twenty-One
Iris

Are we having fun? Is that what this is? The thought makes my face flush, and I realize I want him to notice it too. *See how fun I am?*

"I have to run to the bathroom," Matteo says abruptly, setting his mug down on the counter and—mercifully—interrupting my thoughts. As he walks away, he calls back, "Feel free to read the paper or, you know, whatever."

"I'm gonna go through all your stuff!" I call after him.

"Good luck finding stuff to go through," he calls back, after disappearing on the other side of the living room.

I catch a glimpse of my own smile reflected in the glass of his microwave and quickly erase it. Because *what am I doing?*

The same thing I always do.

It's like Phase One was initiated the second I decided not to wallow over his comment about us not being friends. Or—more to the point—the second the apology meal showed up at my door.

Matteo isn't a mean person, or even a bad guy—but boy, he wants people to think he is.

And I want to know why.

You're doing it again, Iris. This is how it always starts.

I shake away the thought and walk into the living room, taking in the space.

I was right about his corner apartment. The windows on two sides of this open space allow in so much sunlight, I might as well be standing outside.

But the apartment is so . . . sparse. *Too* sparse.

I study it for a few long seconds, wondering how he can live in such a sterile environment. It's like his grandpa took every personal item with him, left behind the basics, and Matteo didn't bother to replace anything.

The kitchen is, not surprisingly, state-of-the-art, all clean lines and things put away, leaving lots of blank spaces.

It needs something. Something homey.

And then, it hits me.

I don't even hesitate to think that it might not be the best idea ever. Or that he might hate it.

I just think *this is brilliant* as I rush out of his apartment, leaving the door open and the newspaper out on the counter.

I hurry down the hall into my space and find what I'm looking for, then rush back to his apartment just as he reappears in the living room from a bedroom that probably smells like a Christmas tree farm.

There's a faint scent of pine or spruce or something delicious whenever he's around, and I have to imagine this smell only intensifies in his bedroom.

Bedroom.

I shake the thoughts from opening *that* door.

"You left," he says as I rush past him. "And . . . you brought the 1970's back with you."

I ignore him, spreading the multi-colored crocheted afghan I made this past summer on the back of his couch. "Don't be ugly. I'm giving you a gift." I turn and find a grimace on his face. "Consider it payment for all the food." I draw in a breath. "It'll make your space cozier."

He cocks his head and points. "Cozy is not what that is."

"It's homemade. Homemade blankets are always cozy." Obviously, this isn't true. When I was a kid, my grandma made me a blanket out of the itchiest and cheapest yarn in the store. But that doesn't support my argument, so I keep it to myself.

"It doesn't go with anything in here," he says.

I shoot him a look. "Anything will go with what's in here because there's nothing in here."

He shoots me an annoyed look, but I ignore it.

"Oh! I made a throw pillow to go with it! Do you want me to go get it?"

"No." And then, after a pause, he says, "Wait, did you say you made that?"

"That's what *homemade* usually means." I quirk a brow, and I see the second he remembers using that exact line on me in Winnie's apartment. "I only use the softest yarn." I reach out and pet the brightly colored granny squares. "It'll be perfect for, you know, relaxing on the couch when you get home from work or if you have a date or something."

What am I saying?

He rolls his eyes and walks into the kitchen, making a clear point of ignoring me. I glance back at the living room, aware that the afghan really does look ridiculous with his modern aesthetic. "So many hard lines in here," I say out loud, continuing the conversation I'm having with myself in my head. "You just need to find something to soften them a little."

He doesn't respond. He's leaning over the newspaper, reading.

"Oh! Yes! Let's do it!" I rush into the kitchen and stand

beside him, leaning over the counter, the same way he is, only I'm pretending I know what I'm looking for.

As if one successful bout with the magic has made me an expert.

"You're way too excited about this," he mutters, eyes scanning the pages. Then, with a quick glance in my direction he adds, "This is why we're here, remember?"

"Right," I say. "All business. All the time."

I pause.

"And French toast *some* of the time."

He gives me a healthy dose of side-eye.

I'm trying to be cautious. I'm doing my best not to be . . . *me*. But, per usual, I barreled in here acting like he and I are exactly what we aren't.

Friends.

I think about what Winnie said—that the world needs my big, open heart—but maybe she doesn't know how easy a big, open heart is to break.

I start scanning the articles, noticing immediately that this edition is different from the one about Winnie. All the articles are about different people, with whole sections of blank space. I don't get it.

After a few minutes of searching, Matteo stands upright and refills his coffee, then leans against the counter.

I feel him watching me, so I finally meet his eyes. "You already found it?"

"Yep."

"It's like a word search." I groan and go back to scanning the newspaper. "I was never good at those." I move over to the other side of the counter and plop myself back down on the stool while Matteo sets his mug on the island and checks on the bread. He pulls a pan from a nearby cupboard then proceeds to put so much butter in it that my arteries clog just watching.

He must sense me judging because he stops moving and looks at me.

I laugh and look away. "That is so much butter."

"Trust me."

"It's a good thing you don't want to be friends with me because my waistline can't handle eating so much of your food."

He quirks a brow. "Your waistline is just fine."

Heat rushes to my face.

"Wait. I didn't . . ." His face flushes.

I try to play it off by saying, "Oh, I know, no big deal . . ." But my inner teenager is back. *He noticed my waistline?*

I inadvertently stand up a little straighter and try to nonchalantly fluff my hair. What else has he noticed? The words on the page in front of me go out of focus as I struggle to concentrate. And this feeling—this gooey, ridiculous, buzzy feeling—is exactly what I've been hoping to avoid.

Never mind that seeing him shirtless this morning just about gave me a cardiac episode.

He moves the butter around the black pan, watching it closely. "Does that mean you don't want breakfast?"

"Heck, no," I say. "I cracked the eggs. I have to see how it turns out."

"Just checking." He picks up one of the slices of bread, and it sizzles when he sets it in the hot griddle. While I can't be sure, I think he's trying not to smile.

I want to ask him why he seems to resist enjoying himself. It's obvious in the way he eats, the way he cooks, that there is passion there. He has to enjoy it on some level.

"None of these articles are about the same person," I say after a few minutes of scanning the words on the pages. "The newspaper with Winnie was all about Winnie."

"Yeah, they're not usually that obvious." He's got his

back to me now. "I think that one was more like the shallow end of the pool. This one's a bit more toward the deep end."

I go back to the newspaper. "How am I supposed to figure this out?"

Now, he turns and leans against the counter, twirling a spatula. "Giving up so soon?"

"No." I turn the page, and Matteo gives me a pointed look. He found whatever he was looking for on the first page. This is probably the only clue he's going to give me.

"How am I supposed to concentrate when it smells like that in here?" I ask, stomach growling.

"Refer back to my earlier comment about patience." He taps the newspaper. "No breakfast until you figure this out. And you're going to want to eat it before it gets cold."

I huff out a sigh. "Fine."

He gets quiet while I go back to searching, and I do my best to ignore the slight sizzling of the bread and just how badly my mouth is watering at the smell. And then, I see it.

A short blip of text, the only thing not written in past tense.

"Aha! I found it!" I say, triumphantly. "Serve it up, Chef."

"Read it out loud," Matteo says, and while he would probably never admit it, he almost sounds . . . excited?

He plates the food as I read aloud:

Joy is a joy, and she needs something new.
Her life became flat when her three became two.
Her confidence is wafer-thin paper mâché
So, if someone could chordially invite her today
(For her balance in life is no work and all play)
A blessing is long overdue.

Look for something noteworthy.

I frown. "That's weird. It reads like a riddle. Plus 'cordially' is misspelled."

"First thing you need to know about the newspaper," he explains, "is that every issue is a little different than the last one."

He points at it.

The rest of the articles, all the words, slowly disappear, leaving only this rhyming blurb.

"So, step one: figure out who the newspaper is talking about—my guess is, someone named Joy." He picks up the two plates and walks them over to the table. "Do you want something else to drink?"

I spin around on the stool and watch him. "Why do you pretend like you're a jerk?"

He ignores me. "Orange juice? Water?"

"Ooh. Orange juice, please." I stand and walk over to the table. "I'm serious. I don't get it. If you were really the awful person you want people to believe you are, you would've kicked me out when you first opened the door." I laugh. "And you definitely would not have made me breakfast."

"I was just saving myself time." He pulls orange juice out of the refrigerator. "I don't know you well—but I do know you wouldn't have left me alone."

I pretend to think about this, then shrug. "Fair."

"And this isn't an act." He hands me a glass. "I'm very careful about who I let into my life."

I want to ask him why. Instead, I say, "Oh, I'm not."

His eyebrows shoot up as he sits, almost like he's surprised I'm admitting this.

"I should be, but I'm not," I say as I start cutting my French toast.

He frowns. "Why should you be? I mean, you said before you like people," he says.

I stop cutting. "Because . . . reasons."

"Oh, yeah, well, that clears it up," he muses.

Because New Iris is trying to be better about volunteering too much personal information. New Iris doesn't want to get close to someone—*again*—only to have them leave. And so far, New Iris has done a decent job. A solid C+.

The problem is, I *want* to tell him everything I'm thinking.

"If I tell you, it'll be a *giant* overshare." I feel like the forewarning makes it okay. Also, I'm a slow learner. A part of me knows this isn't the way to get someone to open up. A part of me knows this is how I run people off.

He douses his plate with syrup, and I take that as permission to do the same. "Okay."

"Okay, I should still tell you, or okay I shouldn't?" I ask, taking the syrup. Because these new rules I've made for myself are getting more and more difficult to interpret. What I know I *should* do is in direct conflict with what I *want* to do.

He shrugs. "It looks like you need to talk about whatever you need to talk about, so . . ."

To me, that's permission.

"I think sharing too much turns people off," I say. "I mean, that's my guess. I have this problem with telling people my whole life's story when they really didn't want to hear it. I think I do it hoping they'll share back?" I pause because sharing about my oversharing is still an overshare. "They usually don't. They usually avoid me like the plague." My laugh is a little self-deprecating.

I mindlessly cut my French toast. "I'm one of those people who doesn't really like a 'get to know each other period.' I dive in. Headfirst. No life vest. I want to be best friends with everyone from the jump, and I want everyone to like me. It's like a sickness." I spear a piece with my fork but don't eat it, and then say, "So when I moved here, I decided to actively *not* be that way."

"To actively *not* be yourself," he says.

I laugh. "I mean, let's be real, I'm a lot . . ." *Too much*, but I don't say so. I glance up and find him frowning at me.

"So, someone told you that you're 'a lot,' and you believed them?" He nods at my fork. "Taste it."

His question hangs in the air as I lift the bite to my lips. Before I eat it, he holds up a hand to stop me from moving.

"Slowly," he says, eyes dipping to my mouth. "Taste every flavor."

I do as he says, chewing slowly, savoring every bite, trying to discern each flavor I watched him put into the liquid before soaking the bread, and for a fleeting moment, I understand why he eats so slowly.

I can safely say that I've never in life tasted something like this. I quickly stab another piece, but he catches my eye, and I resist the urge to snarf.

The textures, the sweetness, the crispiness of the outside with the velvety custard inside . . . it's amazing.

And it's just bread.

"I lied before. *This* would be my final meal," I say, after I've swallowed the bite.

He smiles. "Good?"

I shake my head in culinary disbelief. "How in the world have I been missing this?"

He flips the towel over his shoulder and starts in on his own. "Good."

"And yes, to answer your question. Someone told me I was a lot. Well, not just 'someone'—several people. More than several. When you're a lot, you're a lot." I look at him. "I'm a lot."

He arranges another perfect bite on his fork. "So, how's it working out for you—this plan to become a totally different person?"

185

"Eh, fair-to-middling," I joke, knowing I'm not exactly succeeding right now.

I take a drink. "I'm just, you know, holding back a little so I don't scare people off."

He looks at me, confused. "If you're scaring people off, Iris, then they aren't the right people."

I force myself not to look away for what feels like a full three hours, and then finally, I glance down at my plate. Because he's right. They're never the right people. But also—why does he make this sound so simple?

I glance up. "Is that why you don't pretend? I mean, you're *really* embracing this salty attitude."

"No." He gives his head a little shake. "I don't pretend because I don't care what people think."

I laugh. "What's that like?"

"It's brilliant." He smirks. "You should try it sometime."

My eating has devolved into devouring again, and I have to physically remind myself to slow down. "I can't relate." I shrug. "I want to be loved." A mental facepalm. "And I didn't really mean to say that out loud."

Good grief.

He makes a face, but I can't quite read it. It almost looks like understanding.

"I think we are who we are. You can't change your personality." He shrugs. "And you shouldn't try. Don't make yourself smaller because you've been surrounding yourself with idiots."

"That's nice coming from someone who doesn't even want to be my friend." I smirk so he knows I'm joking, but I'm joking because I don't know what to do with his kindness.

"Yeah, about that . . ."

I set down my fork, paying attention with my whole body.

"I was a little quick. I'm not used to"—he points to me—"someone who's a lot." He smirks. "Would it make you happy if I said we could be . . . friends?" He says this in his most annoyed tone, like this really is a giant inconvenience, and yet, I hear the tease in his voice, and *that* is what I latch onto.

A smile crawls across my face. "Yes."

"Fine," he says. "But only because I'm genuinely afraid to let you feed yourself anymore."

I pump my fist. "Woo! I knew I'd wear you down."

He shakes his head. "And I take it back. Not friends, sorry. Too weird."

I look at him, mocking shock.

He looks back.

And we laugh.

Chapter Twenty-Two
Iris

I HAVE A NEW FRIEND.

He's a hot chef.

Teenage Iris, who takes up far too much space in my brain, is kicking her feet and trying not to giggle. Phase Two has been activated, and I didn't even force it to happen.

It's a step up from "rude neighbor," but I have to remember this is strictly platonic.

Don't romanticize this, Iris.

I know if I start getting too emotional, I'll sabotage this fledgling friendship before it ever really begins.

"So, if we're friends," I say, wishing it was the beginning and not the end of my meal, "does that mean—"

"Still no personal questions," he says, cutting me off.

I groan. "Oh, come on. Just one?"

"Nope."

"I just want to know how you do it," I say.

"Do what?"

"Stop caring what people think."

He ponders this. "Okay, I'll allow that one." He leans back against the counter. "It's not like I don't care what *anyone* thinks. I have some people whose opinions I value. Like my grandpa. And Val. People who matter."

"Ah, okay. So my first step is to find people who matter . . . got it." I laugh, mostly to keep from sounding like a loser. How is it possible that this guy, who is purposefully being a grump, has people and I don't? "I'm really not as pathetic as I sound. I just maybe . . . latch on to the wrong people? I don't know." I don't know why I made that sound like a question when it's a proven fact. "I've gotten burned—a lot—so I guess I'm trying to, you know, care less."

"So what you're saying is you want to be more like me," he says.

"Whoa, hang on," I say, holding up my hands and standing. I stiffen, hunch over a bit, and in a low, gruff voice, I say, "*I don't want to be friends! Custard takes time! This needs more salt!*"

At that he laughs. "*That's* your impression of me?"

I chuckle, then make a show of screwing up my face. "Nailed it."

"If that's what you see, then I need to work on a few things. Like my posture," he smirks. "You made me look like Quasimodo."

I sit back down. "All I'm saying is there has to be a balance between your way and my way."

He nods. "Probably."

We eat in silence for a few moments, and I search my brain for a way to change the subject. But then Matteo says, "Maybe the solution isn't to care less but to find people worth caring about."

I meet his eyes and freeze. Because even though it makes no sense, there's one simple question racing through my mind —*Are you one of those people?*

"In my experience, those people are really hard to find." My gaze dips back to my half-eaten French toast, and I stab another piece with my fork. "I thought maybe I'd control what I can control. That way, you know, I won't get hurt so much."

He holds my gaze. "That—I do understand."

And I wonder, for the millionth time, what his story is. "We're both going to end up old and alone if we aren't careful," I add in a joking tone as I take another bite. "The newspaper will have to send someone to save us."

"Eh. I'm okay being alone." He shrugs.

"I don't think I am," I counter.

"How so?"

I set my fork down. "So . . . because you're asking, it's okay for me to talk about stuff, right?"

He makes a face. "Yeah, that's kind of how conversations work."

It's an invitation. It would be rude to shut down now, right? "Okay. Here it is. When my parents got divorced, everything sort of changed for me."

I think about the day my dad left after quietly falling in love with a woman in his office named Ginny. And her family.

They got married the following year, and I spent the next several years trying to figure out a way to convince him I was still worth his time. I don't think I ever succeeded. He had a new wife and stepkids who he was really trying to impress.

I reach for my coffee and take a drink, then pull one leg up underneath me. How much do I tell him?

"When I was in high school, I had this art show." I turn the warm mug around in my hands, the memory of it forming in my mind. "It was my senior year, and it was a really big deal. I was up for this state-wide scholarship, and they were hosting an art show with a ceremony to announce the winner."

And then I'm back there, standing on that stage, searching the crowd and finding the seat I'd saved for my dad empty.

"I'd been working all year on perfecting my portfolio, and it had been a huge process trying to decide which pieces to submit. I really wanted to win." I'm there, in the memory of it all. "I sent my dad an invitation in the mail. When he didn't respond, I emailed and called, and finally, he told me he'd be there. I made it so obvious how important this was to me, and I was so sure that if he could see me there, in my element, doing something other people thought was really good"—I shrug—"I guess I thought then he'd think I was really good too." My hands are cold at the memory. "I really thought he'd come." I look down. "He didn't."

My mom made excuses for him, clapped twice as hard and cheered twice as loud, as if that could make up for it. We both knew the truth. He'd moved on.

"It's such a cliché," I say on a wry laugh. "I mean, the absent father doesn't show up for his daughter? The empty seat in the auditorium? The daughter who is wounded and spends years dealing with her abandonment issues? It's like an episode of *One Tree Hill*." I pause. I need a second to step out of the memory.

I don't look at Matteo, aware that I've probably shared too much.

But then he says, "So, did you win?"

I meet his eyes, and the heaviness lifts. "Actually? I *did*." I smile at that. "I got a ton of new art supplies as part of the prize, which was even better than the scholarship. At least to me." I clasp and unclasp my hands, then turn my ring around on my finger. When I find him watching, I stop. "The worst part was that after the art show, my friend, Charlotte, convinced me to go to the basketball game. Our school was playing its crosstown rival, and she said it would be a fun distraction. We got there just before half-time and squished into the student section, and after about ten minutes of sitting there, I saw my dad in the stands, cheering for the other team."

I look up, and I don't even bother to pretend it doesn't still make me sad.

"His new wife's daughter was a cheerleader," I say. "They were there for her." I pause. "I never told my mom that part. I think it would've killed her."

At my side, Matteo goes still.

I brighten, hating that I've dragged the mood down. "So, there you have it! It's so far in the rearview mirror, and I'm an adult doing the adulting things, but . . ." I give a *ta-da* gesture. "Now you know exactly what kind of person I am, and why I do the things I do."

He frowns. "I don't think it's too much to expect the people in your life to show up for you."

I look at him, surprised. "You don't?"

A shrug. "No. That's basic human decency. Especially family."

"Right? I always thought so," I say. "But you'd be surprised how hard it is to find decent people out there." A thought hits me. "Maybe your way *is* better. You know, push everyone away? Make them think you're a terrible person? The only problem with that"—I give him a look—"is making sure no one finds out you're really a decent guy."

He shakes his head. "Don't try to be like me, Iris. The world needs way more of your type than mine."

All of a sudden, the newspaper, which we've laid out flat on the counter, rolls up into its original shape and flips twice on the counter.

"Oh, back again, are we?" I say to the newspaper. "We need to have a talk, you and I."

"You . . . talk to it?"

I look over at Matteo, giving him a knowing nod. "Yep.

Quite the personality, I'd say." I stand, hands on hips. "So? Now what? More chimes?" I say to the newspaper.

The paper spins on the counter, and then breaks up into a thousand shimmering pieces, weaving back and forth, until propelling toward Matteo's fridge. The mass of golden shimmering pieces billows, creating a breaking sound of hundreds of chimes as they hit the front of the refrigerator, slowly dissipating, leaving just the cutout article about Joy behind an Aria magnet.

"Well. That's new," Matteo says, shocked.

We share a look.

"Looks like we've got our marching orders. Let's get a plan to help Joy. Whoever she is."

I nod in agreement but point to his plate. "But first, are you going to finish that?"

Chapter Twenty-Three
Iris

SUNDAY MORNING, I wake up to no newspaper alarm, thankfully, but with an intense craving for French toast.

Matteo has ruined Pop-Tarts for me forever.

As I make my way through my morning routine, filling the carafe with water and brewing my coffee, there's a knock at my door.

My heart skips.

It's not even eight. Is this payback?

And why am I excited at the thought?

That excitement quickly turns to dread when I remember that unlike Matteo, I don't look like a walking billboard when I roll out of bed.

I catch a glimpse of my reflection in a small mirror on the wall and wince. I pull the elastic from my messy bun and shake out my hair, but I'm bringing "casual" down to a whole new level. I carry my mug with me as I walk to the door, and when I pull it open, I find Matteo wearing the slightest hint of a crooked half-smile that makes me feel fuzzy on the inside.

"Please tell me you were still in bed." His expression holds.

"You wish!" I blurt. "You're going to have to get here before seven if you want to catch me still in bed."

His mouth twitches, and I feel the heat rush to my cheeks.

"I mean—I didn't—" I press my lips together, but I can't think of any way to erase the visual I've just created.

He just stands there, smirking.

I turn around, leaving the door open, and walk back into my kitchen, mentally flogging myself for being so awkward. I can't help it—this is the first time he's sought me out. It feels buzz-worthy.

And I'm definitely buzzing.

I walk into the kitchen and pull out a mug, aware that he's closed the door and followed me inside. I turn and find him looking around.

"Are you getting hives just being in here?" I ask with a quick glance around my apartment, which looks like a "before" photo on *The Home Edit*.

"It's . . ." His eyes scan the space. "Very you."

I frown. "That doesn't sound like a compliment."

He shrugs. "It looks exactly like I pictured."

"Considering how neat your apartment is, I'm taking that personally."

"It's not an insult, I promise," he chuckles. "Is the artwork yours?"

I look around at the brightly colored canvases I've hung on the walls. "Yeah. I don't paint much anymore, but I hung them to remind myself that I can." I wonder if my smile is wistful or sad.

His expression doesn't answer the question. "You're good."

"Well, thanks," I say, feeling a little self-conscious. Probably because I unloaded my pathetic art show misery on him. Seeing it through his eyes has me rethinking every piece of mismatched furniture and every crocheted granny square.

"What you're seeing is the result of every bad break-up of my adult life."

Matteo's eyebrows shoot up in an unspoken question.

I set down my mug, walk into my living room, and point to a throw pillow. "Peter. College boyfriend. Told him my whole life story on our first date. Thought for sure we'd end up together. When he started his job at a fancy law firm in Boston, he met Ruby and fell in love. Peter said Ruby's *energy* was a better fit for him." I pause for effect. "I learned to crochet because I needed a distraction."

I walk over to the coffee table and point. "Brian. Post-college. Met him at a coffee shop. Brian's mother came to his house to pick up his laundry every Saturday morning, then brought it back all neatly pressed and folded—which *might* have been a red flag, you know, because he was twenty-five, but I somehow convinced myself I could help him make that leap into adulthood. In the end, he said it was too much pressure, and I stressed him out."

I lean down and pat the table. "Found this on the side of the road the day he broke up with me and decided to teach myself to refinish furniture because I needed the distraction."

I point at a cactus. "After Brian, there was Bryan with a *y*." I look at Matteo, who winces. "Yes, really. He was an adult with a real, adult job. But because I wanted him to fall for me *so badly*, I did just about everything I could to make his life easier. I got his groceries. I tidied his apartment. I even picked up his dry cleaning."

Matteo purses his lips, like he wants to say something but doesn't.

"And oh, yes, he let me do all those things. Pretty soon, he expected them. And I became less of a partner and more of a personal assistant." I pull a face. "The worst part? I'd probably still be with him if he hadn't decided I was smothering him." I scoff, then pick up the cactus. "I learned all I could about caring for succulents because I needed a distraction."

"So you keep all these? Don't they make you think—"

"Of what a relationship destroyer I am?" I finish his thought for him. "Yes."

"That's not what I was going to say, but okay."

I shrug.

"I was going to say 'don't they make you think of how wrong they were for you?' Why would you even keep them around?"

I shrug. Names and memories are attached to nearly everything in my apartment.

Ceramic vase? Hunter. Three dates and he'd had enough.

Macrame wall hanging? Timothy. Little bit longer but felt like we were still "moving too fast."

Button art? Jason. Turned out he was gay. Oh, well.

The hobbies, like the men, didn't stick around either.

And that's a brilliant question. Why have I kept all this stuff? Why am I putting it on display, like some Broken Hearts Museum?

I don't look at Matteo. "I think some people who have divorced parents think they're never going to fall in love or get married. They've seen what a mess it can be—and my parents' divorce was messy." I inhale a slow breath. "But for other people—" I go quiet then, because it hits me all at once that I'm realizing this as I'm saying it out loud.

And I'm saying it to Matteo, which is probably a mistake. Is he *really* the person I should be confiding in?

"For other people?" He presses for me to finish the thought.

I shake my head. "Ah, nothing, it's dumb."

I expect him to take the out. To tell me why he's here and

refocus this conversation on something productive—the magic. So when he sits down on the edge of my vintage couch closest to me, it catches me off-guard. "For other people . . .?"

I scrunch my face. "You don't really want to hear this."

His eyebrows shoot up. "I don't?"

"Do you?"

"Just because I don't like to talk about myself doesn't mean I don't want to listen."

I study his face for a long moment, searching for some sign that he's placating me. I don't find one.

It's different, talking to someone with a genuine interest in what I have to say.

Huh. Another real-time revelation.

"For other people . . ." I clasp and unclasp my hands. "It makes the whole concept of a family that much more appealing. It's a glittery, shiny thing I've never really had." I pull my legs up under me. "I think I chase after it because I've romanticized it, but so far, that pursuit has only brought me—"

"Ugly furniture?"

I bark out a laugh and swat his arm. "It's not ugly."

He makes a face that says, *You sure about that?*

"You said it was very 'me,' so you're basically calling me ugly." I mock-glare at him.

He shakes his head. "No, I'm not."

My mind instantly locks on a meaning he probably didn't intend, and when it does, I have to look away. "What about you?"

"What about me?"

"Do you want the whole wife, kids, family dog life?"

There's a flicker of sadness in his eyes, and I see the second he shuts down. "No questions, remember?"

I groan. "Come *on*! I've practically told you my whole life's story! How is that fair?"

"Are you always this . . . open . . . with people you've just met?" he asks.

"*Yes.* You finally get it. It's one of my fatal flaws." I stand and walk back into the kitchen. "Do you want coffee?"

He glances at my drip carafe and winces. "We need to get you a French press."

"It's just coffee, fancy pants," I say, pulling a mug out of the cupboard and pretending like the coffee he made yesterday wasn't the best coffee I've ever tasted.

"I don't think it's a flaw." He's moved from the couch to the other side of the kitchen island, and I'm thankful there's a little space between us. "I just don't share like that."

"Really?" I say, mock-surprised. "This is breaking news."

He rolls his eyes.

I laugh. "Well, be glad. It usually makes people run the other way." I take a mug down from the cupboard and pour him a cup of coffee. I know he takes it black, but I also know it's going to taste like sewer water compared to what he's used to. "I'm working on it."

"This is one of those things you're trying to change," he says, remembering.

I nod.

"Don't."

The word hangs there, in the space between us, and I want to reach up and grab it.

"It's . . . nice," he says. "You know what you want, and you're going for it. That's not something to be embarrassed about."

I've never looked at it that way.

"But my baggage?" I say, as if I need to pull it out of the closet and wave it in front of his face. "Nobody needs to see that on day one. Or day thirty. It's too much."

He shrugs. "For the right person, you won't be too much."

He says it so simply. Like it's the easiest thing in the world.

Nobody's ever said that to me before. Not like that.

It's the second day in a row Matteo has been kind to me, and I wonder if kindness means more coming from an unexpected place. I'm starting to see why the magic picked him.

He takes a drink of the coffee, and his face contorts. "This is terrible."

I laugh. "Was waiting for that."

"This is your *real* fatal flaw." He pushes the mug back toward me. "From now on, you're not allowed to make coffee."

"Oh, really?" I frown. "Are you going to be my caffeine dealer every morning?"

"If it means saving you"—he points at me—"from that"—he points at the mug—"then, yes."

I laugh. "Fine. I get up early. And be prepared for a jump scare when you open my door, because pre-coffee I'm prehistoric." I smile from behind my cup. I like that he's here.

More than I should.

I know what he wants. I know it's not what I want. And just because he listens and is way more decent than I thought does not change the fact that I really don't know him at all.

Yet.

"What are you doing today?" he asks.

"Trying to figure out your whole life's story, probably," I say.

"Can you put a pin in that?"

"Make me a better offer." I walk over to my pantry closet and pull out a box of Pop-Tarts.

"Don't eat those in front of me," he says.

I turn back. "My apartment, my rules."

He shakes his head. "I'll come back later."

"I'll be eating Flamin' Hot Cheetos with cream cheese later," I say. "That's my plan for lunch."

He lets out a groan and stands. "Is this your way of getting me to cook you breakfast again?"

I smirk at him and set the box aside. "I mean, if you're offering. I did have a dream last night that I was being chased by a giant piece of French toast." I sit down at the little two-seater table I've got in the corner of my kitchen and watch as he opens my refrigerator.

He winces at the lack of ingredients. "We're going to have to go to the store."

"We can't do that on Slow Sunday," I say.

He frowns. "Slow Sunday?"

"It's a me-day. A day where I can go slow. I'm sure you can relate, right? You're completely tapped, I'm guessing, after a huge night at the restaurant. I'm with children for eight hours a day, five days a week."

I hold out my arms and show off my outfit, presentation-style. "Slow Sunday."

He leans against the counter and crosses his arms over his chest, and I have a fleeting thought that he looks really good in my kitchen. "You might need to make an exception today."

I frown. "Why?"

"I'm going to give you a magic lesson."

My brain goes into overdrive with the words *give, you,* and *lesson.*

"Oh." I stand, trying not to let on that I'm suddenly warm. "You are?"

He shrugs. "The sooner you learn everything I know, the sooner I'll be done with the magic." A pause. "Or maybe it's the magic that will be done with me."

I give a definitive nod because *of course* that's what this is about. I already knew his feelings on the subject, so I can't be hurt that this "friendship" is conditional.

And once the magic officially passes to me—I don't know if I'll like what comes after.

Chapter Twenty-Four
Iris

"Okay, boss," I say, trying to sound more excited about this than I feel. "Where do we start?"

"With Joy," he says. "I know who she is."

"I assume you're going to tell me how you figured that out," I say. "If you're going to mentor me, you have to share all your secrets."

"Grab your coat and come with me," he says, pulling his own coat back on.

I look down at my pajama pants, then at him with a *this is what you get* look.

"Oh, we're not leaving the building. Well, not leaving the grounds."

I'm confused.

"You'll see. But you'll probably want shoes."

I grab my shoes, pull on my coat and follow him out into the hallway and then down the stairwell.

I do a really good job of not asking a bunch of questions on the way—go me—and we reach the ground floor and step into the lobby, then walk into the courtyard.

The courtyard was one of the things I loved most about

the building when I first moved in, but I only now realize I haven't spent any real time out here.

Even though it's too cold for sitting by the empty pool, I spot two older women on a bench near the fountain, a blanket over their laps, bundled in coats and holding two mugs of what I assume is coffee or tea—but judging by the way they're cackling and carrying on, it could just as easily be brandy.

"What are we doing out here?" I ask, as Matteo makes a beeline toward the women. "Wait! I'm still in my pajam—"

Before I can finish, one of the women calls out, "You're back!"

"Oh! And you brought a *lady* friend," the other one says, clearly interested.

I object to the word "lady" but don't say so.

"This is Iris," Matteo says, indicating me. "She's new to the building."

"Not that new," the first woman cracks. "She's been here since August."

"Works at the elementary school," the other woman chimes in.

"Hasn't had a date since she's lived here but appears to be single," the first one says.

"Buys a lot of yarn."

They both stare at me, like they might have to describe me to a sketch artist one day.

"Uh . . . that's right," I say, frowning.

"What do you make with all that yarn?" the first woman asks.

"It depends," I say. "Lately, I've been crocheting these little stuffed animals, but I've done blankets and scarves and . . ." I lose steam, but add a quiet, "Other things."

They turn to one another and mumble and nod, a smattering of *oh, yeah, see, I told you, yes, you were right's,* like they had a bet on my yarn usage.

Matteo motions toward the first woman, who is wearing thick, black-framed glasses. "Iris, this is Roberta." He pivots slightly and points to the other woman. "And her sister, Rhonda."

Both are gray-haired, wearing big, puffy coats, stocking caps, mittens and have matching red lips.

"Rhonda doesn't live here," Roberta says.

"I'm here for the coffee." Rhonda holds up her cup.

"And for my sparkling personality." Roberta snorts.

"And for this one's cannoli." Rhonda nods at Matteo, who's standing there with his hands stuffed in his pockets. It's not lost on me that he looks like the top result of a google search for "hot Italian chefs," and I'm still in my pajamas.

"We would've talked to you without the cannoli, you know," Rhonda says. "But it was a nice touch."

Matteo trades information for cannoli. Smart. Use what you got, I say. Which makes me wonder—what do I have? A partially crocheted jellyfish?

"Roberta. Rhonda. Will you tell Iris what you told me about Joy?" he asks.

"Oh, right," Roberta says, her Boston accent coming through thick. "So one day last month, I was standing at my sink, doing dishes—my husband Harold is terrible about rinsing the pan after he cooks, so I had to put a little elbow grease into it. I mean, really, what is so hard about rinsing a pan? It would rinse right off if he did it right away, but—"

Rhonda smacks her sister in the arm. "Get on with it!"

Roberta holds her hand up in surrender. "Geesh, I was just saying—"

"Okay, but just *say* the thing he asked you to say! Nobody cares about Harold's pans."

In her accent, "cares", "Harold", and "pans" all sort of rhyme.

Roberta doesn't miss a beat. "So, there I am, washing away, when I see a woman wandering around the building, holding onto a little girl's hand like they don't know where they're going. Of course I couldn't get a good look from my window, so I dried my hands quick, bagged up the garbage, and started for the dumpster, mostly because I didn't want to, you know, make it obvious I was spying."

"No good spy makes it obvious," Rhonda interjects, dryly.

"Right." Roberta pats her on the arm, and Matteo, who's presumably already heard this story, must see this as an opening to speed her along.

"Tell Iris the part about how Joy lives here now with her daughter because she's—"

"Divorced." Roberta whispers this, sounding like *divawced*, like it's something we don't say out loud.

"Getting divorced," Matteo finishes his thought, with a nod toward me. "She's going through a divorce."

"Temporarily here," Rhonda says, clearly clued in on the gossip. "Not sure her husband is going to come through on the alimony, and she hasn't worked since she had her daughter."

"So. She needs a job," I say, with a glance toward Matteo.

"And some hope," Rhonda says. "You wouldn't believe how sad she is all the time. And that little girl." Rhonda presses a palm to her chest and shakes her head. "Bless her sweet little heart. Oh, but you probably know her, Iris. She goes to your school."

And that's when I put the dots together. "Wait. Is her daughter's name Alice?"

"Bingo," Roberta says, pointing at me. "Joy moved in here so Alice didn't have to change schools."

My mind spins back to the day I met them in the hallway,

coming in late. Joy mentioned there was "a lot going on at home." No wonder Alice has been so sad.

"She's been out job hunting," Roberta continues, "but not getting anywhere, and at night, she comes down here and plays that guitar. You might've heard her."

I shake my head. "I haven't."

"She's wicked good," Roberta says.

"Can't make money that way, though." Rhonda shakes her head, like she's got proof to back up this opinion.

"Right," I say. And then, I get an idea. I give a quick nod to Matteo, then back to the sisters. "Thanks, ladies. It was so nice to meet you."

"Nice to meet you too, Iris Ellington of Apartment 3D."

"How do you . . . ?"

Roberta grins. "I know *everything*."

I take a few steps back, slow-nodding and grabbing on to Matteo's arm. As we turn to go, I hear Rhonda say, "I'm glad he's back on the horse, even if she's not at all who I pictured him with."

"The important thing here is that he's dating again," Roberta says. "After what he's been through, that's all that matters."

"Small miracles," Rhonda says.

I turn back, wondering if they realize we can hear them. They wave at me, smiling in unison, seemingly oblivious to how loud they are.

I glance at Matteo, who has picked up the pace and is darting out of the courtyard, clearly uncomfortable, and a thought occurs to me.

If Roberta and her sister know things about me, then they know things about him too.

"So. Confidential cannoli informants," I say as we walk toward one of the doors that leads back inside.

"Whatever works." He shrugs. "They're out there every

Sunday morning like clockwork. Lots of weekdays, too. More often in the summer."

I nod like this is key information I need to know.

"She wasn't lying. They really do know everything," he says.

I narrow my gaze. "Except the fact that we aren't dating."

"Oh, no," he says. "They know that too. My guess is they wanted to see how we'd react."

I frown. "They're like the Fates or the Muses or something. Magic building, crafty old women . . . is this actually Hogwarts?" I joke.

"It'd be easier if it was. More people to take care of things instead of just me."

"Just *us*," I correct him.

He inhales. "And hopefully soon, just you."

I get it, I think. *You don't have to keep reminding me that's all this friendship is.*

"Oh, and they're still watching us."

I pretend to laugh and look back, and yep, Rhonda is craned over from behind Roberta, still watching us walk back into the building. "Remarkable."

"They're bored and observant and invaluable when the newspaper is cryptic," he says. "Which is often."

"And they're kind of fun."

He pulls the door open and looks at me, something close to a frown on his face. "You think?"

I walk inside. "Yeah, I do. I want to have coffee with them."

We reach the lobby and stop. I wonder if this is where we go our separate ways because the magic lesson is over or . . .?

"Do you want to figure out a way to help Joy, or do you need to get back to rotting on your couch?" His question cuts off my mental ramble.

"What about Slow Sunday?" I ask.

"Sacrifices must be made for the magic, Iris."

I watch him for a second, then say, "For someone who doesn't like doing this, you're awfully good at it."

He shrugs. "I've found that the quicker I figure out what it wants me to do and do it, the quicker I can go back to my life."

"And it couldn't be that underneath your cranky exterior, you actually *like* helping people?" I ask.

"Absolutely not," he says with no trace of irony.

If I didn't know him better, I'd believe him. "Uh-huh." I shoot him a look and push past him toward the stairwell. "Fine. I'll go change. Meet me in half an hour?"

"Just come to my apartment when you're ready," he says, "I'm going to run to the market to get a few things."

I eye him for a long moment. "You're going to feed me, aren't you?"

"I'm going to save you from the Pop-Tarts, yes."

"Can you save me with pancakes?" I ask.

He groans. "You're getting to be really high maintenance."

"You kind of knew that." I stare.

He stares back.

After a beat, he says, "Fine."

I push open the stairwell door and step inside, not concealing my smile. "You know what this means, don't you?" I say, holding the door open, knowing he's not going to follow.

He raises his eyebrows in a question.

"Four meals, several cups of coffee, and the sharing of magical secrets?" I pull my arm off the door and take a step back. "I think you secretly like being my friend."

The door closes before he can respond, and I smile because now *he's* the one on the other side.

Take that.

Chapter Twenty-Five
Matteo

"I HAVE one rule for this meal," Iris announces as she pulls two plates out of my cupboard like she lives here.

I glance up from the griddle. "Okay."

"You can't analyze every bite you take."

I look up. "Why?"

"Because."

I squint at her, and I instantly know it's useless to argue. "Fine."

"Fine?"

I go back to cooking. "I mean, yeah, I'll try. But I'm a chef, it's kind of what I do. How about if I asked you to not share every thought in your head?"

She starts to say something, then stops herself. Then, she smiles and holds out her hands. *See? It's easy.*

I shake my head at her, concealing a smile.

It stirs something inside of me, and I have the fleeting realization that I feel lighter when Iris is around.

I'm not sure what to do with that.

"One of the R Sisters said something about Joy playing the

guitar," Iris says. "I wonder if she knows anything about music."

"One of the R Sisters?"

"I don't remember which one is which." She winces. "They look exactly the same."

"Don't tell them that," I laugh. "Roberta says she's 'the pretty one' and Rhonda is 'the smart one.' But Rhonda said the same thing in a less complimentary way."

Iris giggles, then her face turns serious. "Should I be taking notes? I mean, you've had a few years of practice, and I don't want to miss anything."

I shake my head. "Nah. It's not that deep."

She cocks her head. "So, when I come knocking on your door during my first solo magic mission, you're not going to tell me I should've paid closer attention?"

I scrunch my nose. "Eh. Maybe you should write this down."

She pulls out her phone.

"First thing? The magic is unpredictable," I say.

"All right. But it's mostly matchmaking?" she asks, phone out, poised to take notes.

"Not always," I say. "Once it had me match a person with a building."

She looks up from her phone. "Explain."

"The newspaper gave me some riddle about a single mom with this great business idea," I say, remembering it so clearly because it was one of my first attempts at doing what the paper wanted me to do. "She was a frequent customer at the restaurant, and I overheard her talking to Nicola about wanting to open a boozy bookstore."

She laughs. "A boozy bookstore? That's a thing?"

"I guess?"

She smirks, then a realization hits her. "Wait. There's a bookstore near your restaurant. Is that—"

I nod. "The next day, the newspaper led me to a space that was about to go on the market, and now we have Books and Brews just a couple of blocks away from the restaurant."

"That's *crazy*," Iris marvels. "So, it's like, anything goes."

"Pretty much." I take a sip of coffee. "And sometimes—most times—it only gives you half the story."

"But why? Why not just spell it out?"

"Honestly? Because I think it makes you pay closer attention. It's almost like *you're* coming up with the answers, making you more part of it." Her phone buzzes in her hand, pulling her attention. She clicks around on it for a few seconds, eyes scanning whatever text or email has just come through.

"No. Way," she says, incredulous.

"What?"

She flips the phone around so I can see her screen. On it is an email with the subject line: *New job posting: Music Teacher—Spring Brook Elementary.*

"Two hours ago, I would've just deleted this," she says. "But because of that little comment the R-sister made . . ."

"You want to show it to Joy."

She nods, excited. "It makes sense, right? Is this how it works? This is it, right?"

I think about it for a second. "Yeah. That's pretty much it. Sometimes more detailed. Other times, less."

"So *nothing* that happens anymore is just coincidence. It's all part of a plan."

"That's one way to look at it."

She pauses. "So . . . why did your newspaper come to my door, then?"

I look at her—her big eyes, her endearing face—and I'm suddenly overwhelmed with a long-buried feeling.

She's part of the plan for you, Matteo.

Whoa. That thought dropped into my head without permission.

Thankfully she answers her own question. "Oh, duh. It's so you can show me all the tricks, then pass the mantle on to me."

I breathe an inward sigh of relief. It's been my working theory all along, but when she says it, I'm hit with a twinge of disappointment.

"Okay, so what are some things the magic has had you do?" She clicks her phone again, presumably to get back to the note she's started.

"It had me hire Dante," I say. "After he tried to steal money from our register."

Iris's eyes go wide. "What?"

"We'd only been open about a year, and Bear caught him and called the cops. The next day, I got a newspaper that had some cryptic message about a kid who'd gotten in trouble but who didn't need tough love. He needed a second chance." I shrug. "It took me a little while to decipher it because I was planning to press charges. Instead, thanks to the newspaper, I gave him a job as a dishwasher. Now, he's part of the family."

She studies me and then starts slowly shaking her head.

"What?"

"You're just like . . . a *really* decent human."

"Okay." I walk the dishes over to the sink and flip on the water.

She grins, then picks up both of our mugs and walks straight into the space beside me, rinsing them out under the faucet. I tighten at her nearness, but she doesn't seem to notice.

I open the dishwasher and file the plates in as she turns off the water and hands me the mugs.

It's mundane, really, but it feels significant.

Having another person in my space, helping with simple things, feeling comfortable around me—*not* reminding me of the past or trying to plan my future—is nice.

I close the dishwasher and turn around. She's standing next to the sink, but without something in her hands, she's fidgeting again.

"Do I make you nervous?" I'm not sure where the question came from, but I am curious why she's always fidgeting around me.

She follows my gaze to her hands, then shoves them in her pockets and turns away. "No. I mean, maybe." She leans against the counter. "Okay, yeah. You're a little intimidating."

I frown. "I'm intimidating?"

"Well, you *were*." She looks at me. "Not as much anymore."

"Yeah. I was a jerk," I say. "I never really apologized for that, did I?"

She winces.

"I am sorry," I say. "That's really not who I am."

In one fluid motion, she lifts herself up onto the counter and crosses one leg over the other. "Okay, so who are you?"

I tilt my head at her.

"I know, I know," she says before I can remind her. "No questions. But I don't care. If I'm going to have a Magic Mentor, I need to know who I'm working with."

My stomach tenses at the comment, mostly because I don't want her to know who she's working with. I don't want the light, easy, new rapport we've got going on to change, and once she finds out the truth, it will.

Just like always.

People find out about Aria, and I become a charity case. It's not a good feeling.

That's why I keep to myself.

I actually kind of get along with Iris. I like being around her. Maybe because in her eyes, there's no pity, no plan—only the quiet question, *Who exactly are you?*

And my own quiet answer that it's better if she doesn't know.

Chapter Twenty-Six
Iris

I SET my alarm a full forty-five minutes early. There's *no* chance of getting woken up with—
THWAP
It's basically torture at this point.
"Yeah, yeah, golden shimmer, *ooh*, it's *so* magical, wowee wow wow." I begrudgingly whip the covers off to find the newspaper, fully opened, hovering about three feet over my bed. The riddle about Joy is in large font now, taking up both the left and right sides of the pages.
"I have a plan," I say to the newspaper, talking to it like it's a person. "And I'm actually excited about it, so how about you quit hitting me in the face?!"
The paper then ripples, the sound a mixture of paper rustling and chimes, and starts to break apart in its typical magical fashion.
The last word to disappear is *JOY*, lingering on that until the whole newspaper is finely dissipated in a cloud of golden sparkles.
Joy, I think. *Let's find some for her.*
It's Monday morning, and I'm heading to work with a

singular focus—to connect Joy with Mr. Kincaid and get her the job at the school.

No idea if she's even qualified. No clue if this is the right thing to do.

But I have a feeling.

I shouldn't be surprised when I walk into the hallway just as Joy is rushing in with Alice. I smile at them, noting that Joy looks even more exhausted than the last time I saw her. I think back to the early days after my dad left, and I feel instant sympathy for her.

It's hard to keep things going when you're falling apart.

"Good morning, Alice," I say brightly. "How was your weekend?"

Alice gives me a little shrug.

"You know what I found out?" I ask. "We're neighbors! We live in the same building."

Joy meets my eyes, an almost scared expression on her face. "Oh, we're just helping my great aunt move into a long-term care facility." She rests a hand on Alice's shoulder. "She's . . . well, she's collected a lot of things over her life, and . . . it's too much work for her, and—" She stops talking, and I imagine what she might've said if she hadn't.

And we had nowhere else to go, maybe?

I nod, but my attention wanders when Charles walks into the hallway.

"Oh, Mr. Kincaid!" I wave toward him. "I wanted to let you know plans for the end-of-year art show are underway, and I think the kids are excited for it."

"Wonderful," he says, then sighs. "At least one of the fine arts departments is doing well."

My eyes dart to Joy, then back to Charles. "Right, yeah, I heard Miss Acker had to move back to Arizona." I look at Joy. "She was the music teacher. Her mother fell and broke her hip."

"Ouch," Joy says.

"Ouch is right," Charles says. "We have a spring concert in just a few months."

"And also . . . a *broken hip*," I say intently and quietly.

Charles winces. "Right! Of course. That too."

I look at Joy. "You don't know anyone qualified to teach music, do you?" I feel a little like an attorney leading the witness, but I have to play this hunch.

But then Joy says, "I don't. I'm sorry."

I frown. "You don't? Are you sure?" Because really—is she sure?

Her slight smile reads as polite. "I'm sure."

"Hmm. I thought . . ." But I don't finish the sentence because what am I going to say? I thought the magic clues were pointing me in your direction because one of the R-sisters told me you play guitar? Maybe I got it wrong.

On the upside, I'll be needing that Magic Mentor a little while longer. On the downside, I got it wrong.

But then Alice tugs on Joy's hand. "Mom, you could do it."

Joy's face reddens. "Oh, no, honey, I don't think I'm qualified."

"But you're teaching me piano," Alice says. "And you sing all the time."

Joy's laugh is nervous. "But I'm not a teacher." She looks at me. "I'm not a teacher."

Right. I mean, being able to sing doesn't make you qualified to teach. I glance at Charles. "Maybe you could hire her as a long-term sub?"

"Now, there's an idea," Charles says. "Are you looking for a job?"

"I have been, yes," Joy says. "But—"

"You'd have the same hours as Alice," I cut in. "And you'd get to see her during the day."

Alice looks up and slips her hand into her mom's. "Do it, Mommy," she whispers.

"If you have the time, we could talk about the job right now," Charles says. "No pressure, I'll just give you the basics so you can make an informed decision."

"Uh, yeah," Joy says. "Sure."

"Great." He gives her a nod, then sticks out his hand. "I'm Charles."

She laughs, but I don't miss the tears in her eyes, and I wonder if the prospect of finding a job that won't require late hours away from Alice is overwhelming. "Joy Standish." She shakes his hand, and a wave of happiness washes over me.

What if this actually works?

"I can take Alice to class," I say with a glance at the little girl.

"Thank you, Iris." Charles motions for Joy to follow him into the main office, and before she goes, she gives Alice a quick hug and kisses the top of her head.

I can practically see the burden on both of their shoulders lifting.

Because I took the time to pay attention.

Alice watches for a second as her mom follows Charles, then looks at me.

"Well, that's exciting," I say. "It would be fun to have your mom in school, wouldn't it?"

And for the first time since I met her, Alice smiles.

It warms my entire soul.

It's enough to set the tone for my entire day. I walk on sunshine through the rest of my classes, anxious to share all of this with Matteo as soon as possible. I think about texting him—this is why I demanded he put his number in my phone before I left yesterday—but decide I want to tell him in person. I want him to hear the joy in my voice when I relay this news because—What in the world?! The magic is legit!

That afternoon, I get caught up working on details for the art show and leave work a little later than usual, so I rush straight to Aria and park in the back because I know they're not open yet.

I turn off the car and stare at the back entrance. There's a sign on it that says "Staff Only," which, I am very aware, does not include me.

I tap the steering wheel. *You don't belong here, Iris.*

But...I have to tell him Joy got the job at the school. That the magic just made her life ten times better. That Alice smiled.

But . . . he won't like me walking through that door.

I pull out my phone and shoot him a text.

IRIS
Hey, I'm in the parking lot with a magic update. Is it okay if I come in quick?

I stare at my phone, waiting for a reply. It doesn't come.

He's right. I'm not patient. I get out of the car, lock it, and walk toward the door.

My phone buzzes, and I freeze, expecting Matteo's answer, but it's a text from Joy.

I *might've* hovered outside Charles's office during my free period trying to hear the outcome of her interview.

When his door opened and I heard the words, "We're glad to have you on board, Mrs. Standish," I *might've* let out a tiny little squeal.

As if I could be expected to contain my excitement over this. I gave Joy my number and told her we'd get together and go over everything she needs to know about working at Spring Brook.

Now, I stare down at the words on my screen, and once again, my eyes cloud over.

> **JOY**
>
> Iris, I can't thank you enough for introducing me to Charles and encouraging me to take the interview. I haven't thought about teaching for years, and I never would've applied without your prompting, but it's the perfect place for me right now. I've been searching for a job for weeks, but everything I've found would require long stretches of time away from Alice, and I just can't do that to her when things are so uncertain. Iris. You're a lifesaver. I can't thank you enough.

I smile. I sit, and I smile, and I feel warm and important and part of something bigger than me.

I tear up at the words as I read them for a second time, then text back:

> **IRIS**
>
> I was so happy to help. And remember, if you have any questions, my door—and my phone—are always open. Let's get together this week, and you've got a standing invitation to eat lunch with me. :)

> **JOY**
>
> I'm so nervous!

> **IRIS**
>
> You're going to be amazing!!

I click my phone off. I know Matteo won't be as excited about this as I am, but this is a big deal! We actually helped make someone's life better. How can he not see what a cool gift this is?

I hold my breath and knock on the door. When no one answers, I give it a tug, surprised to find it open. I'm expecting chaos in the kitchen, but instead, I'm met with near-silence and an empty space.

It hits me then that it's about a half an hour before they open.

Family dinner.

My body tenses, fight or flight, feeling like I'm somewhere I shouldn't be. Like I'm searching through someone's desk and they're about to walk in and catch me.

I hear clinking dishes and the low hum of chatter coming from somewhere beyond the kitchen.

I don't leave. I listen.

The muted laughter, the sharing of stories, the ease and familiarity—I wonder what it's like to have people to eat dinner with every night. I let myself imagine it, and a wave of nostalgic loneliness washes over me.

Then, suddenly, the kitchen door swings open and Val walks in, freezing when she sees me.

"Oh! Shoot! Hi!" I try to make my voice sound as pleasant —and non-stalkery—as possible. "I'm so sorry, I was, uh . . . looking for Matteo, and I knew you were closed so I came in through the back. I tried texting, but—"

She waves me off. "No response, right?"

I shrug.

"That man never has his phone." Val shakes her head, then grabs a pan from the stove. "Have you eaten?"

I don't bother reminding her that this is not dinner time for normal people. It's impossible to walk into this kitchen and not want to eat. Still, I didn't come looking for free food. I won't tell Matteo, but I've got a frozen pizza and a Caesar salad waiting in my apartment.

"I'm fine, I promise," I say. "If you could just grab him for me real quick, I'll get out of your hair."

"Don't be ridiculous!" she says, beaming. "Come eat!

We're all dying to find out more about the girl who put a smile back on Chef's face."

Wait. What?

I laugh that off and shove my hands into my pockets. "Oh, I don't have that kind of power."

"I beg to differ." Val raises one eyebrow and stares me down. "I know Teo better than anyone, and trust me—there's been a change recently. You're the only new thing in his life, so . . . you do the math."

"I think you're giving me too much credit." I lean in. "I think I really annoy him."

She laughs. "We'll see." She starts toward the door, and when I don't budge, she glances at me. "You coming?"

This is probably a bad idea.

But, for some inexplicable reason, I follow her through the door and into the private room off to the side of the restaurant.

The laughter fades as I step into their space. Matteo's back is to me, and as they all go quiet, he turns.

Our eyes meet, and I expect annoyance. Frustration. Anything to tell me that I've crossed a line.

To my utter shock, he almost smiles. "Iris?" He stands. "What are you doing here?"

All eyes are on me. And Matteo. All eyes are on *me and Matteo*.

"I'm so sorry. Hi, everyone, hi." I give a little wave.

There's a slight pause, and then the room explodes in *Heyo's!* and *Benvenuti!* and *Iris!* and several stand to come over and hug me.

Over the din, I try to tell Matteo, "I just wanted to give you an update about that mom in our building." I say this with a hint of *you know the one I mean*, almost like we have a secret. Because we sort of do. Which I pause to acknowledge because I *like* having a secret with him.

There's a wave of overlapping comments about sitting me down and getting me fed. Val wraps an arm around me. "That's great, but first, we're going to feed you." She looks at Bear. "Grab her a chair, would you?" Then, to everyone: "Make room! Come on, come on, for Iris."

The chatter resumes. I catch Nicola's eye, and she smiles, giving me a wink and a wave. They scoot around the table, easily, like they always do this—happily shifting positions to make room for one more person.

Me.

It's a small thing that feels very, very big.

Because for the first time in a long time, I feel like I belong.

Chapter Twenty-Seven
Matteo

VAL GIVES me a knowing look as Bear slides a chair next to mine.

I know what she's thinking.

Maybe the look on my face when Iris walked in gave her hope. Because when I saw her, I didn't feel annoyed or bothered or put-out. I felt . . . happy.

It's been so long since I've felt that.

"Sit, Iris!" Val says, much louder than necessary. She pats the empty chair between us, and I catch the look on her face. Her eyes go wide, communicating, as usual, in a silent language I don't recognize.

But then I find Iris, unmoving, seemingly waiting for permission to join, and it's clear the only approval she cares about is mine.

I motion toward the chair. "Please."

"Are you sure?" she asks, quietly.

"Val cooked tonight," I say, as everyone else in the room hoots and hollers to Val bowing her hand like the queen. "You're going to love it."

She smiles, then slides into the seat beside me. Val reaches over and wraps an arm around Iris's shoulder. "We're so glad you're here!"

Iris's cheeks flush, and I know that it'll only take one meal for these people—my people—to knit themselves into her heart. Normally there would be warning bells and red flags, but for some reason, there aren't.

Part of me—the curious part—is louder than the part of me that's cautious.

It's clear that Iris has never been to an Italian dinner. Her eyes are huge, taking in the impressive spread.

The *antipasti* is just meats and cheeses, but two platters full. We've already started in on those. The *primo piatto* is homemade ravioli, stuffed with a delectably rich Bolognese sauce, still steaming in the pans. The *secondo* is *pollo al mattone*, or Italian herb-roasted chicken with grilled vegetables (baby potatoes, zucchini, bell pepper) and the finale, the *dolce*, which in this case is homemade pistachio *gelato alla crema*.

Once everyone has resumed their conversations and dug into the food, Iris gingerly picks up her fork and leans toward me. "This is a *huge* amount of food."

"Yeah, I think Italians have dinner figured out." I tell my face to relax, but I'm not sure it listens.

"This is getting a little out of hand."

"What is?"

"My freeloading," she says. "I really should at least be allowed to do the dishes."

"Don't worry about it," Val says, eavesdropping. "There's plenty."

"It all looks amazing," Iris says. "Where do I start?"

Val beams, takes Iris's plate, and starts loading it up with a sample of everything.

I see Iris's eyes get even bigger, and I wonder if the others will get as big a kick out of how she eats as I do. I'm guessing her enthusiasm will be very welcome here.

Val hands Iris her plate back, now about twenty pounds heavier. Before she digs in, she meets my eye. "Joy got the job." She's practically radiating. "At the school."

Another ping of happiness. "Seriously?"

She nods, excited. "Yes. I'll tell you about it later, but that's why I came by—to give you the update. It was *perfect* timing. She came in as my boss was walking down the hall, I mentioned music, and the rest is history. It was practically . . . magic." She grins and takes a bite.

And that's when I lose her.

"Oh. My. Gosh," she says with her mouth full.

Val glances at her.

"Nobody talk to me for the rest of the meal," Iris announces. "I don't want to get distracted from this food!"

"Wait till you taste dessert," Bear says with a nod toward Nicola. "Homemade gelato."

Iris lets out an eager groan. "Shut up. This food isn't even fair! Val, are you trying to kill me here?"

Everyone laughs. Even me, though it's fleeting.

"Can I at least pay for it?"

The whole room voices their disagreement—loud and in unison.

"I know how you can repay us," Nicola says, quieting the rest. "Tell us what Chef is like when he's not working."

Now a chorus of agreement, some even clink their glasses and laugh.

Iris swallows her bite. "Fine, but then you have to tell me what he's like when he's here."

A chorus of *ooh*s! around the table.

"Can we talk about something else?" I say dryly.

"I'd love to know more about you, Iris," Val says. "Where you're from. What you do. Why you're hanging around this guy—" She nods at me.

I wish I didn't know the answer to that last one, but I do.

She needs to figure out the magic. Otherwise, I doubt she ever would've put up with my bad attitude.

"Oh, well . . ." She dabs her mouth with her napkin, and my gaze trips on her lips. I quickly look away.

"My story is pretty boring, but I'd love to know more about all of you," Iris says.

Val squeezes her hand, then smiles warmly at her, the way only she can. "Guaranteed there's nothing boring about you, Iris. We can't wait to get to know you better."

This is Val's superpower. She's only a couple of years older than me, but she's the mama bear. She pulls people in and makes them feel safe in a way that only she can.

"We'll start with an easy one," Nicola says. "Where did you grow up?"

Between bites, Iris talks about growing up in a suburb of Boston, telling stories from her childhood, answering questions, entertaining them. She glosses over her parents' divorce and the pain it caused, keeping her tone light and upbeat.

One quick scan around the table and I see it—she's winning them over. Including everyone, engaging with everyone. And while these meals are usually loud, with everyone talking over each other, Iris has captured everyone's attention.

Including mine.

When she finishes, she seems to shrink at the realization. She looks at me, then at Val. "But enough about me. I really want to hear more about all of you. Where did you all meet?"

Nicola looks at me, as if she knows that talking about culinary school could lead to talking about Aria, and that's not a topic we discuss, especially not at family dinner.

"I can tell you how Bear and I met," Val pipes up, drawing Iris's attention and steering the conversation out of uncomfortable waters like the pro she is.

Iris is as visibly smitten with them as they were with her,

and as the conversation picks up and volleys from one person to the next, that natural overlapping starts happening, along with an increase in volume and laughter, and I zoom out and take it all in. I can practically mark the moment Iris becomes one of them.

One of us.

The mutual connection is rare. The kind of spark you just know is going to grow and turn into something real. The kind I've only ever seen when it's—my face heats as I look at Iris, laughing at something Val said—*magic*, my brain says, quicker than a rumor.

But that doesn't make sense. I didn't get a newspaper telling me anything about Iris. She's never been the target, and neither have I. Connections like this probably happen outside of the magic all the time.

I just don't look up often enough to notice.

"Now that I think of it, it was Matteo who introduced us," Val says, pulling my attention back to the table.

I find Iris watching me, a quizzical expression on her face.

"He set us up," Val says. "He sort of has a gift for knowing when two people belong together."

"No, I don't," I say. "I was just tired of listening to you both whine about your bad relationships."

Bear chuckles. "I was insufferable before I met Val."

She looks at him. "The perfect match." Then, back to me. "And we would've never met if it wasn't for you."

"He introduced me and Danny, too," Nicola says. "Remember?"

Iris looks at me, and I can hear the question she's not asking—*Was it the magic?* I give my head the slightest shake.

Because it wasn't. Danny is one of our vendors who's been coming to the restaurant every week since we opened. I'd known him for years, and when I hired Nicola, I just had a feeling they'd hit it off.

"He tried to pretend it wasn't his idea," Nic jokes. "But he's not that smooth."

They all laugh, and I pretend to be annoyed, even though I'm not. The truth is, sometimes, during meals like this, with these people—it's the only time I feel truly alive.

Until I remember.

"What Chef will never tell you, Iris, is that deep down, he's a hopeless romantic." Val waggles her eyebrows, and everyone around the table nods.

"Not true," I say, shaking my head.

"Whenever he finds out someone is celebrating an anniversary, he comps dessert," Nicola says.

"And it's the only time he goes out to talk with the customers personally," Dante adds.

"Remember that sweet old couple last week? The ones who were on their first date?" Val makes a *weren't they so cute* face, and I roll my eyes.

Bear points at me. "Yes! You talked to them forever, Chef!"

"She lives in my building." I turn to Iris. "It was Winnie. She and Jerry came in after they went square dancing."

Iris beams. "What?! You didn't tell me that."

"I didn't? I thought I did," I say. "Yeah, they definitely hit it off."

Her smile holds. "That is amazing. I'm so happy they found each other."

Something passes between us—maybe the quiet knowing that we have a secret. Or maybe something else? I force myself to look away, and when I do, I find several pairs of curious eyes trained on me. Watching.

I clear my throat and go back to eating. "This is good, Val," I say curtly.

The spell breaks, and there's a lull until Nicola speaks up —thankfully.

"He's always been that way," she says, wistfully. "Rough around the edges with the biggest heart. Especially when it comes to true love."

"Blame that on his grandparents," Val says. "Those two were inseparable. Best friends until the day she died."

Everyone raises a glass in honor of Grandma Vivi, even though only a few people around this table knew her. There's a framed photo of her and my grandpa by the front door, so in some ways, her legacy lives on.

Iris clinks her glass against mine, and we both take a drink. Then, I set my glass down and push my chair away from the table. "You guys are way off. I stopped believing in true love a long time ago."

"See, that's what I thought, but the evidence suggests otherwise," Iris says, a tease in her tone. "Maybe you just haven't met the right girl."

The room goes quiet, and everyone looks away.

Iris frowns, looking around, confused. Then, she immediately realizes. "Oh, no. What did I say? I take it back, whatever it was." She sets her fork down, and quietly adds, "I forgot this was a sore spot for you—"

A thread tugs at my heart. She has no idea. It's like she's being punished for something that's just not her fault.

I can't explain it. I sometimes can't even think about it. Instead of doing what I *should* do and talk to her, I stand.

"I've got to get ready for service."

I can practically hear the questions that must be rolling around in her head, but it doesn't matter. I need some space.

Val follows me into the kitchen and stands behind me as I grab my apron and tie it on. Finally, I look at her and shake my head. "Don't."

She presses her lips together, then takes a step toward me. "She's really great, Tay."

"It's not like that."

"I know," she says. "But if that changes—"

"It won't." It can't. I'm already too aware of Iris. Too invested. I look at Val with a raised brow, then say, more firmly, "It can't."

Tears burn just behind my eyes, but there is no way I'm going to let them fall.

She holds my gaze for a long moment, then says, "Yes, Chef," and walks away.

Chapter Twenty-Eight
Iris

I'M STOPPED in front of my door, looking down.

There's a rolled-up newspaper on my welcome mat.

I'm just home from the restaurant, just home from the most delicious meal of my life, just home from feeling like I was becoming part of something amazing. Something that *almost* felt like family.

They welcomed me in. They wanted me there. It was so opposite of how I've felt for so much of my life. That girl who clambered to fit in, to belong—she was nowhere to be seen. Instead, there was just me and loads of open arms.

And I ruined it. *Maybe you just haven't met the right girl.* Seriously?!

Clearly there's a story there. A story I don't know. My joke about him having his heart broken did *not* go over well.

How could I go there again?

I wanted to talk to him—to apologize—but he was busy, and when I left, he barely looked up from what he was doing. Which is why, on the way home, I decided I need to keep my distance. Until I have a legit reason to bother him again, I will stay away.

Focus on work.

On the art show. On helping Joy get acclimated to her new job.

But there's a newspaper on my welcome mat.

I take it inside and set it on the counter. Maybe it's time for me to do one on my own. I practically handled Joy all by myself. I turn it over and find his name on the label, just like all the others.

I turn it back over, hiding his name. "I can't bother him! I overstepped. And I don't trust myself around him!"

The newspaper vibrates in place, enough to roll over and reveal the label again.

Matteo Morgan.

I laugh out an "Oh, oh, okay. Fine. *Great.*" and turn to walk into my bedroom when I hear the distinct sound of shimmering chimes.

I stop and slowly turn back.

There, on my counter, are now thirty newspapers, spelling out M-A-T-T-E- O.

"Very subtle," I groan.

The newspapers then roll together into one pile, and with a *sploof* of golden misty shimmer, disappear, leaving one lone newspaper in its place.

"Fine. *Fine.* But I'm going to try to figure it out on my own *first*, if you don't mind."

The newspaper pops open and lays flat.

"So helpful," I say sarcastically.

Hours later, my resolve has crumbled. I can't find what it wants me to see. No articles in a different tense, no rhymes or riddles, nothing out of the ordinary.

And I can't be sure, but I seriously think that when I reread parts of the paper, they're different the second time through, like words have switched around.

I have no idea what it wants me to do.

I fold it up and sigh, knowing I have no choice but to ask for help. Also knowing that I'm not going to sleep until I figure it out.

I take a breath, open my front door, and walk down to Matteo's apartment. I knock, but there's no answer.

I spend the next two hours stalking the hallway for any sign of human life. At one point, I hear a door and rush out of my apartment into the hallway. I come face-to-face with my new neighbor, Cash, who is wearing scrubs and holding two bags of garbage, presumably on his way to the dumpster.

"Sorry." I wince.

He gives me a friendly smile and keeps walking.

I go back to the paper. Still nothing.

And this time, I *know* it's switching things around, because on the first eight times reading this one part, the story was about a dry cleaner, and the next time, it's about a shoe store.

"You're doing this on purpose, aren't you?" I say out loud, not even pausing to note how weird it is that I'm talking to a newspaper.

It doesn't talk back.

"Yeah. That's what I thought."

Magic sucks.

A few hours later, I hear something in the hallway, and I leap to my peephole.

I see the fish-lensed side of Matteo's face as he passes my door, and I whip it open and jump out with a "Hey! Hi!"

He jumps away from me, arms up, with a "WHAT THE —!" and after realizing it's me, he puts his hands on his knees and breathes a few deep breaths. "You scared me to death."

I'm not sorry. I've been waiting for his sorry butt for, like, four hours.

"I've been waiting for you to come home."

235

It's then I notice the haggard look on his face. He looks exhausted.

"Tough night?" I ask.

"Long night. Followed by a near heart attack." He stops. "Why do you look like that?"

"Like what?"

"Like if you don't blurt something out it's going to jump out of your chest."

I hold up the newspaper.

"Another one? So soon?" He starts walking again, and I follow him, aware that he's probably way too tired to talk about this right now.

That should stop me, but it doesn't. I feel energized. Excited.

I follow him, and he unlocks his apartment and walks inside, leaving the door open.

I take that as an invitation.

As I open the newspaper, I say, "Look, I wasn't going to bother you, but I need your help with—" I stop. There, right on the front page, is a lone article. The rest of the newspaper is completely blank, except for four large-font centered lines of text.

**Sophie Stewart, Apartment 1C, needs dirt.
Lots of it.
For the rooftop garden.
Four bags should do it.**

And that's it. No rhyme, no riddle, it's about as plain and straightforward as you can get. And absolutely does not need input from the man who is currently standing in front of me.

I look up to find Matteo looking at me. "You need help? Is it a riddle? It likes to test your brain. Here, let me—" He takes the newspaper from me before I can stop him.

His eyes scan the words for three seconds, and then he looks at me. "This was too hard for you?" He frowns. "Four bags of dirt. Seems pretty easy."

"That's not what it said before! It kept changing the words around and—"

"Maybe you're not the right person to hand this off to," he jokes.

"It's not my fault! It's the *magic's* fault. It's playing tricks, it's—"

He reaches over and puts his hand on my forehead. I freeze at his touch.

"What are you doing?"

"Checking to make sure you don't have a fever."

I swat his hand away, grateful for the tease. I grab the paper back from him, crumple it up into a wadded ball, and chuck it into his kitchen.

Mid air, the wadded up ball *pops* in a puff of gold mist back into a normal newspaper shape, and lands right on Matteo's immaculate counter.

I hold out a hand at it.

"See? *SEE?!* It's mocking me!"

Matteo laughs and says, "Maybe you're the one who's exhausted. You need a good night's sleep."

I slink over and slump onto his couch. "I've about had it with this magic. Sometimes it's all warm and fuzzy and 'oh my gosh, Joy has a job—yay!' and other times, it's . . ." I clench both fists and shake them in the air.

Matteo sits down across from me in the chair. "Now you're starting to get it."

I frown. "You're so ready to be done with this, aren't you?"

"It's not all bad." He shrugs. "Besides, I'm used to it."

"And apparently really good at it. At least according to your entire staff."

He pushes a hand through his hair, leaving it disheveled

and sexy. "Don't pay attention to them. They make stuff up all the time."

I grin and pull my feet up under me. "You were matching people even before the magic *forced* you to match people." I blow out a breath. "I'm onto you, Morgan."

In the lull, I think about my careless comment at dinner. I want to apologize even though I'm unclear what the story is, but if I bring it up again, I'm scared he'll kick me out.

And I really don't want him to kick me out.

I pick up the remote control from the shallow container on his coffee table and flip on his TV. "The best way to unwind after a long day at work . . ." I click around on the screen, open up Netflix, and scroll until I find *The Great British Baking Show.*

"You want me to take a break from running my restaurant by watching a show about cooking?" He looks at me.

"Baking," I say. "It's totally different."

He makes a face that seems to concede, then moves from the chair to the couch and turns his attention to the screen.

"Trust me," I say. "It's the most relaxing way to spend a night."

About twenty minutes in, he's clearly hooked. It's the lady with the Scottish accent. Has to be. Every time she speaks, I can practically feel the stress melting away. After all, this show is magic, too.

Twenty minutes after that, I glance over and see that Matteo's jaw has gone slightly slack, and he's breathing in and out in a quiet rhythm.

He's fallen asleep.

My heart squeezes at the sight. There's something quietly intimate about falling asleep with somebody. And I love that he feels comfortable enough with me to do that.

Though, he may just be *that* tired.

Still, I take the opportunity to look at him in a way I can't when he's awake.

His olive skin is a perfect contrast to his deep-set brown eyes and a jaw so chiseled his perfectly trimmed beard does nothing to soften it. My gaze travels down to his chest, then lingers on strong, sturdy hands, resting on his stomach.

He really is a beautiful human.

But also, he's kind. Surprisingly so.

He keeps that side of himself hidden for a reason I haven't uncovered but really, really want to.

Maybe my comment was thoughtless, but that doesn't make it wrong. Maybe Matteo really hasn't met the right person to make him believe in true love.

Maybe . . .

Don't do this, Iris. You know better.

But maybe this time will be different.

It *feels* different. Doesn't that count?

I should go.

The longer I stay here, the more I do what I always do—imagine that this relationship is something more than what it is. And that's a great way to make everything awkward.

I turn off the television, then pick up the crocheted granny square blanket and spread it across his lap. I lean over to adjust it, and as I do, Matteo shifts and reaches for my arm, catching it in his grasp.

"Wait."

My breath catches in my throat, and I go still, thinking maybe it was a reflex or something. But then, I notice his eyes are open, and he's watching me.

Seeing me.

My heart pounds so loud in my chest, I'm sure he can hear it. His grip around my wrist loosens, but he doesn't let go. Just searches my eyes, and I force myself not to look away. A whole conversation happens in that moment and neither of us speaks a single word.

I sink into the space next to him as he shifts and wraps a hand around mine. My mind tries to catch up to my heart, racing in a direction it does not have my permission to go.

Is he going to kiss me?

I press my lips together, begging my overactive imagination to *calm the heck down already*, but there's no sense in trying to be logical right now. I'm already halfway down the aisle in a white dress holding a bouquet of tulips.

Matteo's eyes drift over to our hands, and he folds his fingers into mine, then brings his gaze back. "Iris . . ." he whispers my name, and studies me with a quiet intensity.

I try—fail—to tell myself he's just exhausted and overworked. Lonely.

I inhale his familiar scent, and my skin feels charged. Like there's an electrical current passing from his body into mine and back.

No amount of reason will convince me that something isn't happening between us right now. And there's not one shred of logic that stands a chance over the sound of my pounding heart.

Slowly, I start to move, wanting him to hear the words I'm too scared to say out loud—*Please kiss me*.

I hold eye contact, another inch closer, my mind spinning. Is this really about to happen? My gaze drops to his lips and—

His gaze falls away.

I freeze. Humiliation rushes to my face, and I quickly stand, "Oh, gosh. I . . . shoot."

I misunderstood. I projected. I—need to go. I try to put my hands on my hips, and they don't feel comfortable there, so I cross them, and that doesn't feel right either. I shift, awkward. Deflated.

Where do I put my hands?!

"I should—" I start and then stop.

I feel so stupid.

"I'm going to go. We can talk about the paper tomorrow. I'm sure you're exhausted." I take a couple of steps toward the door.

He stands. "Iris—"

I shake my head. "Sorry. I know you're tired. I shouldn't have bothered you tonight."

"No, it's fine. You didn't bother me."

At that, I dare to meet his gaze.

"I just—" He blows out a breath, turning away and pushing a hand through his hair. "I can't—"

"It's fine, really," I say, not wanting him to feel like he has to let me down easy, especially when nothing really happened. I start toward the door.

"Hey. Wait."

I stop, and I can feel myself start to fidget.

"Stop by the restaurant tomorrow," he says. "We'll, you know, figure out how to get Sophie her, uh, dirt and—"

"Perfect." I cut him off, turning to walk toward the door. I stop before I pull it open. "But you're not feeding me again," I say, desperately trying to find an ounce of levity here.

He shrugs. "We'll see."

I stand there, awkwardly, for a beat too long, knowing I'm going to have to work really hard not to replay that moment on the couch on a loop in my head.

Even now, my face is on fire just thinking about it. I'm *such* an idiot. I don't know what I was thinking. I am obviously not what he wants.

I slip out the door, close it behind me, and before I get back to my apartment, I burst into tears.

Chapter Twenty-Nine
Matteo

I STAND, staring at the door Iris just closed.

I lean forward and let my forehead fall against it.

Out loud, I ask one simple question. Aimed directly at myself. "*What* are you doing?"

I wanted to kiss her. My desire for her was so overwhelming, I almost gave in. And it's been years since that was a battle I had to fight.

This is why I stopped dating. This is why I don't let myself get close to people. This is why I am better off alone.

Watching her at dinner, the way she slipped so seamlessly into my life, it changed something inside of me. Seeing the way my people gravitated to her. The way both Nic and Val found me after family dinner and gave me all the reasons I needed to *make sure* I didn't screw this up. Two nosy sisters who swear they know what I need better than I do.

"She makes you happy."

"You're *you* again."

"She's just so fun. Like sunshine. Heck, *I* might be in love with her."

"We're all in love with her."

In love with her. The words feel strange as they pinball around my mind for the rest of the night. People use the word so casually, but love—real love, the kind I don't believe in anymore—there's nothing casual about it.

And on the day of Aria's funeral, I promised myself . . . never again. I was content with that promise. I *am* content with that promise. Because if I ever have to go through that kind of pain again, I won't survive.

Besides, Iris needs someone who likes to share emotions and feelings and all the crap I suck at. I don't see that changing.

The next day, when she shows up after work and Val loops an arm through hers and insists she stay for family dinner, the attraction doesn't wane.

If anything, it only grows.

And somehow, we get past the awkward near-kiss moment without ever addressing it, which is not very adult, but I'm not going to complain.

Days turn into weeks, and Iris and I settle into a strange new rhythm. I suppose most people call it "friendship," but it feels slightly foreign to me.

She comes by after work, eats with us, charms everyone, then leaves. I find her waiting for me when I get home from work, usually with a new newspaper and five different theories about what it wants us to do next.

Us.

People say it takes twenty-one days to form a habit, and we're well on our way.

Winter has lost its chilly grasp on the air outside, and things are starting to wake up. It's been three weeks since I almost kissed Iris, and we keep getting closer.

And I still haven't told her about Aria.

It's a weight I need to unload, but I haven't found the right time. I don't *want* anything to change. The light feeling I only feel when she's around. The way she doesn't see me as broken. The quiet laughter she tends to coax out of me.

When she's around, it's like I'm collecting a list of things I like about her—the trail of freckles across her nose. How excited she was to give a wonky-looking crocheted jellyfish to one of my servers who is pregnant with her first baby. How she pulls a chair up to the opposite side of my counter and tells me stories about her day while I work. She's so animated when she talks about her job, I feel like I know all of her students. And her co-workers, whom she's brought to dinner several times.

Val and Nic take to them immediately, and twice I've let them go home early so they could all go out for "girls' night," which, I found out later, was just going back to Iris's apartment to watch chick flicks and eat leftovers from the restaurant.

For whatever reason, Iris isn't put off by my attitude or my tendency to hold myself out of conversations. She's content to do most of the talking. She asks plenty of questions, but she spaces them out, probably worried I'll shut down like I always do.

Her approach is working. Little by little, I'm opening up to her. I tell her stories about summers with my grandparents and the way I discovered how much I love to cook. I tell her about studying in Italy with a chef my grandma knew and about starting the restaurant.

Still, I do not tell her about Aria.

The newspapers seem to be on a fairly regular delivery

schedule now, like we subscribed and whoever's sending them wants a five-star review.

They're still all addressed to me, still all delivered to her.

In the three years I've been doing this, I've never had such frequent deliveries. And every time we solve a riddle or meet someone new or connect old friends, Iris is thrilled she gets to help another person.

I've started to appreciate something that used to be such a burden. And I know that's because of her.

She beams as she plans a singles event in the courtyard to connect two young people over their incredibly specific and unique love of guacamole.

She giggles as an animal lover just so happens to be in the right place at the right time—standing next to Iris and me at the coffee shop—when she overhears us talking about a new dog park that's opening and they're looking to hire new people.

She shines as she gets permission to hang a community bulletin board by the mailboxes, where people can post when they have a need or can fill a need—just in time for an elderly woman to post about a faulty dishwasher and the middle-aged plumber to offer his services for free.

It turned out that the plumber and the woman's son were best friends when they were ten, but because of a move, they lost touch. Magically reconnected and friendship rekindled.

She practically dances as she forces me back to Winnie's on a Sunday afternoon for Jerry's goulash, which he insists I'm going to want to put on my menu.

I don't.

We work out the riddles and carry out the magic's demands, and every single time we're successful, it's like she's won gold at the Olympics. She's so invested in every person, so committed to seeing it all through.

She's so happy to help people she doesn't even know.

And unlike me, once she's helped, she doesn't disappear. She stays in touch. She knows all their names.

I can practically see the ripple effect she's having on this community.

Dante is now dating Iris's co-worker, Brooke. I'm not convinced that was magic, but it *was* Iris.

I'm starting to think the two are the same thing.

Last Wednesday, after family dinner, my hostess, Jenna, got sick and had to go home. Iris jumped in without a beat of hesitation. She was so good at it that several of my customers tipped her. She filled in two more nights until Jenna came back, and while everyone loves Jenna, I got the sense that most of my staff was sad when Iris left right after we cleared the plates from family dinner.

When she's not around, I think about her. Check in on her. I've started carrying my phone just in case she texts me.

And every day, it gets harder and harder to deny that my feelings for Iris aren't going away. I'm doing exactly what I said I wouldn't do.

I'm falling for her.

Guilt nips at my heels every time I'm with her. Every time I laugh. Because isn't letting myself have feelings for Iris a betrayal to the woman I promised to love for the rest of my life?

Iris thinks I'm still anxious to be rid of the magic, but the truth is I'm dreading the day one of the newspapers shows up at her door with her name on it and not mine.

Chapter Thirty
Iris

So, I'm like a wizard now. A star student. A magician.

I've gotten really good at sorting out what the newspaper wants me to see, even without Matteo's help, but it's way more fun to work on it together. We sometimes have competitions to see who can sort it faster. I've actually beaten him twice, and I'm *pretty* sure my victories were legit.

More than that, I've started to see ways for us to help people, even without the magic. Like, last week, I convinced him to take his day off and help me plan a date night for Val and Bear. We spent the afternoon at the restaurant—him in the kitchen and me in the dining room, setting up a special dinner just for the two of them. While they ate, Matteo and I hung back in the kitchen, also eating, and by the end of the night, the four of us were laughing over a spread of desserts we pulled from the refrigerator.

Liz and Brooke got tired of me talking about my "new friends" and demanded to be introduced, so we met at Aria for dinner and ended up having so much fun, we had a girls' night.

I'm still trying not to get attached. Not only to Matteo, but to his friends.

But they're making that incredibly difficult.

When I'm there, I feel like they *want* me there. They want to know about me, about my life. They make me feel like I fit in.

And I haven't fit in anywhere in . . . maybe forever.

I survived the near-kiss by avoiding the topic and pretending it never happened. But I imagine the "what if it *did* . . ." more often than I will ever admit.

These fantasies are made worse by the fact that I've put myself in a similar situation several times over the last few weeks, practically waiting for him in the hallway so I can show him our new magic assignment, then sticking around while he unwinds after his very exhausting day.

Which is why I'm here now, on his couch, pretending to watch *The Great British Baking Show* when all I'm really doing is thinking about how our thighs and shoulders are practically touching.

Am I trying to recreate the moment? Maybe.

Am I a glutton for punishment? Definitely.

Will I regret it if something does happen? Probably yes, but maybe not.

That pretty much sums up how I make all my decisions when it comes to Matteo.

Will he turn away from me again? Probably yes, *but maybe not.*

Should I leave his apartment after he falls asleep? Probably yes, *but maybe not.*

The episode ends. My cue to go.

Beside me, Matteo shifts.

It's a familiar pattern, but we both seem intent on avoiding the awkward moment, usually by not looking at each other when I leave.

I am in the friend zone. But at least I get to be around him. That's good enough, right?

I pick up the remote and mute the TV, then glance over, surprised to find him watching me. I smile. "I told you your guy would be safe." I nod back toward the TV, but my nerves are buzzing.

"I'm not convinced you haven't watched this whole season all the way through," he says.

I gasp in mock-horror. "I would never."

"Uh-huh. Sure." He stretches, then sinks a bit deeper into the couch.

"I do wonder what it's like for you to watch it with your knowledge of cooking versus me watching it with—"

"No knowledge of cooking?"

I lean back and angle my body slightly toward him, trying not to read into the fact that he doesn't seem to want me to go. "You could teach me. I mean, the French toast was a big success."

"I could," he says.

"You could teach a whole class," I say.

"Eh."

I frown. "Why not?"

"Too many people," he says.

"I think you're better with people than you give yourself credit for. I mean, look at us. We're thick as thieves." I exaggerate the comment, then glance over, expecting him to make some crack about how I'm always around and he can't get rid of me, even with a cattle prod, but instead, I'm met with *that look* again.

The one that seems to say more than he's ever said out loud.

My heart stalls. My face heats. All these days of being back here, and this hasn't happened again . . . until now.

I don't want to think about how I shouldn't let myself feel

all the things. I have big feelings . . . so what? I have to believe that one of these days, feeling them isn't going to come back to bite me.

What if this time is different?

Matteo shifts and sits up, eyes locked on to mine.

I've dated men. I know what this moment looks like, the seconds before everything shifts, the moment before the relationship changes.

It's the heartbeat before I fall in love.

It's familiar and entirely new all at the same time.

"Tell me what you're thinking," I say, because honestly, I need to know.

"I don't want to think," he says. "And I don't want to talk anymore."

I swear I hear the distant tinkle of chimes from somewhere faraway as the world turns in slow motion. He moves toward me, eyes intense and flush with a desire that matches my own. He reaches for me, and when his hand lands on the back of my neck, I go completely still, except for the cartwheels turning in my stomach.

His eyes search mine as he moves even closer until our faces are only inches apart. He pauses, silently asking for permission to give in to whatever it is that's happening between us right now.

Once he's got it, it's like the dam breaks—like whatever had been holding his desire back simply disappears.

The second his lips are on mine, my body rises to meet his.

I lean back against the arm of the couch, and he follows, hovering over me as I wrap my arms up around his neck and fully give in to this kiss.

He deepens the kiss, and my head spins, swirling with thoughts I couldn't articulate if I tried. I'm sure of one thing, though—Matteo Morgan knows how to kiss.

His lips are so soft yet so firm, and I inhale slowly so I can engage every one of my senses. He's so in control, and while I sense the urgency in the kiss, there's gentleness too.

Is this really happening? Am I actually kissing Matteo?

I clear the mental clutter and focus on the only thing that matters in that moment—him. I shudder when his tongue brushes across my lower lip, sensing the urgency in his shallow breaths, still knowing he's in full control.

And I feel myself slipping deeper. Heat rushes to every nerve in my body, pulsing with a kind of desire that makes me want to ignore reason, to embrace reckless abandon.

In my mind, every past hurt falls away. None of them matter because they all led me here—to him. Which is exactly where I want to be.

He pulls back suddenly, and my stomach sinks.

He searches my eyes. "What are we doing?" His voice is low and breathless, his forehead pressed to mine.

I inch back and squint at him. "Do you really want me to explain it to you?"

He smirks, but his expression turns serious. "I want to be straight with you," he says. "I really don't know what I want . . ." His shoulders slump ever so slightly, and he looks away. "I promised myself I wouldn't let myself feel this way again."

It's the open door I've wanted to walk through. I want to know why. Only now that it's here, my feet are like cinder blocks holding me in place.

"I don't need promises," I say quietly, mustering the courage. "I know that neither one of us can predict the future. But . . ." I wait until he looks at me. "I do want to know the truth."

He looks away, and I feel the weight of whatever it is he's carrying.

"But only if you're ready to tell me." I pause. "Fair warning, though. I'm not very patient."

His smile is fleeting. "Honestly, I kind of like that you don't know."

I frown as my brain tries to fill in the blanks of what it is he isn't willing to talk about, running through a list of worst-case scenarios that start with a felony record and end with a secret identity. "Why?"

He stands, his hand lingering in mine for a moment, and then he walks into the kitchen, pulls open the refrigerator, and takes out two bottles of water.

I follow him, wanting to give him space but also wanting him to know I'm not going anywhere. I take the water when he offers it, open the bottle and take a drink. I get the sense he needs to process this moment in silence, so that's what I give him.

"I was married," he says.

I'm mid-drink when he says this, and it catches me so off-guard, I forget how to swallow.

He doesn't elaborate.

After a beat, I finally say, "A lot of marriages end. I hope you know I would never judge you for getting divorced . . ." Though I am a little surprised nobody mentioned it until now, especially at the restaurant.

But then, he shakes his head, looking at me behind slightly glassy eyes. "Not divorced."

I frown. And I pause. And then I freeze. "Not divorced," I repeat.

"Widowed."

"Widowed." My voice is so small, I doubt he even heard me. My heart squeezes, and I can feel tears push at the corners of my eyes.

Don't tell me you're one of those guys who got his heart broken . . .

My stomach sinks as all the pieces shift into place. My comments must've seemed so flippant and careless to him. How could I be so stupid?

"So that's why you keep people at an arm's length," I say, putting it all together.

"Pretty much," he says. Then, through half-gritted teeth, says, "And because it's *really* hard to talk about. When people find out—especially women—they want to fix me."

Right. The feminine urge to swoop in and save the broken man. I'm familiar with that. All at once aware that I'm squeezing the water bottle a little too hard. I set it down on the counter.

"I liked that you didn't know," he says, half-looking at me. "It was nice not to feel like someone's project. But I also know that if you don't know about this, you'll never really know me." A pause. "And I want you to know me."

My heart flip-flops. "You do?"

He sets down his water, then moves around to the other side of the island. When he pulls out a stool, I think maybe I should pull out the other one and prepare for a heart-to-heart, but before I can, he takes my hand and tugs me closer, pulling my body in between his knees and wrapping his arms around me in a tight, warm hug.

There's something so sweet in the wordless way he does this that makes his pain feel almost palpable. I hold him and let myself be held, clinging to him as the picture of who he really is finally becomes clear.

Minutes pass, and I don't move, because something tells me it's been a really long time since Matteo let anyone hold him.

Also because it's been a really long time for me, too.

I pull back, slightly, not ready to let go. "Thank you for telling me."

He nods, slightly, then presses his lips together. "Thank you for not treating me like some pity case."

I hug him close again, and I realize I'm so at ease with him. I don't know when or how it happened, but I don't feel like I need to impress him or be someone I'm not. I don't even feel like I need to make him like me.

I lift my chin, studying him for a long moment. "Tell me about her."

He holds my gaze, and while I expect his body to go rigid at the question, it doesn't. Instead, he seems to soften, eyes glazing over in what I can only assume is a memory.

"Her name was Aria." He looks at me. "We were supposed to open the restaurant together."

I move away slightly and prop myself on the other stool, but I don't say anything, hoping my silence encourages him to go on.

"She was a pastry chef, like Nicola," he says. "We all went to school together—me and Aria and Nic and Val . . . and then Bear, once they got together . . ." He half-laughs. "Aria and I hit it off right away. She was funny and upbeat, and she didn't take any of my crap."

"I like her already," I say.

He reaches for his bottle of water, uncaps it, and takes a drink. "You two honestly would've hit it off, and it would've annoyed me to no end." His smile is wistful. "She was the life of the party. The exact opposite of me."

I force myself to stay in the present with him, to not go down the road of pity, which is exactly where he doesn't want me to go.

"Not long after we met, we were inseparable. We were . . . best friends, really. And our little group was so tight, it was hard to imagine anything messing that up." He presses his lips together, and I can see the moment reality sets in. I imagine this is why he doesn't talk about Aria very often. Not because he wants to forget her, but because reliving it is too painful.

I reach out and take his hand.

He's cautious. The way I was trying to be.

Heartbreak will do that to you.

"We got married young, and I thought that was it. We'd start our restaurant, have a couple kids, maybe get a dog . . ." He looks at me with a smirk. "*Definitely* not a cat."

At that, I laugh, glad for the break in the tension.

He helplessly shrugs. "I knew that was the life I wanted. I was convinced it would be forever."

But life doesn't work out the way you plan it.

"What happened?" I ask, quietly. "And you don't have to tell me if you don't want to."

"It's okay. I want to tell you." He pauses. "I haven't really talked about it at all. With anyone."

The weight of that isn't lost on me.

"She was driving home from work," he says on a tired exhale. "It was dark and icy . . . and . . ." He draws in a slow breath. "She lost control of the car. Skidded off the road. It wasn't anyone's fault, it was just an accident." He drags a hand down his face. "There wasn't even anyone I could blame."

Oh.

I stay quiet, not sure what to say, wishing I had the exact right response. Instead, I squeeze his hand, hoping that in the absence of words, he feels that I'm here.

"It was unimaginable." He shakes his head, and I see tears pooling in his eyes. "The cops showed up at my door, and I thought it had to be a mistake. There was no way—" He stops, overwhelmed.

I hold his hand and wait.

He sniffs, letting go of my hand to wipe his cheeks with his palms. "But then I tried calling Aria. When she didn't answer, I called her again. I'll never forget the sound of the line just ringing and ringing and then her happy voice on the recording."

He goes still. "I'd just talked to her right before she left." A pause. "I didn't know that would be the last time I'd hear her voice."

I picture every second of that moment, easily feeling the pain of it, my heart hurting at his loss, and because I don't want to be another person who doesn't give him what he needs, I only say, "I can't imagine what you've been through."

He's quiet for a beat, then says, "It's strange how different we are, isn't it? You jump into new relationships, wanting to know everyone and not caring at all about the risk of getting hurt, and I—"

"Hold yourself back because you never want to feel that pain again."

I take his face in my hands, use my thumbs to wipe away what remains of the tears that escaped his eyes, and place a gentle kiss on his lips. "Take as long as you need to realize that this"—I flick my hand back and forth between us—"is worth the risk."

"I think that's what scares me most of all."

Chapter Thirty-One
Matteo

"Okay, Chef. What's going on?"

It's Tuesday morning, and I'm pulling ingredients to prep for lunch when both Val and Nicola corner me in the storage room.

"With what?" I grab a bag of flour from the top shelf.

"Matteo." Val is using her stern voice. "You were whistling." And then, as if I didn't hear her the first time, she repeats, "*Whistling*."

"So?" I frown. "Is that against the rules?" My cheeks are hot, and I wish they'd go bother someone else. I turn to go, but Nicola blocks the exit with her hand up against the door jamb.

She's playfully glaring at me. "You really should just tell us because we're going to find out."

"There's nothing to tell." I'm not sure I'm being convincing.

"Don't ever play poker, okay?" Val quips. "You'll lose everything you have with that face."

"It's Iris, isn't it?" Nicola says.

"No." But even as I say the word, I know it's not convincing. I push past Nicola but hear the tiny squeak that ekes out of both of them as they rush to follow me.

"Oh, my gosh, did something finally happen?" Nicola asks. "Please say yes! We placed bets on how long it would take, and if you tell me it happened within the last week, I'm totally going to win."

I frown. "You placed bets?"

"I already lost," Val says. "I thought you'd realize it two weeks ago."

"Realize what?" I set the flour down at my workstation.

"That you're falling for her," Val says. "Like, really falling for her."

"I am not." I use an exasperated tone, but the truth is, I *want* to talk to them about Iris. I just . . . don't know how. It's been so long since I've had any romantic feelings to sort through, I don't even know what to say.

Which is exactly why I want their help. I don't know what I'm doing.

"Chef," Nicola says. "You've been trying not to love that woman since she followed you to work *weeks* ago."

"And then, you doubled down every time she showed up here—unannounced or otherwise." Val's expression is pointed.

"She's just my neighbor. It's not—" Their matching glares stop me, and I suck in a breath, certain I'm going to regret this. "Fine. Yes. I like her."

The squeals sound a lot like screams this time.

I hold up both hands. "Nope. I'm not talking to you guys if you're going to . . . do all that." I scrunch my face in disapproval.

They start a smattering of *Sorry! We won't! We'll be quiet! Tell us everything!* And I turn toward my station. "I have to prep."

The door swings open, and Bear walks in. "Whoa. What's going on in here?"

Val's eyes go wide. "Teo. *And IRIS—*"

"What about them?" Bear's like a lamp set on the dimmest setting.

"We don't know yet," Val hisses. "Stop talking so we can find out."

He frowns and looks at me. "You and Iris, what? Like, finally . . ." He gives his shoulders an exaggerated shrug and widens his eyes.

I shrug back, as if to say, *I mean, kind of?*

Bear nods and grunts a reply that says, *Cool*, then continues nodding, but in a *she's hot* sort of way.

I pull a face—*I know, dude.*

"Oh my gosh, *what* is happening?" Nicola shakes her head. "It's like some weird primal form of Morse code."

"Are you two finished?" Val glares at Bear, and he walks away but not before he throws a thumbs-up over his head on the way out.

Both women turn the weight of their full attention back to me.

"Spill," Nicola says.

I'm not getting out of this, that much is clear. "Fine. Yes. I like her. I kissed her. And . . . I told her about Aria. No, I don't know what's happening next. No, I'm not sure when I'll see her again, and no, I don't want to discuss it with either of you."

More overlapping reactions—*Wait! What? Whoa! I've got questions! Where is she now? Does she feel the same way?*

And once the initial response dies down, Val goes still. "You told her about Aria?"

I nod.

"How'd it go?" Nic asks.

"It sucked," I say. "It was like running through a crowd of people wearing nothing but an apron and having it broadcast on the internet."

"That's oddly specific," Nicola says.

"Recurring nightmare," I say with a shrug. "But she was great. I mean, really great. I know she felt bad for me, but not in a pathetic way. It was like, all about me—not about her."

Val groans. "Sad how many people don't get that."

"Remember Elise?" Nicola's eyes go wide.

Val and I both groan.

"Who could forget?" Val says.

Elise was the first and last straw. She found out about Aria and decided to make a plan so she could "bring me back to life." She wanted to document our entire relationship on social media and turn my pain into a launch for her "counseling" business.

Never mind that she had no education, apparently just putting it on social media makes you an expert.

"So," Val says. "How are you feeling now?"

"Actually? Fine."

Not fine.

I pull out a large pot and fill it with water.

"You're freaking out, aren't you?" Val asks.

"Good lord, yes." I flick off the faucet and drop my head. "So bad."

They jump into high gear, both of them poised and ready for action. Whatever problem I'm having, they're going to solve it.

"What's the problem? The main problem?" Nicola asks.

I set the pot on the stove and turn on the burner. "You know the main problem." I look at Nicola, then at Val. "I don't know if I can do this again."

"Look, it's totally normal to be wary," Val says. "Anyone in your position would be."

"But Iris is good. And good *for* you," Nicola says. "She makes you smile. Smiling is not your default setting."

I shoot her a look.

"Stop proving my point," she quips.

"Plus," Val says, "When you're around her, you seem lighter. Happier."

"Last week you came out and *talked* to the customers," Nic chimes in. "You haven't willingly done that in years."

The door swings open, and Dante walks in, freezing at the sight of the three of us just standing there. "Is everything okay?"

"Everything's great." Nicola raises her eyebrows. "And you owe me twenty bucks."

His face lights up. "Yeah! Get it, Chef!"

"Go back to work, Dante," I say, a little sharper than I intend to. He doesn't seem fazed. He gives me a peace sign and hits it on his chest twice as he backs out of the room.

"What does that even mean?" I frustratingly ask.

They both shrug, shaking their heads.

"You too. Back to work. We don't need to stand here and talk about my love life," I say.

"I kind of feel like we do," Nicola says.

"We don't." I wave them off.

They look at each other again, and I wait for them to get the point. The subject is closed. At least for now.

Nicola sighs and walks away, but Val stays behind. "Just go slow, Tay. And remember—you deserve to be happy."

As the commotion of the day resumes and I get back to work, I sit with that.

Do I really deserve to be happy? I *was* happy once. *So* happy.

Is anyone lucky enough to feel that way twice? And isn't it selfish to want to?

As if by some cosmic coincidence, my phone dings and I see a text come in from my grandpa. He's not great with texting and always prefers to talk on the phone . . . unless he's sending a photo.

I open the message, and I'm met by his smiling face, off-center and slightly out of focus. It's a selfie of him and Elena, and he's grinning. In the background, I see a huge Italian spread, and I can practically taste the entire meal.

Underneath the image, Grandpa has texted:

> **GRANDPA**
>
> I hope you know the joy of a beautiful night with beautiful company and a full belly. Let's catch up this week! Elena says hello!

He's sentimental, and it makes me smile.

And somehow, losing my grandma made him appreciate his time here on earth, while losing Aria made me resent mine.

Half a world away, and he's still taking me to school.

I try to focus on the tasks in front of me, but I'm mostly counting down the hours until Iris is off work and I get to see her again.

When she shows up, Val and Nicola sweep her back into the storage room, probably to get the play-by-play of everything that happened. When Bear interrupts them, they push him out and slam the door. He looks at me, and we both shrug, because women will never make sense.

After another loud and raucous family dinner, I pull Iris into my office, close the door, and press her up against it. "To make sure nobody comes in."

She smiles and wraps her arms up around my neck while my hands circle her waist and I kiss the heck out of her, because I've pretty much been thinking about her skin since I woke up this morning. My goal here is to leave her breathless and weak-kneed, but my plan backfires when I'm the one who has to pull away and calm myself down. "You're . . . really good at that."

"You're really easy to kiss." She grins. "But now you need

to get to work, and I'm working on some art show details tonight." Her eyes light up. "Hey, would you maybe cater it?"

"Cater an elementary school art show?" I ask.

"Yes! It would be amazing, I want it to feel sort of fancy for the kids," I say. "Not like your usual cookies and punch kind of event." She shrugs. "I want it to be special. High class. An experience!"

I love this about her. Most people would do the bare minimum of what's expected of them, but that never occurs to Iris.

She is not halfway.

"Why are you looking at me like that?" She tilts her head and studies me.

"Just thinking those kids are lucky to have you," I say.

"*Au contraire*, my friend. I'm the lucky one," she says. "They're such great kids. I told them we're going to dress fancy and eat like kings and queens."

I smile. "Happy to make sure the food fits the occasion."

"Yes!" She kisses me, quickly this time, and it's so soft and familiar, it leaves me undone.

When she breaks contact, she gives me a quizzical look. "You good?"

I nod. "Really good."

And I am.

Surprisingly good.

And I'm starting to wonder if that happiness my grandpa's found after deep heartache might actually be available to me, too.

Chapter Thirty-Two
Matteo

WE MANAGE a lot of stolen moments over the next few weeks.

Little by little, Iris is knit into the fabric of my life, even more than she was before.

Our routine is pretty much the same as it was, only the newspapers have stopped coming so frequently.

It doesn't stop Iris from loving them every time, though.

Hiding a business card for a struggling florist in the coat pocket of a bride-to-be.

Facilitating a blind date for two older single people who find out they grew up blocks from one another in the same suburb but never met.

Then there was the dog match. Iris and I secretly helped a young single woman adopt a dog from a local shelter. That wasn't the magical part, though. The magic came when the woman took the dog to the local dog park and the dog slipped off the leash. He was corralled by the only park employee—a single guy we helped get the job there in the first place.

The two hit it off right away and have been dating ever since.

Through all the magic, the papers are still, inexplicably, delivered to her but addressed to me. The magic still doesn't make sense, but maybe it doesn't have to. Maybe we're the lucky ones for knowing we live in a world where magic exists. And maybe that's enough.

Slow Sundays have become our sacred time together. The only uninterrupted day of the week when neither of us has work. Because of that, we sometimes go out, but only in the slowest way possible. We get breakfast at local restaurants to support fellow chefs and make a game out of ranking every coffee shop in Serendipity Springs.

Last week, she convinced me to try one of Winnie's square dance classes, something I deeply regret, though seeing Winnie's reaction to the two of us when we walked in holding hands almost made up for my humiliation.

Almost.

Today's Slow Sunday has us shopping for "the perfect birthday gift" for her co-worker, Brooke. We're in a boutique a few blocks from the restaurant, and while Iris sets off in the direction of bath and body junk, I hang back and pretend to be interested in a wall of wacky socks.

A saleslady asks if I want to see anything, and I shake my head. "I'm just looking, thanks."

I'm scanning the wall, chuckling at the ones with little guitar-playing avocados and the caption "Guac 'n Roll!", when I hear someone say my name.

"Matteo?"

I turn around in the direction of the woman's voice, and all at once, I'm looking at the world through a foggy lens.

"Lynn."

Her face lights up, and tears spring to her eyes. She looks mostly the same, hair a little grayer, maybe a little thinner, but every bit as poised and put together as I remember.

"It's been . . . years. How are you?" She takes a step toward me. "You look good. You look like you're doing good."

I feel trapped. Caught. I don't want to be here.

"I am, uh . . . how are you—?" I give a cursory glance around the store, silently praying that Iris is busy and I can figure out a way out of this conversation before she gets back.

"We're good. Don's good. Everyone's—" She stops. "Did you get my invitation?"

"Uh, invitation?" I repeat. "No, I don't think so?"

"For the dinner? The birthday dinner."

I don't remember an invitation, but I put together what she's talking about. A flood of emotion and memories pour into my mind's eye.

She studies me, head cocked to one side. "For Aria's thirtieth birthday?"

"I've been bad about getting the mail lately," I stammer, tossing a look over her shoulder. "But I'll check."

"It's next Sunday," she says, cautiously. "We just wanted to, I don't know, celebrate her life. We didn't want the day to go by without acknowledging her. Nicola and Val are both coming, and we'd love to have you."

At that exact moment, Iris walks up, carrying a stuffed animal.

"Look at this!" Her face is bright. "It's *perfect!* It's an emotional support sloth. Ha! A sloth! You put it in the microwave, and—" She sees Lynn and her expression shifts. "Oh, I'm so sorry—I didn't know you were in the middle of a conversation." She beams, always excited to meet someone new.

Lynn's smile is kind. "No, we were just saying hello."

There's an awkward pause.

"Hi, sorry, I'm Iris." She holds out her hand to Lynn, who takes it and says, "Lynn. Nice to meet you."

Then, Lynn turns to me. "Hopefully we'll see you next

week, Matteo." She pats my arm, then nods at Iris. "Feel free to bring a friend."

She takes a step toward me, lowers her voice and adds, "The more people who remember her, the better."

And with that, she walks away.

"I'm so sorry I interrupted," Iris says, visibly curious.

"You didn't," I say. "It's fine." But it doesn't feel fine. It feels awful. It feels like I've just been caught doing something wrong. Like I've betrayed a trust I promised to never betray.

"Who was that?" she asks.

I sigh. "That"—I watch as Lynn walks out of the store—"was Aria's mom."

"Oh." There's a beat of awkward silence, and then Iris puts a hand on my arm. "Are you okay?"

I turn to her and paste on a fake smile. "Yep. You ready?"

Her face falls.

"Matteo."

"I'm fine," I say briskly. I don't want to talk about it, and I definitely don't want to feel like this anymore.

She studies me, and then says, "Okay. Well, let me just buy this and then we can get some food."

I take a breath. "Actually, I'll walk you back, and then I'm going to head to the restaurant," I say. "I've got some paperwork I forgot about."

It's clear by the look on her face that she isn't buying it. And why would she? I'm lying.

I expect her to call me on it, to be upset that I'm bristling, to do what most people would do and make this about her feelings, and I wouldn't fault her if she did.

Instead, she slips a hand in mine. "If you need to be alone, just say so. I promise I won't be offended." She squeezes. "And when you're ready to not be alone anymore, I'll be here."

She goes up on her tiptoes, kisses my cheek, then walks away.

Chapter Thirty-Three
Iris

OKAY, I'm starting to worry.

When I told Matteo I'd be here when he was ready, I meant it.

I just thought it would be something like—he'll go to the restaurant, spend a little time alone, then find me for dinner.

But he doesn't.

I don't hear from him for the rest of the night—and my texts the next day go unanswered.

I know what Matteo needs most right now is distance, but "giving others space" isn't my specialty. Still, I'm determined not to mess this up.

Which is why, after weeks of the same routine, I don't go to the restaurant for family dinner on Monday. Or Tuesday. Both Nicola and Val text to find out where I am, and I lie and say I'm "under the weather."

Still no word from Matteo.

Wednesday night, I pace my apartment around the time he usually gets home. When I hear the stairway door open, I hold my breath as I look out my peephole, praying he stops at my door. I hear his footfalls moving closer, and though they slow as he passes by, he barely pauses before moving on.

Tears spring to my eyes as I imagine the worst—that this man, this wonderful, beautiful man, has decided not to let me love him. That this is it for us. That I let myself fall for him, and it's all blowing up in my face.

Just like always.

Because people leave. People *always* leave.

Logic says that it can't be that. Any bystander looking at this situation would say it's not as big as I'm making it out to be. He just needs a little time. He's got a lot of very real feelings to sort through.

But my brain isn't always logical.

I know this isn't anyone's fault, but I also know it's not easily fixed. He was honest about his fears—about the fact that he never wanted to feel the kind of loss he felt when Aria died. And I imagine seeing her mom only stirred up all those emotions again.

Seeing her when he was with me probably stirred up other things too. Things that cannot be solved with a simple conversation.

I slump to the floor, back against my door, head in my hands.

And history repeats itself.

I don't like to wallow, but the moment seems to call for it. I want to grab the pint of mint chocolate chip ice cream I always keep in my freezer for emergencies or PMS and go wallow on the couch for days.

I also want to shirk my big feelings because right now, they're painful.

I'm mid-sob when something hits my feet. I pull back, startled, and see a rolled-up newspaper on the floor in front of me.

I dry my cheeks with the sleeves of my sweatshirt. "Not now."

It rolls away slightly, then back toward me, straight into my feet, landing with the label facing me, his name on full display, like a taunt.

"I said, not n—"

It rolls away and hits my feet again, only this time with a mini explosion of golden shimmer.

Then, in a flash, I'm transported, as my mind is whisked away, memories of all the things we've done playing out before me.

I can see all the people we've met, all the connections we've made, all the happiness I've been a part of, all the lives we've changed—it's almost as if I'm watching a montage in reverse. A movie of my life rewinding in slow motion.

It spins me slowly back through the young couple at the dog park, the long lost friends, the flower shop, the bags of dirt, Joy, Alice, Jerry, Winnie, the newspapers filling up my apartment, all fly through my mind, until I remember the very first time I saw Matteo open his door to me, dripping coffee down my arm, holding the very first newspaper up to him to take it.

I blink. And I'm looking at my floor again.

I look at the newspaper.

And one last thought occurs to me.

I stand, wipe my eyes, and walk down to Matteo's apartment.

Matteo

Iris is standing outside my door.

I've only been home for a few minutes, but I can see her through the peephole.

My heart swells at the sight of her.

Man, I miss her.

But it's not fair. It's not fair to her for me to have so many conflicting feelings while we're together. She deserves better than this. To be with someone who isn't carrying a load of baggage. I just . . . haven't found the courage to tell her yet.

When I open the door, she looks up at me, and I can tell she's been crying.

I look away. I'm such a jerk. "I'm sorry I haven't called, I—"

But she holds up a hand, and I go quiet.

"I'm not here to make you feel bad or anything." She stands. "Just to let you know that I'm not going away. I understand you need space, and I will give that to you." She presses her lips together, and I can see her determination behind her eyes.

"I know that for a lot of people, I'm too much. I get it. And maybe me telling you that I've hated not being with you the last couple days is going to feel smothering or annoying. But I don't care. Because I have hated it. I also hate that you're hurting. And I hate that you won't let me help."

"Iris—"

"Just let me finish."

I nod.

"I think you're amazing," she says. "And I think this terrible, awful thing happened to you. And you didn't deserve it. No one deserves something like that." She pauses and takes a deep breath. "And I know you're scared."

The words are like a drill, straight to my heart.

"I'm scared too," she says. "And I think because I was scared, I held myself back. I did what I thought you would want instead of what I want, which is to be here for you. I don't want to give you space. I want to be a sounding board and a safe place for you to sort through the messy, awful feelings you don't share with anyone else. And wanting that has gotten me in trouble in the past." She presses her lips together and inhales a slow breath. "But you're the one who told me that for the right person, I won't be too much."

I look down and see that she's holding a newspaper in her hand. I didn't notice that before.

"And these past few months have been . . ." She laughs. "The most *magical* of my entire life. Not just because we helped all those people, not just because friends found each other or a dog got a new home, but because this"—she holds up the newspaper—"this . . . brought me *you*."

I don't say anything because I'm afraid if I do, my voice will crack. I think I am finally beginning to understand what magic really feels like.

"So, I guess, what I'm saying is . . ." She steels her jaw. "You need to figure out if I'm the right person. You need to decide if I'm too much. Because even though I know I have a lot of flaws, loving people too deeply isn't one of them." She goes quiet, and I want to reach for her. To pull her straight to my chest and hold her until the sun comes up tomorrow.

And every single day that follows.

But she doesn't give me the chance.

She looks at me for a long moment, nods a period on this conversation, and then she walks away.

I just stand and watch her walk back to her apartment and close the door.

I stand there, dumbly, wanting to go after her, but still so conflicted over the strange feelings seeing Aria's mom brought to the surface.

Sadness. Guilt. Grief.

That simple interaction reminded me of everything I'd lost while simultaneously making me feel like I'd done something wrong in moving on.

I don't know how to square that.

After a sleepless night, I get out of bed early Thursday morning, feeling more clarity than I have in days. If I'm going to make things right with Iris, there's something I need to do first.

Something I maybe should've done a long time ago.

Something I don't want to do at all.

I pull out my phone and send a text to Val:

MATTEO
Can you handle lunch service today?

VAL
Yes, Chef.

MATTEO
Thanks

VAL
Where will you be?

MATTEO
There's something I need to do.

VAL
Hopefully it's getting your head out of your <peach emoji>

MATTEO
<eye roll emoji>

VAL
xoxo

Then, I type out a simple text to Iris.

MATTEO
I heard you loud and clear last night. I'm sorry for being distant.

I'd like to see you, but I have to take care of something first.

Then, I add:

> Don't give up on me yet.

And my thumb hovers over the button before I take a breath and send it.

Am I asking too much?

An hour later, I'm sitting in my car outside a distantly familiar bungalow on a quiet street in Serendipity Springs.

Aria had an idyllic childhood here, and when we talked about our future together, I knew this was what she imagined. It was easy to go all in on a dream with her—her excitement was infectious. And when she died, those plans and hopes died, too.

But I didn't.

And I'd forgotten that.

I get out of the car and walk up to the door, but I hesitate before I ring the bell, thinking I should've called to make sure it's okay for me to be here.

I turn a circle and blow out a breath, giving myself a silent pep talk. I seriously contemplate leaving when the door behind me opens and Lynn appears.

There's a mix of confusion and surprise on her face, but after a beat, both are replaced with warmth and kindness. "Matteo? Hi?" I hear the question in her voice.

"Sorry to just drop by." I push a hand through my hair.

"Don't be silly." Lynn opens the screen door wide. "You're still family—you don't need an invitation." She moves aside and motions for me to move as she says, "Come in, come in!"

I take a deep breath and step inside, where I'm greeted by the smell of cinnamon and vanilla, a combination that will forever remind me of Aria.

"Don's out playing pickleball, but do you want some coffee?" She turns toward the kitchen, and I follow her.

"Uh, sure," I say. A framed wedding photo of Aria and me catches my eye. I packed all my photos away a long time ago, and seeing her face, frozen in time and full of so much joy, stings.

But not as deep as usual. Not like it used to.

I feel guilty for that. Shouldn't I mourn her for the rest of my life? Isn't that what she deserves?

"Come in and sit." Lynn motions toward the small table in the eating area off the side of the kitchen, and a vivid memory invades my mind. The night I came over without Aria to tell her parents I wanted to marry their daughter and to ask for their blessing.

That night, with my whole life stretched out in front of me, I thought I knew how everything would play out. I was excited about the life we were starting and about the person I got to start it with. I had goals and dreams and . . . hope.

Lynn sets a hot mug of black coffee on the table in front of me, then sits down, her own mug quite a bit lighter in color than mine.

This makes me think of Iris.

"I didn't expect to see you today," Lynn says. "How've you been?"

"Honestly?" I say but can't say anything after. I just shake my head.

She leans back. "Yeah. Some days are like that."

I nod.

"I like the beard."

I absently scrub a hand over my chin. "Thanks. Aria would've hated it." My smile is sad.

Lynn's isn't. She laughs. "She absolutely would've hated it. She was not a fan of your facial hair." She takes a drink, and I get the impression she remembers how much I hate small talk, so she doesn't make any more. I'm not here to discuss the weather or my favorite football team or anything equally as mundane, and I think Lynn knows that.

"I want to apologize for not coming by sooner," I say, eyes locked onto my mug of coffee.

"No need to apologize for that," she says. "I know it's been hard."

I nod, swallowing the lump in my throat. "It's been brutal."

She reaches over and covers my hand with hers. "How are you *really* doing?"

Slowly, I lift my gaze to meet hers. "Not great. Part of me doesn't know how to function without her."

"You've been functioning," she says. "Winning awards and running a successful restaurant. We've eaten there a few times, you know?"

I go still. "I didn't know."

"We wanted to be respectful," she says. "So we kept a low profile."

I shake my head. "You shouldn't have. You're always welcome. That place wouldn't be here if it wasn't for Aria."

She smiles. "Then we'll be sure to come back in soon."

"Good."

There's an awkward pause, and I know I need to say what I came here to say, and yet, the words aren't there.

Lynn must sense this. She's still watching me. "Your girlfriend is very pretty."

"Oh, she's—" But I stop myself. I don't want to lie. "Yeah, she is."

"Does she make you happy?" There's no trace of judgment in her eyes. And I make sure of that before I respond.

"She does," I say. "Is that okay?"

She's taken aback. "Okay?"

"It feels unfair," I say. "Like, why should I get to be happy when Aria's—"

"Matteo," she says. "You get to be happy because you're still here, and if she was still here, I'd say the same to her."

"But why?" I ask. "Why am I here and she's not?"

She shakes her head. "I've made my peace with the question 'why,'" she says. "There's not usually an answer to that one. I've mostly accepted it. Mostly."

I'd love to find out how she did that.

She goes on. "I remember the first time I laughed after the accident. I felt so guilty. Like, I didn't deserve to laugh. I'm a mother who lost her child, that's who I am now—what is there to laugh about?"

"That's how I feel," I confess.

"But then, I realized, Aria *loved* to laugh. She loved to make other people laugh. And to see the people she loved happy. She would not be okay with all of us moping around, carrying some cross in her memory. That's not the way we should honor her."

"But how do I move on?" I ask, my voice breaking. "I promised her forever."

"You promised 'till death did you part,'" she says quietly. "You kept your vow. And so did she. But we're still here, Matteo. And there is room in our hearts for more love. Our love for new people doesn't dull the love we had for Aria. You have a lot of life left to live, kiddo. Live it. And live it well. *That's* how you honor her memory."

I blink to keep myself from crying, but my eyes are clouded over, and the lump in my throat is back.

"Thank you, Lynn."

She stands, then motions for me to do the same. When I do, she pulls me into a warm, tight, motherly hug. "It's time to let go, Matteo. It's okay." A pause. "Let Aria go."

As I stand there, wrapped in the quiet comfort of a familiar embrace, I think of my wife. I think of how much I loved her, how much I will always love her.

And then I think maybe Lynn is right. Maybe it's time for me to finally, finally, remember that I'm alive.

Lynn pulls back. "Can you stay for a little while? Catch me up on your life?"

I nod. "I think I can do that."

"Good," she says. "I've missed being in the loop."

I steady my gaze as I let out a shaky breath. "I'm sorry about that, Lynn. I'll do better."

She squeezes my arm. "Nothing to apologize for. I'm just glad you're here now." She sits, motioning for me to do the same.

When I do, she smiles at me from behind her mug. "So . . . tell me about Iris. And don't leave anything out."

I take a deep breath. "Where do I begin . . .?"

Chapter Thirty-Four
Matteo

AN HOUR LATER, I leave Lynn's house and call Val to make sure the staff is okay without me. She sounds irritated that I'm questioning her again and tells me to leave her alone and take the rest of the day off.

For the first time since I opened Aria, I don't argue.

The talk with Lynn settled something inside me. Like untying a knot.

As I drive back toward my apartment, I know there's one more thing I need to do.

I guess this is what they call closure.

I drive out to the edge of town to a place I loathe.

The cemetery.

I wish I could say I'm one of those guys who has a standing date here or a folding chair tucked behind a big oak tree like Rocky Balboa at Adrian's grave, but the truth is, I hate the reminder and the sadness and the emptiness of visiting this grave.

So many memories I'd rather avoid. So many "lasts" and so many "finals."

None of us were ready to say goodbye, but we didn't get the choice. Our only choice was to grieve.

After talking with Aria's mom, I see it a little differently now. Grief can only exist as a result of great love. You can't have one without the other.

For the first time, pulling into this place, I don't resent it.

I park the car, get out, and start walking. Lynn picked out the headstone because I was too much of a mess to make decisions. When I reach the grave, I brush a few dead leaves from the top of the headstone, letting my hand rest on the cool marble as I stare at her name. *Aria Morgan—beloved wife and cherished daughter, fierce friend and lover of delicious food.*

A knot ties itself at the base of my throat.

"Hey." I look around, feeling awkward standing here talking to a piece of stone but also feeling like this is something I need to do. "Sorry I haven't been around much." I suck in a breath. "I hate it here."

With the exception of the sound of a few cars in the distance, the cemetery is quiet.

Silent as the grave, I guess.

"I saw your mom," I say, feeling a bit awkward, talking out loud. "She's good. Misses you." A pause. "We all miss you."

I shove my hands into my pockets and look around. There are flowers on a few of the headstones, but I see no other signs of visitors. "I should've brought flowers," I say quietly. Absently.

I kick at a pinecone on the ground. "I've been having a hard time moving on," I say. "Your mom thinks I'm punishing myself just for, I don't know . . . being alive, or something."

I don't want to feel any of this again.

How can I stand here, looking at her grave, and *not* remember every bit of it? The pain of being told she was gone. The pain of putting her in the ground. The pain of going home and realizing she'd never be back in my arms.

But even as I think through those painful memories, others come in right behind them. The joy of dreaming with her. Her goofy smile when I was being too serious. Riding in our car with the windows down—and her with her bare feet on the dash—on warm summer evenings. Trying new recipes. Feeding each other samples of pastries she was perfecting in our kitchen. Dreaming about our restaurant.

So much joy preceded all that pain.

And I erased all of it with a broad brush.

"We had some good times, didn't we?" My eyes sting with hot tears. I don't want to say what I'm saying, but I think I need to. *Have* to.

"Aria, I think . . . I think I have to get back to the land of the living." I screw my eyes shut, and the tears fall. "But that might mean letting you go."

I have a hard time getting the words out, but once I do, I close my eyes and think of Aria's smile. "Man, I miss your smile."

I open my eyes. "I miss you. And I will always love you, you know that. But . . ." I tap a fist on the top of the gravestone. "I met someone. She's sort of great. She's making me remember to love things again, bringing me back to life, I guess?"

I think of Iris, struck by how deep my feelings for her are and how strange it is that those feelings and my deep love for Aria can co-exist.

"You'd like her," I say. "You'd probably get along really well. She's funny, and she loves to laugh." I kick at a rock. "I know you're gone, and you've been gone. But part of me still feels like—" I kneel down and clear away a few more dead leaves. "Like I was always supposed to be yours. Like it's wrong for me to imagine a life with someone else."

There's a chilly breeze, and I inhale the cool late-winter air.

"I guess I just needed to come here and tell you that I'm sorry. I'm sorry I don't let myself think about you so much anymore. It hurts to imagine where our life would be if this hadn't happened." I shake my head. "I get so mad at how unfair this is, and I want to know why. If you'd left an hour earlier, or if I'd come and picked you up or . . ."

I go still.

"It's stupid to ask questions I know don't have answers."

I force myself to feel everything I'm feeling right now. I've been hiding from my emotions long enough, and I'm finally starting to realize all the ways it's been bad for me.

I kiss my fingers, then press them to the headstone.

"So, I'm going to live. And I'm going to do my best to be happy." I stumble a little over the words, wanting them to be true but knowing it's going to be a while before they are.

Not knowing what else to say, I turn to go. I start to walk, aware that my cheeks are wet, and when I'm almost back at the car, I whisper, "I'll never forget you."

I'm about to get in, to drive off and figure out a way to keep my new promise to live my life when, without warning, the sky opens up and it begins to snow. Big, fat flakes that instantly stick to the ground.

With one hand on the door handle, I turn back and look at the headstone, and I have to wonder if Aria would've believed in magic.

I drive back to my apartment, wishing I felt lighter having unloaded so much of the burden I've been carrying, but mostly I feel heavy from the sadness of letting myself feel things again.

I park in the garage and walk inside The Serendipity. Iris will be at work for a few more hours, but when she gets home, I'll be waiting. It's about time I'm the one to sit outside her door and put it all on the line.

While I still need to work through some things, I'm certain of her.

Of us.

I walk up the stairs and through the door to the third floor. I'm only a few steps in when I see something on the floor in front of my apartment.

There's a rolled-up newspaper on my welcome mat.

I glance at the mat in front of Iris's apartment—no newspaper.

Curiosity and worry simultaneously land in my stomach.

What is going on?

Why now, after all this time, would the newspaper land back at my door?

I pick up the paper, confused by the change and hoping for some logical explanation.

Yeah, I think, *because this newspaper is always so logical.*

I walk inside, drop my keys in the bowl on the table near the door, hang up my coat and take the paper into the kitchen. I turn it over and see that this newspaper, like all the others, is addressed to me.

Delivered to me and addressed to me. Just like they were before Iris came into my life.

I open the newspaper and lay it out on the counter, giving it a quick once-over, hoping whatever it is the magic wants from me, it's obvious from the start. I don't have the bandwidth to go searching right now.

I scan the first page, reading historical articles about the dorm's first co-ed dance and engagement announcements for two girls who got engaged to twin brothers right here in this building.

I flip over to the second page—a rundown of a football game, an announcement for a new science center being built on campus and—my eyes zero in on a photo of Iris. My heart stops when I read the headline: *Iris Ellington Will Meet Soulmate Tomorrow.*

I react as if I were punched, stepping back, trying to unsee what I just read.

I lean in again, and there, clear as day, is the same headline.

Iris Ellington Will Meet Soulmate Tomorrow. Underneath is a photo of Iris, zoomed in on her face, looking over her shoulder at the camera.

She looks stunning.

In a sudden reaction, I grab the paper, ball it up, hard, and throw it across the room.

"*Will Meet,*" it read.

Future tense.

As in, "has not met yet."

I turn a circle, hands on my head, and storm out of the kitchen and into my living room, pacing back and forth at the realization of this.

The whole idea that Iris was never meant for me is infuriating. All that agonizing, all the wondering, all that trying to do it right and make sure I can be the guy she deserves—all for nothing.

I hear the distant jangle of chimes, like they're coming from outside.

I walk back into the kitchen and there, on the counter, is a rolled up newspaper.

I storm over to it, snatch it up from the counter, and am about to rip it in half when I feel it vibrate in my hand.

As it does, it flips out of my hand back onto the counter, where it opens and unfolds in a *poof* of golden shimmer, back to the same article—but this time, it's a different photo of Iris. In this photo, she's making a face and pointing down.

This time, though, all the other articles disappear—leaving a paragraph underneath the headline that I didn't read.

A pang of sadness hits me square in the chest. I could say it's good that it's her turn, that she deserves happiness, that maybe I'm just not ready to be who she needs, but I'd be lying. I don't care about any of those things. And the thought of losing her—really losing her—only makes my feelings for her clearer. Like how flipping a coin reveals what you really want.

What I really want is Iris.

An inevitable apprehension seeps in as I read the words under the photo.

It's been years in the making!

Tomorrow, at the Spring Brook Elementary Art Show, Iris Ellington will at last meet her soulmate! They will connect over a child's painting of his favorite meal, even though the painting will be quite the mess.

Make sure Iris is near the appetizer table for this serendipitous encounter precisely at 6:05 p.m.

Your presence is required to make this happen.

My presence is required to make this happen.

My mind spins. Iris is going to meet her soulmate tomorrow night at the art show. The one I agreed to cater.

And that soulmate is not me.

Chapter Thirty-Five
Iris

I'M SO EXCITED, I could square dance.

The kids have been working on their projects for this art show for months. Some have chosen charcoal, some colored pencils, and still others clay relief and forced perspective. These kids have created some absolute *stunners*, insanely realistic for their ages, and I couldn't be prouder.

And even though my personal life is a hot mess, I owe it to my students to give them my very best—the most professional, memorable experience possible. A night to celebrate their creativity and let them shine. That's what I promised them, so as I get ready, I'm determined to put everything else aside and be here in this moment.

Yesterday, Val called to finalize the catering details Matteo and I had already worked out. When I asked her why he didn't call—hopefully not being too obvious or pushy—she told me he was out for the day.

I assumed she was covering for him, but I didn't say so. Val is now my friend, but she was Matteo's friend first.

A part of me wonders if he's passed the whole event off on

his staff to handle. He might not even show up, which might be what he needs.

Even though what I need is a full rundown of where his head is right now.

His last text to me gave me a shred of hope, but the more time that passes, the harder it is to hold onto it.

I check my bag for about the hundredth time to see if the rolled up newspaper is still there. This morning, for the first time, I found one in front of my door that was addressed to me.

My heart immediately sank when I saw a sticker on the plastic sleeve with my name on it. I tried not to let my mind spiral, but I failed.

If it's addressed to me, does that mean the magic is done with Matteo? That what he suspected is true, and it's fully passed to me?

One thing I didn't consider before is that Matteo might forget all about the magic the same way Brooke and Liz forgot.

My stomach feels hollow at the thought. If he forgets the magic, will he forget everything we've done over the last few weeks?

I reach in my bag and touch the newspaper. I was too scared to open it and rushing out the door anyway, so I just stuffed it in my bag and drove to the school. When I got here, there were parent volunteers waiting for me, and I was thankful for the distraction—but it was like having the telltale heart beating rhythmically in my tote bag.

Every time I glanced over at it, I thought I heard chimes.

Now, about an hour before the art show is set to begin, I've changed into my dress, a floral sage green maxi dress with sheer long sleeves and a cinched waist. It's flowy and makes me feel pretty.

Sometimes a pretty dress can change your whole mood.

Not tonight, though. Because when Dante and Bear came to set up the food table—without Matteo—it was just another reminder that my time with him might really be over.

I think about the sweet, tender moments we've shared. All the ways he showed me he was good and kind. And how much it will hurt if I have to walk away.

I'm standing in my classroom, trying not to cry, when I pull the paper from my bag. I make sure my own name and address are still on the sleeve before pulling the paper out and unrolling it on my desk.

Instantly, my eyes land on a photo on the front page. It's me, with a goofy look on my face, pointing down at a short caption below it. Above the picture is a headline:

Iris Ellington Will Meet Her Soulmate.

Wait. Wait.

Will meet?

As in I haven't already?

My heart drops.

Under the photo is a short caption.

It's been years in the making!

Tonight, at the Spring Brook Elementary Art Show, Iris Ellington will meet her soulmate!

She needs to be on the lookout for a man wearing red. He might appear a little messy at first, but rest assured—he holds the key to her heart.

I lean back. Matteo doesn't own one red thing.

And messy?

If it's possible, my heart sinks even lower.

"He's the least messy person I know," I say to the newspaper.

I quickly snatch up the newspaper and re-read the caption.

"I don't want a soulmate if it's not him," I say in my most

forceful, *I mean business,* teacher-tone. "Do you hear me? I don't want it."

I slam the newspaper back down on my desk, angry tears spilling down my cheeks.

I'm done with you, magic.

Done.

"Hey, there you are!"

I wipe my cheeks and look up to find Brooke standing in the doorway.

"We're about to open the doors." She takes a few steps closer, then gives me a quizzical look. "Oh. Hey. Is everything okay? Did something happen?"

I shake my head, then fold up the newspaper.

"You look upset," she says.

"No," I sniff. "I'm good. Promise." I tuck the newspaper back in my bag.

"You also look hot," she says.

A laugh escapes as I come out from behind my desk and meet her by the door. "Thank you for helping today."

"Of course," she says. "That's what friends are for, right?"

The words hang in the air, and I grab onto them with both hands.

Friends.

I have friends now. Good friends. Today, Brooke and Liz spent the entire afternoon helping me set up, hanging artwork on the walls of the gymnasium, hanging pipe and drape around the space so we could hide the fact that it was a gymnasium, rearranging furniture to give kids and parents places to sit and talk about the art pieces. We also set up blank canvases with paint supplies for anyone who wants to try their hand at creating a masterpiece—an idea I came up with that I hope will be really fun.

I couldn't have done any of this without them.

We walk through the hallways, and when we reach the

back doors of the gym, Brooke pulls the door open and leads me inside. White twinkle lights illuminate the space, and jazzy instrumental music plays quietly through the speakers.

Liz is standing over by the food table with Nicola and Val. We start walking toward them, and Val lets out a low whistle. "What a knockout!"

I shimmy and do a little turn, ending with an awkward curtsy that I instantly regret.

"You look gorgeous," Nicola says. "It's so great that you're going all out for these kids! They are *never* going to forget this."

"They were so excited to dress up, I couldn't let them have all the fun." I glance at a few of the third-grade boys, who are in mini suits, vests, and ties. One of them has a fedora. It's absolutely adorable.

"There's a whole crowd of people waiting in the lobby," Liz says. "Iris, this event is going to become an annual tradition."

"You've done an amazing job," Brooke adds. "I can't even believe it. We should all look for ways to celebrate our students more. I'm inspired." She gives a little shimmy. "Plus, who doesn't love a chance to dress fancy?"

My friends are all looking gorgeous in their semi-formal attire. Val is wearing dress pants and a sparkly sweater, and Nicola is in a cute blue cocktail dress with her hair swept up and away from her face. They're both stunning, and it's fun to see them out of their usual uniforms.

"Thank you for coming. And for going along with the fun of it," I say.

"Are you kidding?" Val says. "We wouldn't have missed it."

Wouldn't have missed it.

Those words are pinned straight to my heart.

She said it like it's the most obvious thing in the world to show up for people who matter to you. And yet, in my experience, the people who show up are so hard to find.

I would've been happy with one or two people who make me a priority, and seeing them all makes me feel spoiled. It's more than I could've asked for, this hodgepodge of people who seem to be mine.

It takes some of the sting out of the realization that one very important person is missing.

"Miss Ellington!" I turn to see Charles walking toward us. I'm growing more comfortable with his first name, which feels like progress. "The crowd is restless! Can we open the doors?"

I glance over to where the appetizers have been set up and see Dante and two other servers. Dante gives me a nod and a thumbs-up. I turn toward Charles and nod. "Looks like we're good to go!"

We move off to the side, and I watch as parents and grandparents filter into the space, being dragged by their excited kids, who can't wait to show off their work.

More than a few of the parents congratulate me, but I assure them that this night is not mine—it belongs to their children. I have no interest in taking any credit here. All I've done is create a space for them to shine.

Brooke and Liz move out into the crowd, seeking out their students as I spot Joy at the back with Alice. She waves, and I wave, and then Alice gives her hand a tug and leads her mom over to the corner where her painting hangs. I watch as Joy kneels down and gives Alice a hug, and I don't look away until I see a smile light the little girl's face, something that's become more common lately.

Excited voices carry throughout the space, and I stand back and survey it all.

Looking for a man wearing red.

After my brief scan, I spot a white-haired man in a red

sweater, a heavily tattooed twenty-something guy who has to be someone's uncle or irresponsible older brother and . . . Charles Kincaid.

My boss.

My stomach wrenches. Charles is ten years older than me, but he is divorced. And he's not *bad* looking. I'm sure he'd be a perfect match . . . for someone else.

Has the magic ever been wrong?

"You did this, Iris."

I turn toward the voice and find Winnie standing beside me.

"Winnie! I didn't know you were here!" I give her what I intend to be a quick hug, but she holds on tighter—and longer—than I expect.

"Of course I'm here," she says. "Do you think I would miss your big night?" She releases me from her embrace.

I smile. "It's really more about the kids."

"Sure, and they all have people to celebrate them and tell them they're wonderful and take them out for ice cream." She flicks her hand in the air. "You deserve to have that, too."

I ignore the instinct to brush it off and let the words fill me up. "Thank you, Winnie."

She turns toward me. "You have a way of making people feel special. It's a gift, really." She takes my hands in hers. "Some would call it magic." She smiles.

Did she . . .

"Winnie, do you—?" but before I can finish the question, she gasps.

"Oh, my, look who it is."

I turn and follow her gaze to see Matteo walking in, carrying a large silver chafing dish.

He's wearing his chef's coat. His *white* chef's coat.

My shoulders drop. "I didn't think he was coming."

I watch him as he makes his way through the crowd, wishing he was here for me and not for work.

And then, our eyes meet.

The world turns to slow motion—not because of the obvious electrical charge connecting us like lightning in the air, but because out of the corner of my eye, I see a tiny, fast-moving black and white blob stumble over one of the sofas.

I slowly realize that the blob is actually Austin Markham, fifth grade whirlwind and class clown, and he has tripped and is tumbling straight toward Matteo.

I call out his name and start waving my arms, but my hysteria only seems to confuse Matteo, not alert him to the fact that he's about to be broadsided by a tiny human, and there's nothing I can do but stand back and watch it happen.

As Austin barrels into his legs, the chafing dish is knocked loose, goes flying backward in the air, spilling pasta and sauce and cheese all over the floor, all over Austin, and all over Matteo.

The noise comes to a screeching halt as people realize what's just happened. I rush over, wide-eyed and a little panicked, not sure what Matteo is going to do, when Austin pulls himself up.

This kid never misses an opportunity when he's got an audience of any size, and this one is much larger than usual.

He swipes his hand through the sauce, stands and smacks it onto one of the blank canvases set up nearby. "Look, Miss Ellington! Food art!"

He swirls the sauce around on the canvas in big, wide circles, and the crowd starts laughing and applauding.

If I don't see this kid hosting the Oscars in fifteen years, it will be a monumental disappointment.

"Good use of found objects, Austin," I say, looking around for Austin's parents when Liz emerges from the crowd. "Come on, Austin, let's find your parents and get you cleaned up." She motions for him to come with her, and I mouth a silent *Thank you*, then turn my attention to the gorgeous man still sitting on the ground in a pile of pasta.

I take a step closer, and he holds up a hand to stop me. "Don't. I'm a mess."

"Yeah, you are." I watch as he struggles to his feet, and only then do I realize that his crisp, white chef's coat is now a very deep but unmistakable red.

Matteo is wearing red.

"You're in red," I say.

He frowns, and he softly flicks a chunk of tomato sauce from his hand onto the ground.

"Yeah, I am."

"You're messy—*and you're wearing red.*" Tears spring to my eyes.

Austin's dad walks up and pulls my attention. "Such a bummer. Baked ziti is my favorite meal." He looks at the canvas of Austin's "sauce art" and shrugs. "Kid's got a great artistic eye, though, right?" He walks off, leaving me standing there, staring at Matteo as he gets up off the floor.

Messy. Red. *Soulmate.*

He cocks his head and looks at me like he's seeing something he didn't expect.

"What time is it?"

"You want to know the time?"

"Yes. Please!" He sounds weirdly desperate.

I frown and glance down at my watch. "Uh, 6:05. Why?"

He looks over at the canvas just as a chunk of pasta falls off and onto the floor.

He looks back at me, eyes afire.

"Do you think that counts as a child's painting of a favorite meal?"

"I'm not sure . . .?"

He takes a step closer, and I'm vaguely aware that the

music is back on and people are chatting again. Dante has found a custodian and they're starting to clean up the mess. But mostly, I'm just looking at Matteo.

Messy. Red. Soulmate.

"I came home last night, and there was a newspaper at my door," he says.

"There was?"

He nods. His face looks bright. "It was addressed to me, and it was about you."

"What did it say?"

He wipes his hands on his black pants, then reaches in his pocket and pulls out a small newspaper clipping. He hands it to me, and I see the same photo that was in my newspaper, but the words are different.

I read the paragraph under the image.

It's been years in the making!

Tomorrow, at the Spring Brook Elementary Art Show, Iris Ellington will at last meet her soulmate! They will connect over a child's painting of his favorite meal, even though the painting will be quite the mess.

Make sure Iris is near the appetizer table for this serendipitous encounter precisely at 6:05 p.m.

Your presence is required to make this happen.

I look up and find him watching me.

"It's 6:05." There's excitement in his voice. He nods toward the appetizer table. "We're near the appetizer table. So I need to know if this counts as a child's painting of a favorite meal."

He takes me by the arms, and I don't even care if my dress gets ruined. "Because there is no way I'm letting some other guy walk in here and claim to be your soulmate."

My eyes fill with tears. "I thought you didn't believe in that stuff."

"I didn't," he says. "But then I met you."

I press my lips together and meet his eyes. "I got a newspaper, too."

His brow furrows, and he inches back, still holding on to my arms. "You did?"

I nod. "It said I was going to meet my soulmate tonight."

"And?"

"And that he'd be wearing red and he'd look a little messy"—I close my eyes to try to keep from crying—"but that he'd hold the key to my heart." I open my eyes and stare at him, so thankful he's looking at me like he feels about me the same way I feel about him.

"I told the newspaper I didn't want a soulmate if it wasn't you." I inch closer. "I was hoping it was you."

Matteo takes my face in his hands and kisses me, so fully I nearly faint, forgetting where we are and who is watching until I hear the shouts and screams of small children all around me. I hear whistles and jeers and the unmistakable, high-pitched sing-song of, "Miss Ellington has a boyfriend! Miss Ellington has a boyfriend!"

The volume of the chatter grows as more kids join in, like they practiced this, and I laugh and take a step out of Matteo's embrace. My cheeks are on fire, and when I turn and see that Nicola, Val, Brooke, and Liz have all joined in the chant, I'm filled with something beyond happiness. Is it joy? Elation? Euphoria?

Whatever it is, I love it. I relish it. I savor it.

It's a feeling I never want to forget.

My life has had plenty of sad moments, but that sadness has only made this moment that much sweeter.

Matteo grins, kisses the top of my head, and says, "I'm going to go clean myself up."

I nod and watch as he goes, waving at the kids to let them know the show is over. Somehow, Matteo managed to keep me marinara-free, which is something of a little miracle all on its own.

Winnie walks up beside me, one eyebrow raised and a wicked grin on her face. "That man looks good in *anything*."

I can't keep from smiling. "He sure does."

"You know, Iris." She puts a hand on my arm. "I've lived a long, full life. Some moments have been beautiful and wonderful and unforgettable. And other moments have been dark and sad and heavy. But through all of those moments, I've found friends who are as close as family."

I look at Winnie, then scan the crowd. I spot Brooke, bending over to fix a little girl's bow on the top of her head. She glances up and makes a face at me.

There's Liz, chatting up some parents. She smiles when our eyes meet and gives me a wave.

On the other side of the gym, I see Val and Nicola, Bear and Dante, cleaning and serving and being loud and obnoxious. Nic catches my eye and gives me a wink.

Friends who are as close as family.

Winnie pats my hand. "I know a little something about life and love and loss, and there's one thing I know for sure."

"I'm listening," I say, eager for her to finish because I will soak up every word.

"I don't believe that soulmates are found. They're *made*." She squeezes my arm and leans in a little closer. "The real magic is when two people make the *choice* to love each other. To put each other first—no matter what. And making that choice every single day, over and over"—she pats my hand—"that is a truly rare and beautiful thing. That's what a soulmate is."

Soulmates aren't found, they're made.

The words are so simple, they're profound.

And I realize that maybe it was the newspaper that

brought Matteo and me together, but only he and I can turn what we have into magic.

I look at Winnie, who I'm now convinced knows more about the magic in The Serendipity than she's telling me, but she only smiles. "I have to go save Jerry from carbohydrate overload. If he eats any more of those tiny pastries, he's not going to fit into his competition pants."

I laugh as Winnie pulls me into one of her hugs. This time, I don't try to shorten it or pull away. I hug her back, thankful she's now a part of my life. Then, I walk out into the hallway to find Matteo so I can kiss him properly without an audience that's all under four-foot-three.

Chapter Thirty-Six
Iris

Cloud nine.

That's where I live now.

It's one thing to help others find magic, it's an entirely different thing to *feel* it for yourself.

After the Art Show, I grin the whole way home. When I get back to my apartment, I change into my most comfortable clothes then trudge down the hallway, and before I can knock on his door, it opens.

Matteo takes one look at me and smiles. A real one. An eye-brightening, cheeky smile that makes me feel like the luckiest girl in the world.

He takes me by the hand and pulls me inside, closing the door and pulling me close until our bodies are flush against each other. His eyes dart around like pinballs, taking in every inch of my face, and his smile lingers.

"You smell like garlic," I joke.

"You look like heaven," he answers.

I give him a playful shrug. "I'll accept it."

"You know," he says. "I didn't get a chance to tell you how beautiful you looked tonight."

At that, my skin warms, and as he brushes a soft kiss across my lips, a tingle runs up my spine. "No," I whisper. "You didn't."

"Gorgeous." He kisses my cheek. "Stunning." Back to my lips. "And I missed you."

"I missed you, too," I say.

He tucks me under his chin and presses me to his chest. I pull him closer, thinking I'd be happy to stay like this for the rest of the night.

"I'm sorry I disappeared for a few days," he says. "It wasn't cool for me to not let you in. And it won't happen again. I had some things to figure out."

I look up into his eyes. "And?"

"I did," he says.

He kisses my forehead, then pulls back and holds my gaze. "I love so many things about you, Iris. Like, how excited you get to help other people. And how you don't really take no for an answer. How you didn't let my bad attitude run you off, and how you called me out on my stupidity. I love how you fit right into my world, and after family dinner you stick around and talk my ear off while I cook. You're a huge distraction." He grins. "I missed that this week."

I don't bother trying to hold the smile in anymore. I couldn't help it if I tried. "I'm not too much?"

He shakes his head. "Not for me."

I pull him close and kiss him full on the mouth, savoring every single breath as a shiver runs down my spine. My body heats as my nerves wake up, and I think about what Winnie said—that selfless love is a choice. If that's true, then I choose him.

He pulls me away from the door, into the living room and onto the couch, where we both lay down, facing each other, me tucked between his body and the back of the sofa. I grab the crocheted blanket and spread it over the two of us, then settle my fist under my chin, my eyes captured by his. I could get lost here.

"So," he says. "You do realize that we were the newspaper's target all along, right?"

My eyes dart away as I think about this. "Oh, my gosh," I say, realization dawning. "We were the target."

"We did some things for other people, but yeah," he says. "That was all about you and me."

"The magic totally set us up!" I think through all the ways the paper pushed us together. All the ways it brought me exactly what I've been searching for—a community, a family, a place where I finally feel like I fit in.

He leans down and kisses me.

"I love magic," I say, kissing him back.

"It's a good thing because when I got home, there was another newspaper at my door."

"Seriously? Where is it?"

"On the counter."

I push myself up and over him, letting the blanket fall in a heap to the floor. I rush to the counter and pick up the paper, still wrapped in the plastic sleeve.

"Look at the address label," he says.

I turn it over and read: *Matteo Morgan & Iris Ellington*

When I glance up, I beam. "Now, we're a pair." I meet his eyes. "Have you looked through it yet?"

"I was waiting for you."

He sits up as I rush back to the couch and plop down next to him. I pull the paper out of the plastic and hold it up in front of us. There, on the very top, above the fold, is a bold headline, an announcement, that is shocking to us both.

"Um, does that say . . . ?" I start.

He pauses. "Yep, I think it does."

I look at him, and he looks back at me. "Can we plan it in four months?"

"I do know a great caterer." He straightens and takes my hand in his.

"I'm game if you are."

A smile spreads across my face, and in the distance, sounding like it's coming from outside, I hear the distinct tinkling of chimes.

THE END

Only Magic in the Building
a whimsical romance series

The Serendipity
Emma St. Clair

The Cupid Chronicles
Courtney Walsh

Petals and Plot Twists
Jenny Proctor

Misfortune and Mr. Right
Savannah Scott

Clean Out of Luck
Carina Taylor

Off the Wall
Julie Christianson

Signed, Sealed, and Smitten
Melanie Jacobson

The Escape Plan
Katie Bailey

Acknowledgments

I am so fortunate to be surrounded by so many amazing people, and without them I wouldn't be able to write a single word.

Always first, my husband Adam. My first reader. My creative counterpart. I'm so grateful for you and the way you never let me quit on myself.

My kids, Sophia, Ethan & Sam. You'll never see this note, so I could really say anything I want... but mostly I'm just really thankful I get to be your mom.

I'm eternally grateful for my sweet writing friends and brainstorming buddies, Katie Ganshert and Becky Wade. What a wild ride it's been...and you guys have stuck like glue through it all. How lucky am I?

Tarah Curry. Just a few months and already making my life so much easier. Thank you for everything!

To my earliest readers: Leslie Brown, Heidi Robbins, Stephanne Smith. Thank you for your eagle eyes, your helpful words and the gift of your time. I'm grateful to you!

To my co-conspirator, Emma St. Clair, who has braved the madness of organizing such a huge project with me. We survived! Now...when is vacation? And to the other amazing authors in this collection, Jenny Proctor, Savannah Scott, Carina Taylor, Julie Christianson, Melanie Jacobson, & Katie Bailey. Thanks for going on this wild ride with us! You all are so gifted...but more than that, you're just awesome humans.

And to YOU, dear reader. I'm SO incredibly grateful to you. Thanks for picking up this book, for reading it, for sharing or reviewing or passing it along. Because of you, I get to talk to myself all day and call it work. What a blessing that is! I'm THANKFUL for you!!

As always, please drop me a note if you want to say hi! I love making new friends. courtney@courtneywalshwrites.com

Also by Courtney Walsh

Holidays with Hart

My Phony Valentine
My Lucky Charm

Road Trip Romance

A Cross-Country Christmas
A Cross-Country Wedding

Nantucket Love Stories

What Matters Most
If For Any Reason
Is it Any Wonder
A Match Made at Christmas

Harbor Pointe

Just Look Up
Just Let Go
Just One Kiss
Just Like Home

Loves Park

Paper Hearts
Change of Heart

Sweethaven

A Sweethaven Summer
A Sweethaven Homecoming
A Sweethaven Christmas

Standalone Novels

Hometown Girl
Things Left Unsaid
Right Where We Belong
Can't Help Falling
Merry Ex-Mas
Christmas with a Crank
The Happy Life of Isadora Bentley
The Summer of Yes
Everything's Coming Up Rosie

About the Author

Courtney Walsh is the *New York Times* and *USA Today* bestselling author of several low spice romance and contemporary women's fiction novels. She is a Carol-award winner, Christy award finalist and seeker of happy endings.

More than anything, Courtney feels compelled to spread joy by writing light-hearted but poignant, character driven stories that provide a sweet, safe escape when life gets a little too heavy.

In addition to writing novels, she has written two craft books and several full-length musicals. Courtney lives in Illinois with her husband and three children, where she co-owns a performing arts studio and youth theatre with her business partner and best friend—her husband.

Visit her online at www.courtneywalshwrites.com

Made in United States
North Haven, CT
25 April 2025